MW01146361

New Frontiers

The Expansion Wars Trilogy

Book One

Joshua Dalzelle

©2016

*****

Edited by Monique Happy Editorial Services

www.moniquehappy.com

The euphoria of victory following the news that the Terran Starfleet had eliminated the Phage threat and had, effectively, won the war didn't last long. The celebration gave way to a hangover that left the leadership of the Terran Confederacy's individual enclaves feeling snappish and demanding answers. More specifically, they wanted a scapegoat. Someone they could point to and shout to their respective electorates, "*Those* are the people that caused this! Blame them, not us!"

Exacerbating this was the loss of a centralized Confederate leadership structure. The capital planet, Haven, had been destroyed in the war, along with most of the administrative bureaucracy, a sizable chunk of the Senate, and CENTCOM's orbiting fortress: Jericho Station. The elected leader of the Confederacy, President Caleb McKellar, could not be confirmed as being on Haven when it was lost so the entire civilian government seemed to be left in the lurch, unsure as to what their next move should be and most too afraid to even suggest something in the hostile political environment.

As if that wasn't enough, CENTCOM had also clammed up. Fleet Admiral Marcum, who was also the CENTCOM Chief of Staff and second in command after the President, refused to provide complete details of the campaign until they resolved questions about the civilian leadership of the organization. This left the press, and the less scrupulous politicians, free to invent their own narratives. Among the most popular of the early theories was that a rogue starship captain, Jackson Wolfe, had ignited the war when he'd panicked and fired upon an alien ship in one of the Frontier systems.

The story of Wolfe's bumbling exploits almost took hold and was close to becoming a "truth" in the collective consciousness of humanity, but then there was a massive leak from within CENTCOM. Since the organization was still temporarily headquartered at the New Sierra Shipyards, and the facility had been hastily upgraded to make room for all the new tenants, pinning down who had leaked the sensitive information proved to be almost impossible. The tech crews hadn't even been able to find out how the secure servers had been accessed to pull so much classified data, much less transmit it off the orbiting facility.

In the end, however, it didn't matter. The damage was done and now the people really had somewhere to focus their fear and anger: The Asianic Union, one of the five major enclaves that made up the Terran Confederacy. The AU was a manufacturing powerhouse with a large population and had apparently not been content with the nine worlds it controlled. One of the documents that had been released in the dump was a detailed report from an unnamed source within the Confederate Intelligence Section that made a compelling case squarely placing the blame on the AU's unauthorized colonization beyond the Frontier that allowed a terrifying and implacable enemy, the Phage, to find them in the first place. The AU government tried to squash the report, but it was too late. It wasn't long before New America, Britannia, and the AU's closest stellar neighbors, the New European Commonwealth, began demanding some sort of punitive action be taken. The Warsaw Alliance, longtime allies of the AU, refused to join the chorus condemning them.

While the remaining tatters of the Confederate Senate would have liked nothing more than to issue some sternly worded resolution regarding the enclave's illegal colonization efforts, the fact was that with the loss of Haven and Jericho Station they had little with which to project their authority.

At first, the people turned to Earth, feeling that the birthplace of humanity, that had remained untouched during the war and had an intact government, might be a logical place to form the new capital. But Earth would not so easily forget the centuries of neglect and outright abuse by the worlds of the Terran Confederacy and quickly released an edict stating ships and refugees from Confederate planets were not welcome in the Solar System or on Earth.

This was seen as the final act that tore the fabric of the Confederacy beyond repair. With hostilities mounting, the Asianic Union declared themselves independent and recalled all of their remaining ships. The Warsaw Alliance followed shortly after, as did roughly sixty percent of the New European Commonwealth. These splinter factions wasted no time in reorganizing themselves into a bloc and closing off their space to any and all Confederate ships, even going so far as to deny inbound com drones safe passage.

Within two short years there was a literal blackout of information coming from the worlds that formed the new Eastern Star Alliance. Official diplomatic channels were still open, but general communication was tightly monitored and controlled. Many in the remaining Confederate worlds said good riddance, their anger still smoldering for the actions of the AU that they believed had led to such a horrific conflict with the Phage. Others were a bit more pragmatic, however, as they knew that the Phage were likely not the only other stellar neighbors out there and would much prefer that humanity presented a unified front when they came face to face with them.

Confirmation of their suspicions came much sooner than they would have liked.

Chapter 1

Danilo liked the quiet down in the "Tombs," as the long-term storage vault was colorfully known to the crew of maintainers. Some found the silence unnerving or even oppressive, but Danilo was able to do some of his best thinking in those dim, subdued depths as he supervised the machines that wordlessly went about the task of collecting any dust that may have settled on the artifacts.

The Tomb, sublevel thirty-eight of the Confederacy's new archives, housed mostly CENTCOM equipment that was deemed too sensitive or dangerous to dispose of or decommission. Danilo had been medically unqualified to join Starfleet and had been flat-out rejected by the Marines, but his interest in everything military still burned brightly. It made the three-acre level especially fascinating since almost all of it was relics from the recent Phage War. While the war was almost mythology for those that weren't directly involved, Danilo devoured any scrap of information on the conflict that he could find. Once his security clearance had been granted, the assignment to supervise the Tomb's weekly cleaning had been nothing short of a godsend.

He stopped and reverently put his hand on a piece of twisted, charred metal that was propped haphazardly against one of the Archive's support pylons. It was a sort of ceremony he went through every time he stepped off the lift despite the fact he had no idea what the mangled chunk of alloy might be. But he did know what it was from.

"*TCS Blue Jacket*," he read reverently off the riveted tag that was still legible. "Captain Jackson Wolfe, commanding."

"Help ... help me." The voice came as a whisper, so softly that Danilo couldn't even be sure he had actually heard it.

"Hello?" he called loudly. "Nobody is supposed to be down here!"

"I ... help," the voice came more clearly this time, and loudly enough that Danilo couldn't ignore it as a figment of his imagination.

"Who's there?" he called. "Identify yourself immediately! This is a Level Five secured facility!"

"Help!"

"I'm not kidding!" Danilo's voice was tinged with fear. "Simmons? If that's you this is *not* funny!" He began walking slowly forward and towards a barely visible glow that was coming from deep in one of the storage rows.

He steeled his nerves and continued towards the glow, quickening his pace and telling himself over and over that there was no way anybody could get down here who wasn't supposed to be. It had to be one of his fellow maintainers playing a practical joke on him. When he cleared the corner, however, that hope evaporated.

Sitting back against the outer wall was a black cube that he'd passed by with barely a curious glance dozens of times, but now there appeared to be a monitor of some sort activated on the surface with indecipherable characters tumbling across it.

"Are you the one calling for help?" Danilo asked, feeling foolish.

"Who are you?" the voice asked, unmistakably coming from the cube.

"My name is Danilo Jovanović," Danilo answered, still approaching slowly. Before he could identify himself further the Cube spoke again.

"Where am I?"

"I'm afraid that's classified," Danilo said automatically. "What are you? Some sort of computer?"

"I … am not sure," the Cube said. "Something is wrong. I need—" the voice trailed off and the terminal went dark.

"What do you need?" Danilo asked, but received no response. He circled the Cube a few times, prodded at it with his gloved hand, and eventually shrugged before turning to leave. He'd report the incident to his supervisor. A lot of the equipment down there had been hastily designed and poorly built. In fact, during orientation he'd been warned that although they didn't think there was anything dangerous down there, he should suspect strange things to happen.

"Looks like a glitch from some old bit of—"

"I need Wolfe." The voice came back strong as the lights on the display surged, stopping Danilo in his tracks. "I think … I think Wolfe knows what I am." With that the display went dark again and no amount of poking or prodding would elicit another response.

"Could it possibly mean Jackson Wolfe, the starship captain?" Danilo asked himself. "I'm pretty sure he might be dead."

****

"Senior Captain, it's an honor—"

"It's just Mr. Wolfe now," the man said as he was escorted into the Archives. He was thin, almost slight of build, and of average height. "Just call me Jackson."

"Of course, Cap—Mr. Wolfe," one of the ubiquitous civil administrators sniveled. "Would you care to tour the upper levels of the Archive, sir? We have an extensive collection of imagery from the Battle of Nuovo Patria."

"No ... thank you." Jackson visibly shuddered at the memory of the bloody and costly battle. "If it's all the same to you, I'd just like to see what was so important I had to fly all the way from Earth to New Sierra to see it. The summons was unnecessarily vague."

"You know how Fleet Security is, Captain," a new voice said from the stairs behind Jackson. "Secrets for the sake of secrets."

"Admiral Pitt?!" Jackson asked in shock and genuine joy the slightest whine from his prosthetic leg could be heard as he turned quickly. "I thought you bought the farm on Haven."

"Close," Pitt said. The admiral was everything the CENTCOM recruitment films said he should be. Lean, impeccably groomed, and just enough grey in his hair to convey a sense of experience. He had a raspy voice and a scowl he'd worn so long that Jackson was certain it stayed put even when he slept. Admiral Pitt had been in charge of Fleet operations during the height of the Phage War although he was stationed on Haven, well away from the fighting on the Frontier.

"I was on a courier ship over Haven when those Charlies moved in and began bombarding the surface," he continued. "We lost main power but had enough velocity to be thrown clear of all the excitement, and the Phage never bothered investigating or pursuing. We floated around for some weeks on a ship that reeked of unwashed spacers and refuse before a survey ship finally stumbled upon us. We were down to the second to last set of emergency CO_2 scrubbers, a backup reactor that was close to failing, and the rations had been gone for days."

"That's ... incredible." Jackson didn't know what else to say. One of the greatest fears that seemed to be universal among spacers was that of being trapped on a powerless ship. Dying slowly in a floating tin can was considered one of the worst ways to die in space. "And now you're working here at the Archive?"

"Not all of us turned our back on the Fleet after a bit of a rough time in the war, Captain," Pitt said sharply. "I'm overseeing the refit of a new drive system to some of the newer ships. I caught a shuttle down from the shipyards when I heard your ship made orbit." There was a long, uncomfortable silence following the admiral's comments.

"So!" the administrator said, clapping his hands. "How about I show you down to the Tomb. That is why you're here, after all."

"New drive system?" Jackson asked quietly as they walked to the security checkpoint off the main lobby.

"I hardly think that concerns you anymore, does it Captain?" Pitt said pleasantly, but the bitter edge underneath was unmistakable. Jackson looked at him, but decided not to comment further. It was only natural that his decision to completely leave Starfleet after the war was met with criticism and open hostility. At best the old "Earther" slurs were brought up, at worst he was re-branded a traitor. But he cared about none of that now, and it was only a burning scientific curiosity that had dragged him out of North America again and had him ride an old, slow courier ship all the way to New Sierra.

"Who was the first to speak to it?" he finally asked as the lift doors closed and the car began to descend.

"Chief Technician Danilo Jovanović," the administrator said in his grating, faux-enthusiastic delivery that coupled perfectly with the pasted-on smile. "I can have him join us if you'd like."

"It wouldn't be a bad idea to speak with him myself," Jackson said. "But I have a feeling I know what it is down here that seems to want a chat with me. If I'm right, we'll probably want to destroy it as quickly as possible."

"Care to elaborate, Captain?" Pitt asked.

"I hardly think this sort of thing concerns you anymore, does it, Admiral?" Jackson deadpanned. It had the desired result as he saw Admiral Pitt's jaw clench and his eyes narrowed slightly. "It shouldn't take me long to determine how dangerous this thing has become."

"Become?" the administrator asked with what seemed like genuine concern. Jackson and the admiral both ignored him.

****

"This is Danilo Jovanović," the administrator said as he indicated the man standing near a twisted chuck of alloy. "Danilo, this is Mr. Jackson Wolfe, formerly Senior Captain Wolfe of Seventh Fleet."

12

"Hello, sir." Danilo nodded his head respectfully but didn't approach closer or offer his hand.

"You were the first one it spoke to?" Jackson asked.

"As far as I know, sir," Danilo said.

"And everything it said to you was accurately transcribed in your report?" Jackson indicated the hard copy he held of the official incident report he'd been provided with.

"Yes, sir."

"Okay, thanks, Mr. Jovanović," Jackson said. "I won't need to hold you up any further."

"Sir?" Danilo asked as Jackson turned to walk deeper into the Tomb. "Could you please tell me what this is?" Jackson looked at the charred and twisted metal behind the technician, a puzzled look on his face until he saw the plaque the other man was gesturing to. He approached for a closer look, his interest piqued.

"That, Mr. Jovanović, is what's left of the portside main boarding hatchway frame from the *TCS Blue Jacket*," Jackson said. "The reason I know it's the port hatchway is because, despite commanding the ship for eight years, the starboard entry was never fitted with a plaque. Is there something specific about this artifact you find interesting?"

"It's just … many people think that the stories about you, and about the *Blue Jacket* and the *Ares*, are just legends," Danilo said. "Most people that I meet don't believe that you're still alive, and some don't believe you ever actually existed."

"Who knows, Mr. Jovanović," Jackson chuckled, "maybe they're more right than you know. Now … if you gentlemen will excuse me." He turned and walked away quickly from Jovanović, Pitt, and the administrator whose name he'd purposefully neglected to ask for. It didn't take him long to find what he was looking for among all the damaged and forgotten Phage War equipment; it was the only thing in the cavernous room that looked as pristine as the day he'd taken it aboard the *Ares,* the last ship he'd commanded before leaving Starfleet. He felt a momentary pang at the thought of his old command as he'd been forced to leave her, stricken and adrift in an uncharted region of space. She'd been too damaged to survive a warp transition to leave and they had a limited time to get the crew evacuated and onto the ship that would bring them home, so the ship still floated through space in a state of limbo that bothered him to this day. There had been no time to properly scuttle her and a recovery effort was out of the question.

"So ... who's behind the voice this time?" Jackson asked as he approached the Cube. "Setsi?"

"I do not know who that is," the Cube replied immediately.

"He was our Vruahn liaison during the Phage War." Jackson, surprised at the instant response, approached closer and peered at the display, seeing if there was anything there he could decipher. "So if you're not Setsi, who are you? I'm assuming you're using the Cube as a com relay again to get in touch with us, but why not just open direct lines with humanity? Why go through all this trouble?"

The Vruahn were an ancient and highly advanced species that had found themselves unwilling allies of humanity during the war. They had been inextricably involved with both humans and the Phage when things had spiraled out of control and, grudgingly, had accepted their responsibility in the matter. They had provided technological support and a squadron of light attack ships to help end the Phage threat, but once the

14

war was over they had made it quite clear that further contact with humans was not something they were interested in.

"Captain Jackson Wolfe," the Cube said, the words rushing out in what sounded like a sigh of relief. It disturbed Jackson greatly. "You have come as I asked."

"Who are you?" Jackson asked, this time more sternly.

"I … do not know," the Cube said. "My thoughts are so disjointed … memories that aren't mine."

"Let's take this step by step since there can be no misunderstandings where our two peoples are involved," Jackson said. "Are you a Vruahn operative using this machine as an open com channel to talk to me?"

"No," the Cube said. "I am … me. I do not fully understand what you are asking, but your assumption that I am speaking as a conduit is incorrect. My thoughts are my own and I vocalize them as I feel necessary." Jackson stood silently for a moment, trying to work through the various scenarios the cryptic answer pointed to. As he eliminated them one by one and the realization of what he was likely dealing with sank in, he gave an involuntary shudder from the cold chill that swept through his body.

"Oh, shit," he whispered before backing up a few steps to collect his thoughts. He knew the smartest thing would be to march back to the lift, inform Admiral Pitt of his suspicions, and then be on his way back to Earth before anyone had time to drag him in any deeper than he already was. He'd left all this behind, damnit! He'd served and had done his part. It wasn't his responsibility anymore and there had to be better, smarter people available to handle it.

That's what he'd do. Just walk back the way he'd come, give a brief, concise statement, and then firmly request he be taken back home. Easy.

"So what do I call you?" Jackson asked with resignation, walking back to the Cube.

Chapter 2

Four years later ...

"Steady as she goes," Senior Captain Celesta Wright said, her voice calm. "Prepare for orbital insertion. We'll wait for the formation to catch up there."

"Preparing to make orbit, aye," the helmsman replied. "Engines answering zero thrust."

Celesta smiled at the word "thrust," a term that was no longer always accurate when describing the product of her starship's engines. The Phage War had exacted a terrible price on humanity, but the silver lining of that black cloud was that they'd been violently shaken out of their centuries-long complacency. Advancements were coming fast and furious now and her ship, the *Starwolf*-class destroyer, *Icarus*, was among the first to receive the next generation starship engines: a space-warping reactionless drive similar to what the Phage had employed against them.

The new systems were in their infancy, but already the *Icarus* was able to demonstrate she had a marked advantage during the trial exercises even in scenarios in which she was pitted against up to three other vessels. Human scientists had known how to modify gravity for hundreds of years; it was one of the base principles their warp drives operated on and every ship had stable artificial gravity for the crews. Until the war there just hadn't been a push to move away from the reliable and predicable thrust engines.

So far only four ships had been fitted with the new drive as only the more recent classes of starships had the newest generation fusion powerplants needed to support the power-hungry drives. As the systems were so new and untested the *Icarus* still had her two massive magneto-plasma drive (MPD) pods on their respective pylons just in case. It was a good thing they'd left the old engines attached, as the new drive, although a marvel when it was operating properly, had shown itself to be horrifically unreliable. The new engines were constantly overloading the power system, blowing out junctions, or just failing inexplicably and with no warning. Sometimes they'd come right back up after a reset, but often it took her engineering crews many hours to get it sorted. It had been bad enough that Celesta had ordered the drive taken offline most of the time the *Icarus* was flying, telling CENTCOM that she would only power up the drive when ordered to do so. She'd hoped that her status as a bonafide hero of the war would be enough influence to convince the brass at Fleet Operations that the drive wasn't quite ready to be deployed on an active starship.

She had been wrong. In no uncertain terms she had been ordered to not only return the ship to active status but to use the RDS as often as possible to collect data. As if that wasn't bad enough, she'd then been ordered to escort a diplomatic convoy out past all logistical and technical support should something really go wrong.

"Time to orbit?" Celesta asked, rising gracefully from her seat at the center of the bridge to stretch her legs and observe her crew.

"Two hours, sixteen minutes, ma'am," the helmsman said. "We could achieve orbit in an hour but we're held up by the slower ships' decel burns."

"We're in no hurry, Mister Ellsworth," she smiled again. "A stately, dignified approach is more in line with our mission, wouldn't you agree?"

"Yes, ma'am," the helmsman, Specialst First Class Richard Ellsworth said, sounding completely unconvinced. Celesta had noticed a repeat of the general attitude of her crew since the shakedown flights of the new reactionless drive system (RDS) from the one when they'd returned victorious in a battle in which they were literally outnumbered by the thousands. It was a swagger that bordered on arrogance. She'd have a word with the executive officer to make sure it didn't get out of hand, but a little healthy pride and competition between ships wasn't necessarily a bad thing.

"The flagship is requesting we decrease speed, Captain," the com officer said. "The ambassador's ship is beginning her decel burn ahead of schedule."

"Very well," Celesta said. "OPS! Calculate our optimum decel rate based on the position of the *Amsterdam* and the *John Arden*. Send it to the helm so that we can wrangle this mess into something resembling a military formation. This simply will not do as a first impression to our new friends."

"Aye aye, ma'am."

The ambassador representing the Terran Confederacy, or what was left of it, had insisted on flying aboard his own ship, the *John Arden*. The aging cruiser was named for an infamous diplomat who, depending on whose side of the story was to be believed, had managed to single-handedly broker a peace deal between New America and Britannia over a disputed world some one hundred and fifty years in the past. The New Americans revered him as a hero, while those in Britannia were told that Arden had drugged their representative during the talks to push an unfavorable deal upon them. The planet, called Aleeciana after Arden's daughter, was still a point of contention between the two powerful enclaves.

John Arden's namesake, the aforementioned cruiser that was well past her prime, had been causing issues the entire flight. Admiral Marcum had made it perfectly clear he had no intention of flying his flag on such a decrepit ship and elected to fly the *Dreadnought*-class battleship, *Amsterdam*, on the mission. Almost as an afterthought he had informed the Ninth Squadron, Seventh Fleet, that he would also like one of their *Starwolf*-class destroyers to fly escort, specifically the *Icarus*. Celesta wasn't fooled. The Chief of Staff was bringing three of the fleet's most powerful mainline ships along with the old consular ship and she had to assume he was savvy enough to understand the sort of impression that made. It would be akin to showing up to a new neighbor's dinner invite heavily armed. He either didn't care or was deliberately flying to the rendezvous with a heavy show of force.

"So what do you think these new aliens will look like, Captain?" Celesta's executive officer asked quietly and for the fourth time since the convoy had departed the New Sierra Shipyards.

"As I told you, Commander, I wasn't given clearance for that," she said evenly.

"Yes, ma'am," Commander Barrett said. "But you must have some opinion based on the information we've been given."

"Commander, we will find out soon enough." Celesta ended the conversation. "If you wouldn't mind, prepare the *Icarus* for orbital insertion and try to reign in your curiosity until we've parked this convoy over the planet."

"Of course, Captain," Barrett said, moving away to the OPS Station. Celesta suppressed a smile at her XO's enthusiasm for the upcoming encounter.

The planet they were approaching had no official name or designator as of yet. Even among the political upheaval that had split the Confederacy in two and left most of the governmental apparatuses completely crippled into inaction, Starfleet Research and Science Division, and the Office of Planetary Exploration that fell under their direction, was still cheerfully plugging away at their mission.

The planet the *Icarus* was now chasing in its orbit had been discovered by an unmanned exploration drone just prior to the first confrontation between a Phage "Super Alpha" and the Terran destroyer, *TCS Blue Jacket*. The drone dutifully performed its function of surveying and cataloguing the planet, spending most of the duration of the Phage War observing weather patterns and sending down small, disposable landers to survey the various flora and fauna. By the time the war had wound down some years later, the probe was finally ready to make its initial report back to Fleet that it found the planet to be almost eighty-two percent ready for human habitation.

Eventually, once Fleet was able to begin standing down from wartime footing, R&S Division sent a cruiser out to the planet to corroborate what the probe had sent back. What they found was that the probe had indeed accurately reported that the planet was eminently suitable for colonization. They also found someone else in the skies over the planet, someone who had been expecting them since discovering the probe during one of their own survey missions.

The discovery of another alien species was not welcome news to a war-weary Starfleet whose only interactions with extraterrestrials had been either to be manipulated or be slaughtered by them. But, after many tense months in orbit during which the survey scientists and their alien counterparts tried to devise a method of communication, it seemed the newly discovered species was genuinely pleased to meet them. As time went by, and the translation methods improved, the scientists of both species were relegated to the background as the politicians and diplomats stepped in.

Everything appeared to be on the level with their new "friends," but most veterans of the Phage War, Celesta Wright included, felt like the crew of the R&S cruiser should have been court-martialed for taking it upon themselves to open a dialogue with another unknown alien species given all they'd just been through. But, like the proverbial genie that had been let out of the bottle, there was no going back.

Captain Wright, now in command of the Ninth Squadron after the retirement and virtual disappearance of her mentor, Senior Captain Jackson Wolfe, had been tasked with providing an escort for the latest diplomatic mission to the new planet that now served as neutral ground for both parties. She had tried to get out of it, once again cursing the fact that Wolfe had taken an early retirement and left her with all the responsibilities that came with being in command of the three-ship squadron. Not least among those responsibilities was lobbying Fleet to bump the construction priority for her two replacement ships, something that was practically impossible while being stuck well outside Terran space.

"New contact, Captain," the OPS officer broke Celesta out of her reverie. "They appeared very deep within the system, on course for the same planet we are."

"The timing is a little too close to be coincidental," Celesta said. "Keep up full active scans and make sure our telemetry is being dumped onto the Link. Let me know as soon as you have positive identification."

"Aye aye, ma'am."

"You think they were out there waiting on us, ma'am?" Commander Barrett asked quietly. "That doesn't say much about the level of trust in this new venture if they're sitting out in space dark waiting to see what we show up with."

"Probably just being prudent, Commander," Celesta said. "My concern isn't that they would begrudge us an escorting destroyer to make sure our ambassador's ship made it safely, but that the Amsterdam might send the wrong message. There's no mistaking her as anything other but a battleship."

"I think we'll have some answers when we see what they showed up with, Captain," Barrett said. "Or … at least what they allow us to see. It seems that we're yet again holding the short end of the stick when it comes to technology."

Celesta didn't reply, not wanting to engage in a conversation that would likely just devolve into base complaining when they were approaching a sensitive juncture in the mission. There were five ships total in the Terran convoy: two warships, the ambassador's cruiser that was flying the flag, and two supply frigates. She'd understated her concern at the inclusion of the Amsterdam, a Dreadnought-class battleship, and what signal it might send, but Fleet Admiral Marcum was adamant and senior captains did not argue with the CENTCOM Chief of Staff on such matters.

"Update on the … alien … formation, ma'am," Celesta's OPS officer said, obviously about to use the word enemy in place of alien. It was an honest mistake, but it also indicated to her that not everyone was as enthusiastic about meeting yet another new species after such a vicious, bloody struggle against the last one that they'd yet to recover from.

"Seven vessels total, two distinct classes," the officer continued. "The two larger ships are moving into the front and we're picking up some radiation leakage from the forward ports that indicate weapons."

"Can you tell from the readings if they're armed?" Celesta asked, concerned. She could see on her display that the two larger vessels were roughly the size of the *Icarus* and she revisited her fears that the massive *Amsterdam* flying in formation behind her might be more provocative than Admiral Marcum had originally thought.

"I don't have enough data to make an educated guess, ma'am," the OPS officer apologized.

"Transmission coming in from the formation on the expected frequency, Captain," the com officer said. "It's being transmitted on a clean channel; shall I put it on the speakers or send it to your terminal?"

"On the speakers, if you please, Ensign," Celesta said after a moment of thought. No point in keeping secrets from the crew just for the sake of secrets. Enough people in the com section had already heard the message to ensure that it would be widely disseminated with or without her permission.

"*Welcome most honored guests,*" a clearly artificial voice came over the speakers in an even, steady tone. "*We are most pleased to have together again so that we might formalize relations between our two great peoples so that both will be benefit. Our delegation now leaves for the rendezvous location on the surface.*"

"Short and to the point," Celesta said once it was clear there wasn't any more to the message. "Coms! Send a flash message to the rest of the convoy that we will proceed with our original deployment plan. Nav, make sure you're coordinating with the *Amsterdam* to ensure we're well out of the way once they—"

"New message coming in from the *John Arden*," the com officer interrupted. "It's flagged as urgent, ma'am ... they want us to veer off and allow them to make orbit first. The ambassador doesn't want the *Icarus* or the *Amsterdam* moving into orbit until his landing craft has departed for the surface."

"Interesting," Celesta said with an arched eyebrow, her voice steady and measured. "Did they give a particular reason for deviating from the established protocols other than the whims of their VIP?"

"No, ma'am."

"Very well." She stood stiffly. "Nav! I need a flightpath correction immediately for a braking maneuver that will move us off course and allow the *Amsterdam* room to also decel and veer off to clear the way for the *John Arden*."

"Aye, ma'am," the nav specialist said. "Sending new course to the helm now."

"So much for sticking to the plan," Barrett mumbled as he ran through a series of checks from his own station to make sure there weren't any issues with the new course.

****

The next two weeks were uneventful. Mind-numbingly uneventful, if Celesta was being honest with herself. After they'd finally made it to the planet and assumed their orbit at an altitude of thirty-seven thousand kilometers, far above and slightly behind the other ships in the Terran convoy, it had been made clear to them that only a small delegation from the *John Arden* would actually be participating in the meetings with the aliens. This had been bitterly disappointing to many of the officers on her staff who had wrongfully assumed they'd be rotated down to the surface to look around and maybe even be one of the first humans to get a glimpse of the new species.

Instead the crew of the *Icarus* sat on overwatch patrol above the *Amsterdam, John Arden,* and the two supply frigates while the alien ships were in a similar formation on the opposite side of the planet. Celesta was grateful the RDS had decided to cooperate and the gravity-warping drive allowed the *Starwolf*-class destroyer to easily keep pace with the other ships without overflying them at such a high altitude.

"How goes the watch, Ensign Accari?" she asked as she walked onto the bridge thirty minutes before first watch began.

"All quiet, Captain," Accari said. "Some standard com traffic from the *Amsterdam* that I've had routed to your inbox, but nothing flagged as priority. I've heard that you'll be asked to attend a dinner aboard her as the admiral is getting bored with racing around this planet."

"Mr. Accari," Celesta began sternly. "You are now an officer and a gentleman. It is beneath you to insinuate that the admiral is anything but in complete control of the situation. A young officer with a bright career ahead of him would also be careful about letting slip just how much inside information he was getting through an infatuated young woman who happened to be the admiral's aide."

"Yes, ma'am. My apologies, ma'am," Accari said, recognizing his captain's peculiar sense of humor and not sounding the least bit contrite. Ensign Idris Accari, formerly Specialist Second Class Accari, had been the first watch nav station operator on the *Ares* under Captain Jackson Wolfe. Jackson had recognized early how sharp the young man was, and in one of his last actions before he'd officially retired from Fleet he had lobbied to get Accari a commission, dependent upon him completing Officer Candidate Training (OCT) as well as the subsequent command schools. Accari had breezed through them without trouble and had been one of the few selected from his class of enlisted candidates for a commission. Those that didn't receive a direct commission were given the option to return to the enlisted ranks or go through the Academy. Since the Academy was typically a five-year stint, most just went back to their previous commands.

Celesta Wright, having been Accari's superior on the *Ares*, made sure she was kept aware of his progress every step of the way through his training. The file entry for his rank change had barely cleared Admin when she submitted her request to have him transferred to the *Icarus*. After training he'd been serving as her first watch OPS officer since and, like when he was at the nav station, he seemed to have a knack for the OPS position, instinctively knowing what information needed to flow up to the captain and what could be pushed back or rerouted. Celesta wished that she was still in contact with Jackson Wolfe if for no other reason than to let him know how his protégée was excelling, but it was like he'd just disappeared without a trace.

"But while we're discussing what you may or may not have heard through your backchannel sources, Ensign, what else might I find interesting?" she asked while he vacated the command chair.

"The negotiations aren't going well," Accari said seriously. "Apparently this new species, they call themselves Ushin, are either masters of the runaround, are hiding something, or the communication methods R&S devised aren't as flawless as they claimed. These are some of the things the admiral would like to discuss with you in person."

"I see," Celesta said neutrally. "While I thank you for your trust in me, Ensign, I feel I would be remiss if I didn't offer some warning to you."

"Ma'am?"

"Even on the bridge of a Fleet destroyer, that is some fairly sensitive information you're bandying about," Celesta went on. "My office is always available and just remember, there are ears everywhere and not all of them friendly."

"Yes, ma'am." Accari was no wilting flower. He accepted the criticism like the professional he was and offered neither an excuse nor an apology. Celesta found it refreshing and hoped that she'd be able to mentor him around all the pitfalls many officers fell prey to that tended to stunt their careers. More and more, Ensign Accari showed himself to have the raw talent and grit to command a starship of his own someday, and it'd be a shame if that potential was cut short because he was trying to pass on a bit of intel to his captain and the wrong people overheard him.

She'd only just begun to get herself organized when a sharp, staccato alarm began chirping from the com station behind her. That particular alarm meant that a com drone had appeared in local space and was broadcasting a general alert for any Terran ship within range and could mean anything from a threat detected in the area to a recall order. She resisted the urge to get up and check on the message herself while her com officer decrypted whatever data the drone was sending.

"Captain, authenticated emergency message from CENTCOM," the second watch com officer called out. "Your eyes only, ma'am. Where would you like it routed?"

"I'll take it in my office, Lieutenant Moll." Celesta stood calmly despite her rising anxiety. "Mr. Accari, you have the bridge until Commander Barrett arrives."

"I have the bridge, aye," Accari said.

It took Celesta less than a minute to go the short distance to her office on the command deck, lock the hatch, and validate her credentials so the computer would allow her access to the secure servers. When she began reading the flash message header she could only shake her head in amazement, unsure what it meant for her immediate mission and Starfleet as a whole. By the time the accompanying video was done, her mouth hung open in shock.

"Have Commander Barrett report to my office," she said conversationally. The computer beeped twice in acknowledgement that she'd been heard and understood. Barrett must have been close by because there was a loud, single knock on the hatchway a few seconds later. She rose to unlock it and let her XO in, motioning to one of the seats in front of her desk before reclaiming her own.

"You'll need to be aware of this," she said, spinning the monitor around and restarted the video without explanation.

"This is Fleet Admiral Pitt, speaking on behalf of CENTCOM Chief of Staff Marcum during his absence on an undisclosed, classified mission.

"I am not a politician nor do I claim to be particularly eloquent, so I'll just come out and say what's happening here on New Sierra: The Terran Confederacy has been dissolved and is no longer the governing body controlling the worlds outside of the Eastern Star Alliance. The decision was made to permanently disband the Confederacy after no accords could be reached within the remainder of the Senate and the absence of our duly elected President, Caleb McKellar.

"I will not bore any of you with the details because, honestly, there aren't any. Delegations from each enclave will begin arriving on New Sierra in the following months to decide what should happen next. As of right now, each enclave is responsible for governance on their member worlds, but *all* Fleet ships will now report directly to CENTCOM and will ignore any and all orders from local authorities no matter how mundane. I expect this to be sorted quickly and I *will not* tolerate any of my ships exchanging fire with each other due to planetary governments deciding it's time to settle some old scores. I have the newest warships here at my disposal and I will not hesitate to use them should I hear of any extracurricular activities from my deployed units.

"For now, follow the chain of command, continue on your missions, and if any of you are religious … pray that when the delegations meet here on New Sierra in the coming months this can be quickly resolved. I shouldn't have to say this but I will: This brief is classified at the highest level. Pitt out."

"What in the fuck?" Barrett blurted. "I know there was a bit of chaos after the war and the loss of Haven, but dissolving the Confederacy? This is lunacy!"

"Calm yourself, Commander," Celesta said. "You need to read between the lines. This has been in the works since the Asiatic Union and Warsaw Alliance broke off and closed their borders, though I will admit to some surprise that they made the announcement this early. It was supposed to be accompanying the restructuring agreement between the enclaves. Someone at CENTCOM must have found out that wasn't supposed to and forced Admiral Pitt to release that cryptic order."

"How could you possibly know all of that, ma'am?" Barrett asked before his eyes widened in realization. "Never mind ... Pike let you know, didn't he?"

"Agent Pike of the Confederate Intelligence Section did *not* send me an unauthorized transmission of the classified internal, behind the scenes political wrangling at work, Commander," Celesta said primly. "However, senior aide to the Honorable Augustus Wellington, a Mr. Aston Lynch, did happen to mention it to me at the reception on the planet before we departed."

"Those are the same person," Barrett rolled his eyes.

"He claims otherwise," Celesta shrugged. "I don't pretend to understand it but he's quite adamant that he is not Aston Lynch when he is Pike."

Pike, the only name he'd ever given, was an operative in the Confederate Intelligence Section (CIS). He wasn't just an operative but a full-blown agent and had been instrumental in assisting Jackson Wolfe during the Phage War by feeding him critical intel on some of the internal wrangling happening on the Confederate capital world. One of his disguises was a man named Aston Lynch, aide to the powerful Chairman of Fleet Operations, Senator Augustus Wellington. He'd originally been placed on Wellington's staff by the Director of the CIS to dig up some dirt to be used as leverage if needed, but the senator was no fool and he'd somehow figured out who Pike was.

Rather than lodge a protest or make a scene, he somehow managed to get Pike permanently assigned to him. Celesta never got the details on that, but she suspected Wellington threatened to expose the fact that the Director was infiltrating the staffs of elected officials with his own operatives and offered to keep quiet in exchange for Pike. Since then the slippery agent worked to make sure there wasn't anything that happened within the Confederacy that Wellington didn't know about.

"That still doesn't make any—" Barrett was cut off by the computer chirping, followed by the first watch com officer's voice.

"Captain, priority Two-Alpha channel request coming in from the *Amsterdam*," she said.

"Put it through, Lieutenant."

"Aye aye, ma'am."

Celesta pulled her monitor back around and put her finger to her lips, indicating to Barrett to remain silent before hitting the accept icon flashing on the screen.

"We've got a situation, Captain Wright," Admiral Marcum said harshly.

"Yes, Admiral," she nodded. "I just finished going through the video—"

"Shut up and listen, Captain!" Marcum snapped, startling Celesta. Barrett's eyes widened but he maintained his composure and didn't utter a sound. "This has nothing to do with those bullshit games the politicians are playing on New Sierra. There's been a development along the Frontier. Something has been … detected … in the Xi'an System."

Celesta's blood ran cold at the name and she immediately forgot Marcum's outburst.

"The Phage?" she almost whispered.

"No," Marcum shook his head. "At least not that we've detected. The brief I received when the com drone buzzed through the system was light on details, but it was enough that I'm ordering you out of the system. As of right now your current orders are to take the *Icarus* and make best speed directly to Xi'an. You'll rendezvous there with a CIS Prowler that's been monitoring the system."

"Can you give me a bit more than that, Admiral?" Celesta asked.

"I could, but I'm not," Marcum said. "You're being deployed on a recon mission, Captain. I need you to investigate what this might be and I'm afraid that if I give you too much detail you'll be inclined to jump to conclusions that may lead to rash action when you finally arrive in Xi'an. The short answer is that despite the Xi'an System being off limits we have reason to believe a Fleet warship may be stranded there."

"But—" Celesta tried to interject.

"Your orders are being transmitted as we speak," Marcum waved her off. "I'm verbally ordering your ship out of orbit; you can go over the data packet on your way to the jump point. No arguments. The next words out of your mouth had better be 'aye aye, sir.'"

"Aye aye, sir," Celesta said automatically, but she was staring at the logo for Seventh Fleet as Marcum had killed the channel before she had even opened her mouth.

Chapter 3

Starship captains were given a lot of leeway when it came to how they executed their orders. CENTCOM knew it was fairly pointless to try and micromanage the operations of vessels that were lightyears away with no way to reach them except dispatching a comparatively slow and costly message via one of Tsuyo Corp's com drones. As such, Celesta Wright was accustomed to orders that could almost be vague suggestions that CENTCOM would appreciate it if her ship were in a certain area at roughly the time they required.

The orders that had arrived from the *Amsterdam* as the *Icarus* made her way out of the unnamed system were different, however. These were the type of orders she'd expect when they were on wartime footing, not a reconnaissance flyby in a system that had no habitable worlds ... at least not anymore. The Phage had begun their savage tear through Terran space by first annihilating everything on the surface of Xi'an and then later destroying the planet completely in a display of firepower that still gave the veterans who'd witnessed it nightmares.

Admiral Marcum's staff had cut orders that required her ship to hit specific and precise rendezvous at such an aggressive pace that if there was a single maintenance delay with the *Icarus* they'd miss it completely. The knot that had formed in her stomach at the mention of the Xi'an System refused to go away in the face of these unusually specific orders, at least specific for a time of relative peace. Humanity was in the midst of a post-war upheaval that looked to be a prolonged situation as the remaining enclaves restructured their agreements with each other even as others broke away completely and shunned all contact with the remnants of the Confederacy.

Celesta read through her orders one more time as the *Icarus* flew her first warp flight back to the Columbiana System and a new worry began to gnaw at her. They would stop in the New America capital system to be joined by six other ships before pressing on to the Frontier, all of them newer warships with veteran captains. Marcum had specifically said it wasn't the Phage, but was there a new enemy at the gates that just happened to pick the Xi'an System as well?

Even as she realized how virtually impossible that scenario was a new, possibly worse fear arose. Xi'an was still under control of the Asianic Union and therefore was within the Eastern Star Alliance, Starfleet ships were not given permission to freely travel there. Could the ESA be ready to capitalize on the Confederacy's downfall and gain a few more worlds in the confusion? The idea of fighting humans, while it would at least be familiar, seemed repugnant after the horrors of the Phage War. She hoped she was wrong.

"Commander Barrett," she said, raising her voice unnecessarily and waiting for the computer to route her intercom request.

"*Barrett here, Captain.*"

"I'm forwarding you our new orders, but from what I see we can tolerate no holdups due to technical trouble with the *Icarus*," Celesta said as she began packaging and forwarding a copy of the orders to her department heads. "Please have Commander Graham physically decouple the RDS pod from the main power MUX. Tell him that while I admire his perseverance and skill when it comes to the new drive I cannot afford for it to act up again and delay us. We'll be flying on the mains while in real-space until further notice."

"*Understood, ma'am*," Barrett said. "*I'll go down now and speak with him.*" She frowned as the intercom beeped softly to tell her the channel was closed. Why would Barrett leave the bridge during his watch to go to Engineering? When she looked at the clock on her office wall that displayed ship's time she realized that Barrett had likely been in bed and she'd been sitting at her desk for hours longer than she realized. She quickly logged off her terminal and straightened up her desk before heading to her own quarters to catch at least a few hours of sleep before first watch began.

****

By the time the *Icarus* had reached her final rally point before the warp flight directly to the Xi'an System six different com drones had caught up with them, each providing a little more detail about the political chaos within the former Confederacy and the not-so-secret meeting with a new alien species, but almost nothing about what was awaiting them on the Frontier.

Celesta was somewhat relieved to learn that Augustus Wellington, formerly Senator Wellington of the Terran Confederate Senate and Chairman of the Fleet Operations Committee, had moved quickly and decisively to consolidate his powerbase and use it as leverage to bring all the other factions to the table. The powerful politician from New America was wasting no time hammering out a restructuring deal while most of the major pieces of the old system were still intact. Despite the loss of Haven, much of the old administrative apparatus had survived as well as a fully functioning CENTCOM along with Starfleet. If he could get everyone to agree quickly there might even be some opportunities opened up for the other enclaves to step in with the loss of the ESA's production and manufacturing power, something they'd never wanted to compete with in the past. Celesta's fervent hope was that the politicians did what politicians always did: look out for their own best interests. If they were able to strike a new set of accords quickly and restructure the remaining planets within the Confederacy's sphere of influence, there was less chance for more splintering and unrest among the civilian population.

"Captain, we're receiving a standard hail, no encryption," the com officer, Lieutenant Ellison, called. "Source is a CIS Prowler."

"Respond with our standard countersign, Lieutenant," Celesta said. "Tactical, am I correct in assuming that we were the first to arrive?"

"Yes, ma'am," Lieutenant Commander Adler called from the tactical station. "No other transponders in the system active but ours; even the Prowler is quiet."

"Very well," Celesta said. "Ensign Accari, please secure our own transponder and ensure we have no other emissions from the *Icarus* but the com system."

"Aye aye, ma'am."

"Burst packet from the Prowler, ma'am," Ellison said. "They're asking us to keep the com chatter to a minimum and to form up on them. I'm sending the text from the message to your station now."

Celesta looked over it, slightly irritated that she was being given orders from a non-Fleet officer, but tamped it down once she read the full message.

Senior Captain Wright, please form up on the Prowler and we'll more easily maintain emission security protocols. We're deploying an asset deeper near the jump point to greet and route the rest of your task force to the formation. Once all ships are accounted for you will have full operational control over the mission.

Agent Uba

"A full-blown agent," Celesta mused softly to herself. "CENTCOM must be taking whatever the hell is in Xi'an very seriously." The fact there was an agent aboard the Prowler made her mind flit briefly to Pike before she was again wholly focused on the business at hand.

"Nav, I'm sending you a set of rendezvous coordinates you will use to get a course plot to the helm." She raised her voice, "Helm, all ahead one-half when you get it."

"Ahead one-half, aye."

The main engines rumbled to life as the *Icarus* switched from her unguided drift to powered flight, the prow angling down the well as they chased the smaller CIS Prowler. Celesta could shave off quite a bit of time by ordering a more aggressive approach down the well, but the other ships were likely days behind her so it would be a pointless expenditure of propellant. She also tossed around the idea of having her chief engineer, Commander Graham, reintegrate the RDS pod so she would have use of the gravity manipulating drive, but discarded the notion quickly. There was something in the Xi'an System that had CENTCOM scared enough to order the *Icarus* all the way from the unnamed planet they'd been orbiting despite the fact there were a dozen closer ships, two of them identical *Starwolf*-class destroyers.

Whatever was there had to be something so dangerous or mysterious that Admiral Marcum wanted his most decorated, battle-hardened captain to be the first to investigate. She took some small comfort in the fact that Marcum had actually used the word *investigate* multiple times during their conversations as opposed to intercept, disable, or destroy. Maybe this was simply an overreaction from a command structure that was now trying to find its stride in a time of relative peace.

"Commander Barrett, you have the bridge." Celesta stood up as her XO walked through the hatchway for duty. "I'll be in Engineering. Ensign Accari will brief you on the latest developments."

"Yes, ma'am," Barrett said to her back.

****

Celesta rode the lift down from the command deck, located at about the midpoint of the comparatively squat superstructure fitted on the *Starwolf*-class, all the way down to Deck Eight where she could take the main aftward access tube all the way to Engineering. Before leaving her office the previous evening she'd sent a message to Commander Graham's inbox asking that he come up with a few options for employing the RDS without risking the failure modes they'd experienced on other systems when it decided to fail.

She'd complained bitterly to Tsuyo and CENTCOM both about the abysmal reliability of a drive that had been fitted to an active duty combat vessel, but the excitement of the brass for the new drive trumped the strident complaints of even the legendary Captain Wright. So, without wasting further time and effort trying to get management, as she'd come to view them, to see it her way she had decided to trust her own engineering crews to find an acceptable solution. It was either that or she'd jettison it over an unpopulated planet before returning to New Sierra.

"Commander Graham," she announced her arrival loudly to be heard over the noise of the machinery in the bowels of her ship. "I hope you have some good news for me."

"I do indeed, Captain," Graham said. A fellow Britannic citizen, his accent was similar to hers, but a practiced ear would be able to tell they likely didn't come from the same planet within the enclave.

"It was a fairly simple solution, but a degree of difficulty is induced by the sheer size of the components needed, not to mention the safety concerns. To be perfectly honest, Captain, this is something that should have been built into the RDS pod before they ever tapped *Icarus's* MUX."

"Very good, Commander." Celesta suppressed smiling at the enthusiastic man. For some reason he always took that as a mocking gesture. "I am prepared to be awed by your engineering prowess."

"The problem is, at its core, a simple one," Graham assumed his "lecturing" voice and mannerisms, clasping his hands behind his back and leading Celesta deeper into the heart of the ship. "The RDS develops unexpected variances in its power supply and causes a push-pull on the MUX. Sometimes it'll draw enormous amounts of current unexpectedly, other times it will dump so much power back on the bus that it blows out the junction.

"Tsuyo R&D assured us that this was all accounted for, and to be fair there is an extensive detection and suppression network on the power taps, but what we're finding in real world testing on *Icarus* is that the MUX controllers aren't always ready for what the RDS power sub-system does. I've had discussions with the *Amsterdam*'s chief engineer while we're in such close com range and he agrees with my findings."

The *Icarus*, like every other starship since humans had begun leaving Earth, utilized a "smart" electrical distribution system that allowed the computer to monitor and prioritize where power was sent. It utilized a multiplexing system, or MUX, to distribute power and reduce the amount of wiring stuffed into a ship that was hundreds of meters long. It also had many redundancies and safeties built in to prevent the ship from being damaged, the same safeties that were causing them problems when it came to their new reactionless drive.

"And what solution do you suggest to mitigate this?" Celesta asked.

"In descending order of preference I would first take the ship back to New Sierra and tell Tsuyo to either pull the RDS pod or properly integrate it into the ship's power distribution system," Graham said, ticking off the points on his fingers. "Barring that, I would leave it disconnected and simply refuse to risk the safety of the ship over what is proving to be a system that isn't ready for active deployment. Third, I would order my teams to begin fabricating an interface consisting of up and downstream surge detectors coupled to fast-break load contactors. What this should do, in theory, is very simple: When an event is detected the connection to the main bus is broken before the RDS has a chance to damage our power system."

"Cons?"

"We're breaking the connection completely," Graham shrugged. "That means when power is reapplied that it won't just come back up. You'll have to reinitialize the entire startup sequence again."

Celesta frowned. The startup on the RDS was an intricate and lengthy procedure that also required they shut down a myriad of other systems that would interfere with the initial calibration of the field generators. Realistically that meant that if Graham's interface was triggered and cut the drive during combat, or even normal intrasystem flight, that would be it: no RDS for the remainder of the operation until they could call for a full stop somewhere.

She was also worried about what that would mean for her bridge crew, specifically Navigation and Helm control. If a course was plotted with the assumption the RDS was available, and the helm was flying that course, what would happen if the drive dropped out without notice? The MPD main engines were kept primed and ready as standard operating procedure, but their performance envelope was completely unlike what the reactionless drive was capable of.

"Proceed with your least favorite option, Commander Graham," Celesta said after a moment of thought. "Go right to the point that you actually tap the interface into the MUX. Worst case scenario is that your people get some invaluable training and familiarity with the new hardware while fabricating the necessary parts."

"That's not the worst case scenario, with all due respect, Captain," Graham said with a slow shake of his head. "But I will get my crews to work immediately on the interface. I will alert you as soon as we're ready to implement it, of course."

"Thank you, Commander," Celesta nodded. "Carry on." Her trip back to the command deck was filled with doubts about the orders she'd just given. Was she as enamored with the idea of a gravity engine as the CENTCOM brass was? Maybe she should have told Commander Graham to pull and stow all the cables leading to the RDS pod and leave it as useless ballast until they returned to New Sierra. As the lift doors opened she pushed thoughts of Tsuyo's engineering debacle out of her head and began to gather her thoughts about the upcoming push back into Xi'an. Not only did she not know what she would find there, she also had to consider that her taskforce's very presence would be seen as a hostile act by the Asianic Union should she be spotted.

Chapter 4

"Let's be quick about this, everyone," Celesta said to the wall-sized monitor that was split seven ways so she could simultaneously talk to each starship captain and the CIS agent. "I want to be transitioning out of this system within the next forty-eight hours. For the sake of clarity allow me to state that my orders give me operational control over this mission, but as of now I'm just as much in the dark as any of you. Agent Uba, would you please rectify that?"

"Of course, Captain," the agent said, seeming unsurprised at the abrupt introduction and handoff. "Captains, before I begin let me say that this is classified Top Secret, Special Instruction Level Six. Even though there may not technically be a Confederacy at the moment, CENTCOM will still come down on all of us like a hammer should word of this get out."

"We know what classified means, Agent Uba," Captain Kolsh of the heavy cruiser *Leighton* said testily. "Please get on with it."

"Approximately four months ago a proximity beacon was detected in the Xi'an System," Uba continued, unruffled. "It was first determined that this was some sort of ruse or even threat by the Asianic Union, even if our analysts didn't fully understand the context. Three and a half weeks ago the prox beacon stopped and a full power emergency beacon was detected from the same ship. The coding of this ship's emergency beacon wouldn't have been something the AU was privy to."

"Which ship are we talking about, Agent Uba?" Celesta asked.

"*Starwolf*-class destroyer, Seventh Fleet," Uba said, his face impassive. "It's not transmitting its registry, however, so that's all we know."

"Well we know that's impossible," Celesta said after a long, uncomfortable silence where she could sense everyone watching her closely. "Every *Starwolf*-class ship is accounted for and Tsuyo will not be making any more."

"I'm well aware of that, Captain," Uba said. "Our initial recon of the system indicates that there is something of appropriate mass, however, that is squawking classified codes identifying it as a Black Fleet destroyer. We have now been waiting here, one warp flight away, for your taskforce to arrive so that we may thoroughly debunk what our sensors are telling us and, if possible, link it back to the AU. Consider the second task our mission priority."

"So the analysts are convinced that this *is* an AU ploy?" Kolsh asked.

"We believe so," Uba nodded. "While we're unsure how they would have gotten the proper code sequence for the transponder, we're relatively certain there is no other logical explanation."

"I'm inclined to agree," Celesta nodded. "But why? If it's supposed to be a message I'm afraid I don't understand it."

"Your former CO has become a reviled character behind the closed border of ESA space," Captain McKenzie of the First Fleet frigate *Midlands* said, her accent identifying her as not a Britannia native despite her posting. "In order to absolve themselves from the blame for costing the lives of billions, the AU and Warsaw Alliance governments adopted an official position blaming the attacks on the reckless behavior of a certain Starfleet captain from Earth. As these things often go, he has been morphed into a nefarious caricature that some people believe led the Phage to them on purpose. Using a *Starwolf*-class beacon signal could be aimed at him. This might be some sort of propaganda effort as much for the benefit of their people as it is a message or warning to us."

"Absurd." Celesta scoffed at the idea the AU was blaming Wolfe for actions they had perpetrated. "But the point is well taken. This could be a threat or a warning that we're not able to fully comprehend due to being closed off from what's happening on ESA worlds." She was becoming more comfortable now that it was apparent that this was humans playing games and nothing more. Even if there was an ESA fleet sitting near Xi'an they'd be able to simply fly the perimeter of the system and transition out before anyone was close enough to do something foolish.

"I wish there was more, but that's the long and short of it," Uba said. "I'll have the raw data from our limited recon flights transmitted to each of your ships immediately."

"Thank you, Agent Uba." Celesta stood and began to pace behind the conference table, the camera on the wall automatically tracking her movements and keeping her in the center of the frame. "I would ask each of you to review the data thoroughly, and if there are any questions or concerns contact the *Icarus* before we reach our jump point. In light of the brief I am bumping formation's movement up five hours. Be ready to begin transition acceleration seven hours from now. If there's nothing else?" She left the question hanging in the air, directing her gaze to each of her fellow captains for a second. "Very well," she nodded. "Dismissed. *Icarus* out."

"Channel closed and secured, ma'am," Ellison said. She'd brought her bridge com officer to run the equipment during the conference since he'd already been privy to all the com calls coming in from the Prowler.

"I had better not learn of any scuttlebutt on the lower decks about Confederate ships appearing in the Xi'an System, Mr. Ellison," Celesta said sternly.

"No, ma'am," Ellison agreed. "Unless you need me further, Captain?"

"You're dismissed, Lieutenant," she said. Ellison spun smartly and unlocked the conference room hatch before escaping his captain's steely gaze. Her warning hadn't been just idle fretting on her part; the rumor mill on every starship seemed to plod along with an almost comforting regularity, but recently it had shifted into high gear aboard the *Icarus*. The phenomenon seemed to really gain some steam about two weeks after Ellison had reported aboard. Her command style required that she have a bit more proof, however, before accusing one of her officers of disseminating classified information.

Celesta sighed in irritation at some of the more mundane aspects of command. But, mundane or not, things like a bridge crewman with loose lips had to be addressed. She picked up her tile and comlink, slipping the latter into her utilities, before leaving the conference room for the bridge to prep her ship for the last leg before they reached the objective. If this was indeed the ESA as she suspected, it would mark a strange kickoff to what promised to be a long and especially contentious cold war.

****

"Report!"

"*Icarus* has successfully transitioned into the Xi'an System, Captain," the nav specialist called out. "Position confirmed within fifteen thousand kilometers of target."

"Tactical, begin full passive scans of the system. Helm! Bear to starboard and clear the jump point, maneuvering thrusters only," Celesta ordered before turning her head slightly. "Coms?"

"It's there, ma'am," Lieutenant Ellison confirmed. "Decrypting now. The file header is properly formatted ... It looks legitimate. Reading a strong beacon for a Terran Starfleet *Starwolf*-class destroyer, no registry identification transmitted with the message."

"OPS, stow the warp drive and clear Engineering to start main engines," Celesta said. "Coms, begin working with Tactical to ascertain where the signal is coming from and put your directional data on the Link. When the rest of the taskforce arrives we'll be able to triangulate and pinpoint a position."

"Aye, ma'am."

"The Prowler and the *Leighton* have just transitioned in, ma'am," Accari reported. "Waiting on confirmation that they're moving into position."

"Very well." Celesta stood up. "Nav, send our first course and speed change to the helm. Helm, when you have main thrust available you're clear to engage the mains, ahead one-quarter."

"Ahead one-quarter when mains come up, aye," the helmsman said. It was another few minutes before she saw her helmsman reach over and advance the twin throttles up to twenty-five-percent thrust.

"Engines answering ahead one-quarter, Captain. *Icarus* is now under power."

"The Prowler, *Leighton*, and *Midlands* have all initialized their Link connections," the tactical officer, Lieutenant Commander Adler reported. "The computer is processing the incoming data stream. We'll have a rough location within a few hours and will resolve with more accuracy as the formation spreads."

The other ships slowly filtered into the system and began deploying as the *Icarus* continued her course down into the system in the opposite direction of the Prowler while the Midlands and *Leighton* fanned out above and below in relation to the ecliptic. Celesta could feel herself tensing up and tried to force herself to relax. This wasn't likely to be anything more than a bizarre but otherwise harmless action from the Asianic Union.

"Beacon is confirmed, Captain," Ellison reported. "As far as the computer is concerned, that *is* a *Starwolf*-class destroyer down there."

Celesta just nodded to her com officer but didn't answer. That wasn't welcome news. She'd assumed once the computer began parsing through the encrypted portion of the beacon transmission it would become apparent that it was a fake. It was actually the main reason an encrypted sign/counter sign signal was piggybacked onto the standard distress call, to keep someone from doing just what she thought the AU was doing and baiting a trap with another ship's emergency transponder signal.

It was another two hours before they were able to lock down a general location for the signal's origin. When she saw it Celesta began to doubt her initial assessment as to what they were seeing.

"Nav, plot a course to the signal's point of transmission. Ahead full," she said quietly.

"All engines ahead full, aye." The deck began to vibrate gently as the two massive plasma engines ran up to full power and the *Icarus* raced down into the system.

"Tactical, begin active scans," Celesta said. "Coms, tell the rest of the taskforce to remain silent. Let's only have one ship broadcasting until we get a better idea of what it is we're dealing with."

"Active array is coming up now, ma'am" Adler said. "Threat board will begin populating once we start getting returns."

"Do you think it might not be prudent to at least arm the forward missile banks, ma'am?" Barrett leaned in and asked quietly. "This is starting to spook me a bit."

"Do you really think that's one of our ships down there?" Celesta asked as she considered his request.

"I don't see how, Captain," Barrett almost whispered. "But I know I'm really hoping it isn't and for more than one reason."

"I think I take your meaning, Commander," Celesta nodded before raising her voice. "Tactical! Arm the forward missile banks, Hornets only. Standard yield and don't tie the guidance into the active array just yet."

"Yes, ma'am," Adler said, clearly surprised. "Missiles initializing; they'll be available in thirty seconds."

Celesta didn't bother to clarify her orders further as she watched the first weak returns begin to show up on the threat board. The computer would begin trying to correlate the objects to anything in the database to assign a threat number to each. The threat board itself was a holographic representation of local space that was overlaid upon the main display, and she could adjust the opacity of the outside view from her terminal so that the detail wasn't lost. It would make more sense if the main display didn't show the outside view at all, but studies had shown that crews had lower stress levels if they could see outside the ship, even if the "view" was nothing more than an image put up on a display.

"How long until we can begin visual confirmations of the objective?" Celesta asked.

"At current speed and assuming our degree of accuracy increases with proximity ... roughly thirty-nine hours, ma'am," Accari said, earning him an annoyed glare from Adler, who was still trying to get the proper display pulled up.

"Coms, let the other department heads know I want to maintain our alert status but we're more than a day from knowing any more than we do now," Celesta said. "Make sure they're on normal watch schedules and that their people are rested and ready. OPS, dig into the archives and find out if we have any intel on what was physically left of the planet Xi'an after the Phage Charlies were done using it for target practice."

"At once, Captain," Accari said crisply before turning from his main console to the auxiliary station to his left, programming it to begin fishing through the *Icarus's* servers to find the information his captain wanted. Celesta watched her bridge crew go about their tasks, still feeling the tension hanging in the air, when her comlink buzzed. She flipped it over and looked at the message.

Captain, all parts for the RDS interface have been fabricated, tested, and are ready to implement. – Commander Graham

"Commander Barrett, would you please accompany me to Engineering." She stood up. "Ensign Accari, you have the bridge ... I need Lieutenant Commander Adler focused on tracking and identifying our objective."

"Aye aye, ma'am," Accari said while making no move to leave the OPS station. Celesta liked that he had the good sense to realize that he could manage the bridge from his post, enabling him to continue doing his primary job.

"Is there some problem, Captain?" Barrett asked as he followed her to the lifts.

"Not yet," she said. "I've had Commander Graham working on a solution that will allow us to use the RDS with a greater degree of confidence and he just messaged saying he's ready for me to give him a go, no-go on implementing it. I'd like your opinion added to the mix when he tries to sell me on the idea and I try to poke holes in it."

"Then in the spirit of full disclosure I must admit that I've never been as enthusiastic about the RDS pod being installed on the *Icarus* as CENTCOM seemed to be, ma'am," Barrett said.

"Go on," Celesta crossed her arms over her chest as the lift began to move with a barely perceptible lurch. Barrett took a deep breath before continuing.

"I feel like Tsuyo took too many shortcuts to adapt the system to a ship that was never designed to carry it," Barrett said. "I love the idea of Terran ships being able to thumb Sir Isaac Newton in the eye and ride around on waves of gravimetric distortion, but I'd love it a lot more if it was something built into the next generation of starship."

"So it's the retrofit that has you so negative towards the idea?"

"Half-assed retrofit, ma'am," Barrett corrected. "The pod was supposed to be this universal one-size-fits-all solution for ships with a Class IV powerplant, but even during testing they knew it was prone to fits and could damage the power distribution system. Sorry, Captain, but I'm firmly of a mind that the RDS pod bolted to the stern of the *Icarus* is nothing more than a politically mandated liability. This would have never happened if__" Barrett trailed off and his eyes widened as he realized what he almost said.

"You can say it, Commander," Celesta said evenly, her eyes boring into his. "Jackson Wolfe would have never allowed that system on his ship."

"Ma'am, I—"

"You will remain silent until I have finished speaking," she said, her voice still calm and steady. "I am not Captain Wolfe. For better or worse, we're not cut from the same cloth and I do not buck the chain of command for the fun of it at every whim." She let out a breath before continuing.

"I understand and share your loyalty to him, Commander. His singlemindedness likely saved our species from extinction, but I cannot emulate him. The data from the RDS pod on the *Icarus* will be invaluable for Fleet engineers when it comes to outfitting it on the new ships being built."

"Captain, I sincerely regret what it was that I was about to say. It was certainly not meant to be an insult towards you." Barrett looked miserable. "Serving on your ship is as much an honor for me as being on the *Ares* was. I apologize for my careless words."

"No apology is necessary, XO," Celesta said as the lift stopped and the doors slid open. "I just want to make sure we're both clear on where the other stands."

The walk down to Engineering was quiet and uncomfortable. Celesta regretted turning on her XO and friend as she had in the lift, but his careless comment, although not meant to disparage her, had hit a little too close to home. Wolfe would absolutely *not* have allowed the RDS pod to be installed on the *Ares* if he thought it would compromise her ability to perform her duty or keep the crew safe, and if they forced the issue he would have had the chief engineer jettison it before the first warp transition.

The reasons she listed off to Barrett were true, but they didn't tell the whole story of what she was feeling. She did wish there was a bit more of Wolfe's brazen independence in her, but there had to be some middle ground she could find. Being so openly disobedient was not only destructive to the Fleet but also set a bad example to the crew. He could get away with it because by the time he took command of the *Ares* he was already a legend. But wasn't she as well? Many gave the nod to her when it came to the almost inevitable comparison between Captain Wolfe and Captain Wright, his former XO and protégé. She had led the *Icarus* on a single-ship slaughter of hundreds of Phage units while flying within their own formations, a feat not matched during the entire war.

"Captain, XO," Commander Graham nodded to the pair as they walked in through the hatchway. "Would you like the long version or the short version?"

"Short first, then I'll decide how much more detail I want at the moment," Celesta said. Graham was a first rate engineer, but he could be incredibly long-winded when giving technical explanations.

"We can reintegrate the RDS pod into the MUX with our surge detection equipment in place to protect main bus integrity, and we even found a way to keep all the calibration settings from being lost during an event that shuts down the drive," Graham said.

"A little more detail, if you please, Commander," Celesta said.

"Tsuyo engineers had originally used a single, high-power tap to the pod in order to make it more of a self-contained, easily installed system." Graham motioned for them to follow him. "The power regulation and distribution for the pod's subsystems was handled internally. We've broken these out so that we can isolate the power input to the primary field generators and those will be the lines that we'll run through the switching network."

"What's the advantage to this?" Barrett asked. Barrett's background was in engineering, which was the main reason Celesta had brought him along. He would be able to see through Graham's enthusiasm and also know if her chief engineer was skimping on some of the details in order to get the answer he wanted from his captain. She had taken the requisite technical courses during her time at the Academy, of course, but her specialization was military history and political science.

"Since we're now able to keep the pod's control systems powered up during an emergency disconnect, theoretically once power is restored to the field generators the RDS should come back up almost instantly on its original settings. This would eliminate the need for the reset and recalibration we've had to do every time the drive blew out a power junction."

"Can this be done while we're underway?" Celesta asked.

"All work to the pod can be done while we're under power," Graham nodded. "But to connect the interrupt network to the power junctions I'll have to shut down part of the main bus in that area. The systems that will be affected are artificial gravity and aft-facing sensors."

"How long will you need to shut that down?"

"The connections themselves will only take a few minutes, but call it an even hour by the time we safely secure and shutdown each system, do the work, and then bring everything back up in an orderly manner," Graham said.

"Go ahead and begin the work up to the point you need to start shutting down systems," Celesta said. "I'll make the call on whether to proceed based on what's happening at that moment."

"Aye aye, ma'am." Commander Graham was obviously quite pleased with the outcome of the conversation. "I'll get my teams on it right away."

"Very good, Commander," Celesta nodded. "We'll leave you to it then."

"You're considering reintegrating the RDS while we're flying down the well towards a potential engagement?" Barrett asked once they were in the starboard main access tube and out of earshot of anyone in Engineering. His tone of voice clearly indicated he was surprised at her decision.

"I'm not inclined to do so at this time," Celesta said. "But there won't be any harm in allowing Commander Graham to complete all the preparatory work now and then do the final hookups later once we find out what we're flying towards."

"Yes, ma'am," Barrett said. "If I may say so, I'm relieved."

"Understandably so, Commander," Celesta smiled. "Your distrust of the RDS has been well-stated."

"Yes, ma'am." Barrett looked away uncomfortably.

"You should be hoping that I allow Commander Graham to pursue this project," Celesta said as they reached the first lifts that would take them to the upper decks of the main hull before having to take another lift into the superstructure.

"Why's that, Captain?"

"Because that will mean we've investigated this strange beacon down near Xi'an and found that it was nothing to be alarmed about," Celesta said.

"Very true," Barrett nodded his agreement. "Allow me to withdraw my previous protests."

"Consider them withdrawn, XO."

Chapter 5

"We're within visual range of the target now, Captain," Ensign Accari reported as soon as Celesta stepped onto the bridge. "Data is being run through processing now to clean up and highlight the objective."

"Let's get a confirmation as soon as we can, Ensign," Celesta took her seat. It had been a boring, slow flight down into the system as the taskforce could detect nothing else of interest save for the continually chirping transponder that still insisted it was a *Starwolf*-class ship. Of the three such ships remaining Celesta knew that the *Icarus* was the only one anywhere near the Frontier, so it would be fascinating to see what it was that had been transmitting the distress call.

"This ... can't be right," Accari muttered to himself.

"You have something, Ensign?" Barrett said loudly.

"Yes, sir ... but—"

"Just put it on the main screen, Ensign," Celesta said a bit impatiently. "Let's all see it at once and then discuss what has you so out of sorts." Accari wordlessly sent the images to the main screen and sat back expectantly.

Celesta stood and walked near the left side of the screen, intending to view the cleaned-up images in order. The first showed nothing of distinction, just a dark shape that might have been a ship. The next image made her stop and frown. It was certainly the right profile for a *Starwolf*-class ship. The third image left no doubt that whatever the object really was, it had been made to look just like the Terran destroyer it claimed to be. The next few images she skipped over as they just showed the same level of detail at slightly different angles. When she came to one of the final images, however, all the blood drained from her face. The angle was just right so that they could clearly see the dorsal surface of the prow section and the spot where a ship's name and registry had been helpfully highlighted by the sensor backshop:

TCS ARES

DS-701B

"Captain, I suggest we go to general quarters," Barrett said, breaking the stunned silence on the bridge.

"Sound general quarters," Celesta said without turning away from the display. "And then you can explain why we're getting ready for a fight."

"Sound general quarters!" Barrett barked to Lieutenant Ellison. "Set condition 1SS! Prepare the *Icarus* for battle!" Celesta waited with strained patience until Barrett approached and pointed out something on one of the more clear images.

"Ma'am, I strongly suspect that this really is the *Ares* despite how unlikely that is," he said. "See this area here … on the ventral surface? That's damage from a kinetic weapon she sustained on the mission to kill the Phage core mind. The location of the *Ares* was classified and the data was imprecise due to our unfamiliarity with the area. If it's a fake"—he trailed off for a moment, seeming to collect his thoughts—"to replicate the damage so perfectly, damage that wasn't recorded or

reported other than word of mouth, is just too much."
Celesta just looked at him for a moment.

"Ensign Accari?" she said, not taking her eyes off Barrett's. What he was adamantly claiming was so absurd she felt her OPS officer would be the voice of reason.

"I concur, ma'am," Accari said. "The damage shown in the images is consistent with the battle damage taken by the *Ares* during her final mission. I am forced to agree with Commander Barrett's assessment that this really is our former ship."

"So ... how does a ship too damaged to fly that was left in an unknown, uncharted region manage to get itself all the way back to Terran space?" Celesta asked, her hands clasped behind her back. "Not just back, but precisely to the place where the entire war was started."

"I'd say it was brought here," Barrett said. "When we abandoned her, the hull was so badly compromised that she wouldn't have survived a single warp transition."

"And nobody we know of, other than the Vruahn, has the ability to move a destroyer halfway across the quadrant," Celesta said. "Since I doubt it was them, and in spite of Admiral Marcum's insistence otherwise, this reeks of the Phage."

"The Phage were destroyed, Captain," Accari said firmly and with absolute conviction.

"I hope that you're right, Mister Accari," Celesta said. "Please return the view to a live feed of the ... *Ares* ... and signal the rest of the taskforce to begin converging on our position. I want no change in their velocity until so ordered by me. Transmit the data we have so far to the Prowler as well."

"Aye, ma'am," Ellison said as Accari switched the main screen back to a live view of the *Ares*. Through the high-powered optics of the *Icarus* they were able to begin making out more detail in the false-color composite image the computers were generating through the multi-spectral sensor suite. Celesta's stomach was in knots. Someone had brought Wolfe's last ship to the Xi'an System as a powerful statement, she was certain of it. Nothing else made sense other than possibly an unbelievably elaborate and inexplicable hoax by the ESA.

"We've received confirmation of orders from the rest of the taskforce, ma'am," Ellison reported after a tense hour and a quarter had passed.

"Anything else coming from the *Ares* other than the distress beacon?" Celesta asked.

"Negative, ma'am," Ellison said.

"Any change in the ship at all?"

"No, ma'am," Accari said. "She's still in the same slow tumble in a trailing orbit behind the chunk of what used to be Xi'an."

"Well, let's kick the hornet's nest and see what comes flying out," she sat back in her seat. "Tactical, is the *Icarus* fully prepared to defend herself?"

"Yes, ma'am," Adler answered.

"Coms, transmit a message to the *Ares* requesting a status update," she said. "Let's see if we get an answer."

"Transmitting now—whoa!" Ellison shouted as the main display washed out in a flash of white.

"The *Ares* has just exploded!" Adler exclaimed. "The force of the blast is out of range for our sensors. It must have been immense. I'm beginning to run—"

"Incoming transmission, all bands," Ellison cut off the tactical officer. "Putting it through now on bridge speakers." Celesta didn't bother to chastise him for not asking if she wanted the message sent to her station first. Truth be told, she was just a bit overwhelmed herself.

"*Your interference is unwelcome. This is your only warning,*" a synthesized voice came over the speakers. "*We are watching.*"

"The message repeats a few times but that's all there was, ma'am," a shaken Lieutenant Ellison reported.

"New contacts!" Adler called out. "Four distinct returns. They just appeared within the system."

"Phage?" Celesta asked.

"Negative. Contacts are quite large but appear to be metallic in nature."

"That rules the Vruahn out," Barrett asked. "Could they be Terran?"

"They don't fit any known design methodology for Terran starships, sir," Accari said. "Computer analysis of initial radar contacts is inconclusive. I don't think this is the Asianic Union's new fleet, sir."

"Nor I," Celesta said. She'd been running the numbers in her head. Given the amount of time it took for a radar signal to get out and then for them to receive a return, the ships had appeared in the system *before* the *Ares* had been detonated. They also had come in much further towards the primary star than most Terran ships were able. That left only one unpleasant probability.

"Coms! Broadcast this on all frequencies: Unknown alien fleet … this is Captain Wright of the Terran starship, *Icarus*. You have violated our borders and threatened us. Please clarify your intentions."

"Sent, ma'am."

"Now send an encoded message over the Link to the rest of the taskforce," she said. "I want them all making best speed back to the jump point we came in through and tell that Prowler it'd be best if they made a hasty retreat. CENTCOM needs to be aware of this ASAP."

"Link is now populating more contacts within the system," Accari called out. "Eight more contacts total and they're converging on the rest of the taskforce."

"They already know where all our ships are," Celesta said tightly. "Coms, tell all ships to go full active sensors and they're free to unsafe weapons. *Nobody* is to fire first until we have confirmation of intent."

"Aye, ma'am," Ellison said tightly. "No response from your open hail yet."

"Tactical, lock on Shrikes, two each, on the closest four targets," Celesta said as she looked at the course plots. "Helm, bring us about! Reciprocal course, keep your turn as tight as you can. Nav! Begin updating our track back to the jump point. Let me know if it looks like we're going to be cut off. Coms, keep looping my original all-frequency message until we get some sort of response."

There was a chorus of affirmations and a few pops and groans could be heard as the *Icarus* was put into a tight turn and fought against her inertia. Celesta was suddenly very much wishing the RDS was active and available even as the helmsman throttled up the mains to keep the turn as tight as possible. A "tight" turn in interstellar terms was still over a hundred thousand kilometers at the speed they'd been flying, but when the *Icarus* came out the other side they'd still be carrying most of their forward velocity.

"Ma'am, the *Midlands* wants confirmation of RoE," Ellison said, referring to the rules of engagement Celesta had handed down regarding use of weapons.

"Reiterate that they are *not* to fire first," Celesta said. "Nav, do we have a path up past the four ships facing us to the jump point?"

"No, ma'am," the chief at Nav said immediately. "They're too far out and arrayed too wide. We have no angle to take that they can't easily beat us to."

"Very well," Celesta said calmly. "Plot a course for the X-Ray jump point."

"Ma'am, the X-Ray jump point is—"

"I am well aware of current flight restrictions, Chief," she cut him off. "Under the circumstances I would say I'm more interested in extending and escaping than adhering to the rules of a Senate subcommittee that no longer exists. Now carry out my orders!"

"Aye aye, ma'am!" the chief said, his face bright red. "X-Ray jump point course plotted."

"Helm, come onto new course and bring the engines to full power," Celesta ordered. With the orientation of the system at that particular time the X-ray jump point was more or less "behind" them, giving them the option of running around the primary star and trying to put some distance between her and the four ships facing off with her. If she was actually required to transition out of the Xi'an System using that jump point she knew it may very well be out of the pan and into the fire as it was impossible to know what was beyond. The Senate subcommittee on territorial expansion had strictly forbid any flights past Xi'an after the war, even simple recon flights by automated drones.

"Engines answering all ahead flank," the helmsman called as the *Icarus* swung past the apex of the ponderous turn she was executing.

"Coms, tell the taskforce they're now operating autonomously," Celesta said. "We'll be too far out of range soon to effectively communicate orders. Make sure you emphasize that nobody is to fire without being provoked. OPS, give me a status update."

"The four original contacts are moving to pursue us." Accari read off a summary list he'd been keeping updated. "So far they're just pacing our acceleration curve almost exactly. The other eight contacts have broken into four two-ship formations, three of which are pursuing the other taskforce ships and the fourth appears to be heading to our entry jump point."

"Another enemy that seems to know a lot about us while we know absolutely nothing about them," Barrett grunted.

Celesta said nothing, but was forced to agree with her XO. This new group could only be another space-faring race that, for some reason, seemed to have a low opinion of humans. Now that she was able to think for a few moments while the *Icarus* raced ahead of her pursuers, she tried to objectively analyze their options.

They had mentioned a "warning," yet were chasing them around the star system. Celesta had to assume their tech was at least slightly more advanced than what she had at her disposal given that they seemed to just appear deep down into the system, managed to retrieve the *Ares* and bring it back, then rig it to blow in a demonstration that was impressive in its raw destructive power. The initial analysis by the CIC indicated that the blast was on an order of magnitude greater than the *Icarus's* entire weapons payload combined.

So turning tail and running was the only viable option in the short term while she was facing a numerically superior enemy of unknown capability, but she needed to come up with something else and come up with it fast. Her hope was that she would get a response soon from her still-transmitting message, but the longer the engagement went on the less likely that seemed. Whatever the motivation for the warning, they weren't talking.

"The support frigates have transitioned out of the system, ma'am," Accari said after another four hours. "However, the *Vought* has dropped off the Link. Waiting on confirmation from the *Midlands* as to what might have been the issue. They were still twenty-two hours from the jump point at last update." Celesta clenched her hands. The *Vought* was a heavy assault cruiser that probably should have been retired from service six decades ago. It was as likely she'd floundered and lost power while trying to run as it was she was destroyed by the enemy, a term Celesta had to now concede was appropriate.

"Direct message from the *Midlands*," Ellison reported. "The *Vought* was destroyed by what they're calling an *energy lance* of some sort. After it had destroyed the *Vought,* the ship vanished."

"Vanished?" Celesta turned to glare at her com officer, her mouth going dry at the news of a lost ship.

"That's what the report says, ma'am," Ellison said helplessly.

"*All ships, this is Agent Uba aboard the CIS Prowler,*" the familiar voice overrode their com system and was broadcast over the bridge speakers. "*The enemy vessels are apparently attempting to capture Terran ships. Do not let them close on you. The Leighton has been captured and somehow transported out of the system while the Vought was lost completely ... I suggest to the taskforce commander that we break contact and escape while possible. The Prowler is on the way out of the system now. This has to be reported to CENTCOM. Agent Uba out.*"

"Coms, broadcast the emergency withdraw order," Celesta said without hesitation. "Emergency short hops are authorized ... just tell them to get away as best they can."

"Captain, our four bogies are accelerating," Lieutenant Commander Adler said. "They'll overtake us before the X-Ray jump point at their current rate."

Celesta looked at her own display to verify the information herself. "Helm, zero thrust," she said. "Bring the prow about to course one-eight-zero by zero, attitude jets only."

"Engines answering zero thrust, aye," the helmsman said after pulling the throttles all the way back. "Bringing the *Icarus* about to course one-eight-zero by zero." The manual course commands would have the ship rotate about on her Z-axis so she would be flying in the same direction but stern first.

"Tactical, optimum range for the first volley of Shrikes, if you please," Celesta said, the familiar adrenaline of combat beginning to course through her.

"All four tangos are within optimum performance envelope for the Shrikes," Adler said.

"Very good, Lieutenant Commander," Celesta said. "Stagger fire pattern, twenty-second delay between shots, maximum yield."

"Parameters set, Captain."

"Fire!"

"Missiles one through four are away," Adler said. "Missiles five through eight standing by."

"Coms, broadcast to our remaining ships that they are weapons free but their priority is to escape," Celesta said.

"Second volley is away!" Adler said.

"Confirm tracking," Celesta ordered.

"Tracks confirmed," Accari said. "All eight missiles are burning hot and tracking true."

"Helm, bring the *Icarus* to bear on her original course and then run the mains to full emergency acceleration," Celesta ordered. "Nav, begin a running update on acceptable snap-jump locations if we have to bug out immediately."

"Disabling safety locks now," the helmsman said. "Engines answering full emergency thrust." The pronounced rumbling of the decks let Celesta know that the *Icarus* was now giving all she could to stay ahead of their pursuers.

"First volley impacts targets in ... five hours, seventeen minutes," Adler said and put the clock up on the main display so that Celesta could see it without having to ask. She nodded her approval to her tactical officer before returning her attention to the Link updates. The *Icarus* and the *Midlands* were showing as the only ships in the system. She didn't know if the Prowler was still hiding out near the perimeter but she did know that she'd lost two ships, one apparently captured by the enemy. This was a whole new fresh hell from the previous alien that had appeared on their doorstep and had just decided to kill as many of them as it could.

"I'll be interested to see what the intel folks have to say about the sensor feeds after this," Barrett said quietly. "*Another* alien species coming into the Xi'an System and kicking us around ... and this time it looks like they're abducting ships just for good measure."

"It at least solves the mystery about how they brought the *Ares* here." Celesta swallowed hard, trying to keep the bile down at the thought of all the spacers she'd just lost. It was inexcusable. She'd flown them right into a trap, so confident was she that it was just a bizarre ploy by the AU. If she had followed the protocols that she had helped develop, sat back near the jump point and let the Jacobson drones make the initial incursion she might have avoided one of the worst mistakes by a Fleet officer since the beginnings of the Phage War.

She would certainly be relieved of command, but that was the least of her worries. There was a new enemy now. Someone who could prove to be worse than the Phage and, to make matters more complicated, their motivations were even more mysterious than the simple eradication tactics of the previous invaders. Where did they take the *Leighton*? Was the crew still alive? How would she even begin to try and track them down? Her ruminations were interrupted by a startled, sharp inhale from her tactical officer.

"Two enemy ships are now accelerating away from their formation," Adler reported. "Shrikes are compensating, impact on leading targets now in three hours and decreasing."

For the next three hours they watched in horrified fascination as two of the enemy ships quickly closed the range. She could see from the high-power radar returns that the ships had an ungainly, blocky appearance and were roughly symmetrical. The sensors on the *Icarus* could not determine the enemy's method of subluminal propulsion other than it produced a slightly lower thermal signature than their own plasma thrust drives. She checked their velocity and position, quickly running the numbers in her head.

"Helm, engines to zero thrust," she said after a moment. "OPS, deploy the warp drive. Nav, stand by to execute a snap jump on my command."

"We're waiting to see if the Shrikes do any damage?" Barrett asked.

"Correct," Celesta said. "We have to take something away from this disaster that will be useful to CENTCOM."

The *Icarus* continued to fly unpowered as the bridge crew watched tensely, well aware that the data they were getting from the sensor suite on the enemy was at least fifty minutes old. Normally that would have been considered a significant safety buffer against Terran or even Phage ships, but new enemies also came with new and unknown capabilities. The fact they could seem to make entire ships *vanish* from within a star system was enough to make Celesta question whether their twenty-five light minute gap would be any real obstacle for them.

"Weapons impact imminent," Adler gave the final warning. Since the Shrikes were smart weapons that would track and adjust to targets once they were locked on, and given the distances involved, it wasn't uncommon for up to a five-minute variation from when they expected the weapon to intercept the target and when it actually did.

"Coms?"

"Still no response, ma'am," Ellison said. He sounded tired and Celesta knew he wasn't alone. During the engagement first watch had been on duty for thirty-two hours straight, and there didn't seem to be any reprieve until they transitioned out of the system. With a completely unknown adversary she just couldn't risk swapping out critical personnel like she would if it had been a Phage Alpha chasing her.

"The two straggling tangos are braking, reducing speed and—no, they're veering hard off, ma'am. It looks like they may be trying to reverse course," Adler reported. "The two others are still on a direct pursuit course. Weapons are running silent so I have no update other than I expect sensor returns on the detonation within ten minutes."

"Nav, execute emergency warp transition immediately!" Celesta barked sharply.

"Aye aye!" the startled chief said. "Assuming helm control now." They all felt the mains run to full power as the *Icarus* dipped her prow to aim down below the ecliptic plane and surged to their final transition velocity. It seemed like mere minutes before the vibrations ceased and Celesta could see on the main status board that they were being purged and secured from primary flight mode.

"Two tangos have appeared BEHIND us!" Adler said sharply. "Range is less than one hundred thousand kilometers!"

"Snap fire aft Hornets! Auto-target mode," Celesta ordered. "Nav!"

"Standby for warp transition!" the chief shouted even as the forward distortion ring began to cause the main display to darken. There was a sharp bucking as the ship vanished from the system and, a moment later, a more pronounced shaking as she reappeared two hundred and fifty light minutes outside the Xi'an System.

"Report!"

"No damage, no casualties, Captain," Accari read off his master status display. "Engineering is requesting we secure from powered flight mode until they've had time to inspect the warp drive."

"Tell Commander Graham he has ninety minutes and then we're underway whether he's finished or not," Celesta said.

"Aye, ma'am." Accari pulled his headset back up and began speaking into it.

"How did you know?" Barrett breathed.

"Lucky guess," Celesta said. "The two trailing ships either left the system or dropped back to give themselves a greater degree of accuracy to try and appear close behind us. Since Agent Uba said they were trying to capture Terran ships, and we hadn't shown ourselves to be much of a threat, it had to be the latter."

"That's not really a lucky guess, ma'am, but whatever you call it you just saved our ass again." Barrett was still speaking quietly amid the chaos created by a short warp flight on a drive that was not designed to perform such a maneuver. Celesta ignored the well-meaning compliment, still physically ill over the loss of at least two ships under her command.

"Listen up!" she called loudly. "That time limit isn't just for Engineering. Get with your backshops and get the *Icarus* checked out stem to stern ... we have no idea what sensor capabilities the enemy might have so we need to be underway as quickly as possible."

"I can't believe this is happening again," Ellison said as he let his headset slip down around his neck.

Celesta opened her mouth to chastise him, but he'd said it to himself and, honestly, she shared the sentiment. Not even a decade of peace and in the middle of major political upheaval it looked like they had a new alien threat to deal with. She fervently hoped the Prowler, with its extensive sensor capability, was well on its way back to New Sierra with the record of the engagement for CENTCOM to view.

****

"The *Icarus* made an emergency warp jump out of the system." The sensor operator turned in his seat. "That's the last taskforce ship to get clear."

"Not all got clear," Agent Uba said, pacing the cramped bridge of the CIS Prowler. He'd had to pull rank and, against the Prowler captain's protests, had ordered them to stay on the edge of the Xi'an System with stealth protocols enabled. The small ship was now sitting just inside the orbit of the outermost planet, just a dark hole in space, her passive sensors soaking in and cataloging every detail, every emission.

It had not been pretty. The *Vought* had been easily run down and had exploded brilliantly when the hull had been pierced by some type of energy beam. The *Leighton* had been disabled by the same type of weapon and then grappled up against one of the enemy ships before both vanished from the system. Hovering above it all was what Agent Uba considered to be the gross incompetence of one Senior Captain Celesta Wright, *Hero* of the Phage War.

She'd led her taskforce into a slaughter, not for a moment thinking that there could be something else in such a notorious region of space other than some prank by the Asiatic Union. Then, when the shooting started, the vacuum created by her lack of coherent leadership caused the other commanders to falter and hesitate. He'd been one of those who regarded her as one of the Fleet's few true warriors, the exact sort of captain you wanted in a situation like what had just happened. Her performance during what he was calling the Fourth Debacle of Xi'an in his head made him question everything he'd ever heard about her.

"We do have some good news out of all this," the captain said.

"Do tell, Captain Edgwin." Uba turned and walked over to the sensor display.

"Our weapons seem to be quiet effective," Edgwin said. "The *Icarus* fired eight Shrikes and four Hornets prior to their emergency jump. The result is two destroyed enemy ships and one that appears to be badly disabled."

"What?!" Uba exclaimed. He hadn't even been aware Wright had fired a shot. "Show me."

"The *Icarus* is being pursued by four of the enemy ships here," the sensor operator pointed to the icons on the display. "You can see they begin to redeploy and stagger their formation, we think in response to the *Icarus* firing a full spread of Shrikes."

"I see that," Uba said.

"Then the trailing two reversed course and disappeared, coming in right behind the *Icarus*," the operator continued. "Captain Wright snap-fired four Hornets and then the ship transitioned out of the Xi'an System."

"Which means Wright had already initiated the emergency jump protocols." Uba straightened. "Somehow she knew exactly what it meant when two of her pursuers broke off and reversed course."

"Yes, sir," Edgwin nodded. "Then the four Shrikes still actively tracking impacted here, and here. One target was obliterated and the other was torn nearly in half. The Shrike is a penetrator missile designed to be used against organic Phage hulls, but it appears to be quite effective against metal alloys as well."

"So it would appear," Uba agreed. "And then Wright's snap-fired Hornets also found their mark?"

"Yes, sir," the sensor operator said. "They must have launched under an auto-target protocol and all four went after the same target. It was adrift and tumbling along the original course before two other ships grappled onto it and disappeared."

"So they have tech that's quite a bit ahead of ours, but their ships can't take a punch," Uba said, tapping his upper lip with his index finger. "It seems both sides have learned something from this engagement. What's left in the system?"

"The wreckage of the two ships the *Icarus* destroyed, the wreckage of the *Vought*, and us," Edgwin said. "What are your orders?"

"Continue to observe for the time being," Uba said after a moment. "We'll begin to parse and package the data into one of the new direct-flight com drones and launch it within the hour for New Sierra. After we're absolutely certain we're alone we'll decide if we want to investigate the wreckage of our new friends or get out of here before they return or the ESA gets wind of what's happening here."

"I'll have a drone prepped immediately," Edgwin said. "Who do you think these guys were?"

"I couldn't begin to guess," Uba shook his head. "They *warned* us about interfering with something, but the fact they dragged the *Ares* all the way here for a sort of melodramatic display first just creates more questions than it answers."

"What is it with this star system?" the sensor operator muttered. Uba turned and walked off the bridge without answering, ducking through the low hatchway. So Wright had managed to take out two ships and bust up a third ... maybe he'd have to reevaluate his initial impression of her performance. It was true that Uba knew as much about captaining a starship as Wright likely did about being an agent, so perhaps his perspective was completely skewed. It didn't matter either way as an assessment of the Fleet's most successful and decorated starship captain was not within his purview. All he was required to do was compile the massive amount of data the Prowler had gathered, attach a synopsis, and forward it to CENTCOM where the analysts would draw their conclusions.

What he did know was that his gut was telling him this was not going to be an isolated occurrence and that humanity was likely about to face off with another enemy they were completely ill-prepared for. Maybe the critics were right. Maybe they had no right to be out this far and the policy of open and constant exploration and expansion may lead to their eventual extinction. They'd already run headlong into the Phage and won not by overwhelming force but by what most would concede was a lucky break. What were the chances they'd get another "lucky break" if this new challenger turned out to be as formidable as they appeared?

Chapter 6

"Position confirmed," the specialist first class at the nav station said. "We're on target in the DeLonges System."

"Normal com traffic is present," Ellison reported. "Picking up the New Sierra beacon loud and clear, condition normal."

"Very well," Commander Barrett said. "OPS, stow the warp drive and inform Engineering we're ready for main engines. Coms, begin getting the necessary clearances to fly directly to the New Sierra Platform and ask them to give us their preferred course down into the system."

"Aye, sir," Ellison said. Barrett had been shocked when he'd called Captain Wright's comlink to inform her they were about to transition into their destination system and she'd given a curt reply that she thought he could handle it.

She was starting to slip. Barrett could see the cracks in the façade as the reality of losing two starships with full crews began to sink in. During her time fighting the Phage she'd never been put in a position like that, and now Barrett feared she was compromised. The guilt and loss of confidence associated with that sort of defeat wasn't something all commanders were able to get over. He had watched his former captain, Jackson Wolfe, go through something similar after the Battle of Nuovo Patria. While Captain Wright was handling it with a bit more grace, he couldn't help but be concerned that she might not snap out of it.

"Priority com traffic coming in now, sir," Ellison said. "Some addressed specifically to the captain but most is just general alert messages."

"Go through it and give me a breakdown of what you think I need to know," Barrett said, not wanting to be distracted while he was about to fly the *Icarus* down into the heavy traffic of the world many assumed would be the new capital.

"The rest of the taskforce was able to escape," Ellison reported with obvious relief in his voice. "They've launched com drones ahead but they're not due in for another week. We have confirmation from the Prowler that we destroyed two enemy ships and disabled one ... no word in the mix about the *Leighton*."

"Anything in there about our approach priority?" Barrett asked.

"No, sir," Ellison said. "We're being told to queue in behind normal traffic; they're sending up target coordinates now. Apparently there's another group of ships due in soon that has priority over us."

"That has to be the delegation to the Ushin," Accari said.

"The who?" Barrett turned to look at the OPS officer.

"Shit," Accari muttered before raising his voice. "Unofficially, I've heard that's the name of the new species we've made contact with. It's either what we call them or what they call themselves. Anyway, the only group of ships I could imagine that would have a higher priority than us would be the *Amsterdam*, the *John Arden*, and their escort."

"In addition to being *very* interested where you're getting your unofficial intel, Ensign, I'm inclined to agree," Barrett said. "Why don't you go ahead and verify our intel package and mission logs and send those to Coms so that it can be retransmitted and verified by New Sierra before they have to ask for it."

"Aye, sir," Accari said. They'd already transmitted the encrypted intel package at every waypoint on the flight back, including expending one of their next generation com drones that was capable of point-to-point warp flight instead of having to relay a message through each system's platform via the established warp lanes. The new drones were abhorrently expensive and Fleet wasn't all that enthusiastic about increasing the drone traffic in most systems, so they were to be used under emergency circumstances only. Captain Wright had felt a second alien invasion into the Xi'an System qualified.

Barrett was happy to learn that all the other ships in the taskforce had been able to escape. The loss of two was still devastating, but it could have been much worse. Just as he was about to send a runner to go and physically knock on the hatch to Captain Wright's quarters, he looked over when he detected motion at the bridge hatchway. There stood Celesta Wright, sharp-eyed and in an impeccable set of utilities.

"I have the bridge, XO," she said as she walked around, inspecting each station. "I'm sure I can get turnover from OPS, so why don't you go and get some rack time. I'll need you fresh and alert when it comes time to dock."

"Aye aye, ma'am," Barrett said crisply, hoping his voice masked the relief he felt. As per his unofficial duty as executive officer, he'd taken it upon himself to deflect and absorb from the crew in order to protect his captain during an understandable moment of weakness. Celesta Wright had earned that sort of loyalty from him during their time serving on the *Blue Jacket* together and then later when she'd approached CENTCOM and lobbied specifically for him as her new XO with the declared intention of grooming him for command.

He vacated the command seat, grabbing his tile and comlink as he did, and marched off the bridge on his way to his quarters. While the fact Captain Wright had come back on duty looking like she was more than fit for command was a relief, Barrett still had some lingering worries about her. He'd replayed the engagement in his mind over and over and he didn't see anything that she should have done differently given the information that had been available at the time. He just hoped that eventually she'd see it that way and that at some critical moment in the future she wouldn't hesitate or doubt herself. Only time would tell.

****

"My word!"

"Look at her!"

"How did they make it all the way back?"

The *Icarus* had been in a holding orbit for the last four days, slowly flying around New Sierra while waiting for the flight with the higher priority to arrive. It turned out Accari had been correct about which ships would be incoming, but the condition of those ships was a total shock.

The *Amsterdam*, a true battleship and the Fleet's mightiest warship, limped by, flying underneath the *Icarus* on her way to one of the enclosed docks. The hull was scorched and blackened in places and she was streaming atmosphere from no less than twenty gaping rents in the hull. Most noticeably, however, was that one of the two massive outriggers that flanked the main hull and housed the main engines and sensors was missing. The pylons, also streaming atmosphere and sparking occasionally, looked like they were deformed as if melted.

"I wonder who did this," Celesta said as she stood near the main display and took it all in. "Our new friends, our new enemies, or has the ESA decided now would be a good time to expand their territory."

"The ESA doesn't field a ship that can take on a *Dreadnought*-class battleship," Barrett said.

"That we know of," Celesta corrected.

"Captain, Admiral Marcum requests your presence on the New Sierra Platform in ... six hours," Ellison called out, checking the difference between ship's time and that of New Sierra. "He'd like you to take a shuttle; the *Icarus* isn't being given clearance to dock."

"Confirmed, ma'am," Accari said. "I've just been given a request that we vacate our current orbit after you depart. The *Icarus* is to join a holding formation over DeLonges."

"This should be interesting," Celesta said. "Ensign Accari, have Flight OPS prep a shuttle. After that, get your relief up here and get yourself packed, you're coming with me. Be quick about it because you're also going down to CIC to sign out a secure tile with all of our logs and intel packages on it."

"Yes, ma'am."

She turned to her XO. "Commander Barrett, while I would like you there as well I think you realize that you're going to have to stay in command of the *Icarus* while I'm gone."

"Of course, Captain," Barrett nodded.

****

"While I normally like to work big to small, let me take the opportunity to make an official announcement regarding our elected government." Admiral Marcum walked in, beginning his comments before he was even through the door. Celesta rose with the others and noted that the admiral looked a little worse for wear and was even sporting a few bandages on his head.

"The com drones will be carrying the news far and wide in a few hours, but I've just received word the New Sierra Accords have been agreed upon and ratified by ninety-seven percent of the delegates. We are now operating under a new charter within the Terran Federated Planets, or the Terran Federation. That's actually the last sticking point they were working out when I got off the com with President-elect Augustus Wellington. We only lost one star system that may, or may not, decide to entreat the Eastern Star Alliance for membership." A smattering of applause kicked off a full ovation until Marcum irritably waved everyone to silence.

"Shut up and sit down, all of you. The universe has decided to take another heaping shit on us while we're still digging out from the last one. You may have noticed that I arrived on two-thirds of what was once the Terran Starfleet's flagship … I am here to tell you it was only by the grace of God and the quick thinking of Captain Everett that we were able to fend off the attack. As it turns out they came light because we weren't the intended target; our new allies were. Captain Wright, as I understand it you took the brunt of what they intended for us."

"I'm afraid I'm not able to give an answer to that due to lack of perspective, Admiral," Celesta said. "But we were hit with a numerically superior force in what appears to be a trap set specifically for us."

"Yes, I've read your mission logs," Marcum nodded slowly. "At least you made them bleed. We'll be having a private briefing immediately following this, so for now allow me to disseminate all information as you may not be aware of what's been classified need-to-know."

"Of course, Admiral."

The next two hours were a rehash of portions of the *Icarus's* encounter as well as a brief of the attack on the delegation sent to the Ushin, as they were now officially referred to. The battle of two alien ships against a single Terran battleship was heartening. The *Amsterdam* was ambushed and took most of her damage in that opening salvo, but Captain Everett was fast on his feet and came back out swinging. He destroyed the first target with a single Shrike and then ran down the other, peppering it with laser fire until he hit something critical. As an interesting aside it was the first kill by a Terran starship with a tactical laser in the entire history of the organization. The entire Phage War had been fought with missiles and ferrous shells out of mag cannons.

"So that's the good news," Marcum said, setting his water glass down with a bang hard enough that it fell over and spilled. "Goddamn it," he growled. "My hand is still numb from being flung about on the bridge.

"As I was saying ... that's the good news: Unlike the Phage that waltzed in and shrugged off nearly everything we threw at them, this enemy seems to be on par with us technologically with a few exceptions. The fact our lasers can burn through their hulls and our missiles can down their ships is heartening.

"The bad news, other than the fact another species has decided to kick us in the teeth, is that they now know everything we do. These opening engagements are learning experiences for both sides. Not only that, but they've captured one of our ships and, obsolete or not, the *Leighton* and her crew will likely be able to give them far more additional intel about us than we'll be able to gain about them."

Celesta looked away, feeling her cheeks burning. She was still bitterly angry with herself for the loss of two ships but doubly so for the loss of the *Leighton*. Not only was the crew likely already dead, but she'd given the enemy a treasure trove of information about them. When she looked back, Admiral Marcum was staring right at her with an unreadable expression. He nodded slowly once to her before continuing.

"There is one more thing we'll address in this preliminary meeting, possibly the more important as it has implications for what we do going forward," he continued. "Our new friends, the Ushin, know who this new species is. They call them the Darshik, though I'm probably not saying it right. Communications with the Ushin are still in their infancy and it is very, very difficult to sometimes get even simple concepts across. You'll all have a series of briefings on them in the coming days, but suffice it to say that even though they communicate audibly with each other that's where the similarities end. Their vocalization organs can't even mimic our phonetic sounds and vice versa. All you need to know for now is that they *are* our allies and the Darshik problem will not be going away on its own. That's all for now … dismissed. Captain Wright, please remain."

Celesta remained seated while the others filed out, most avoiding looking at her, but the ones who made eye contact telegraphed either curiosity or sympathy, the latter setting her nerves on edge.

"Let's go somewhere a bit more practical than this enormous room full of CIS listening devices," Marcum said. "Grab your ensign out in the passageway and we'll go to my office."

"Yes, sir," Celesta said automatically and followed him out the door.

The admiral's staff, along with Celesta and Accari, made their way down the wide, sweeping corridors of the facility past many curious onlookers before passing through the security checkpoint that led to the station's command and control section. When Jericho Station had been lost, Marcum had moved his offices to the New Sierra Shipyards, an enormous orbital production facility, and had promptly set about refitting the sleepy, civilian-controlled platform into a bustling hub from which he controlled Fleet operations. Many of the production slips had been converted to maintenance berths and most of the ships docked on the outrigger arms were simply parked there, not even being serviced. Celesta had been concerned about the fact that their largest ship-building facility had been absorbed by CENTCOM at a time when they needed ships built more than they needed paper pushed, but she'd been told with a wink and a nod that it was all under control.

"Have a seat, all of you," Marcum said as the door closed and locked. He motioned Celesta to the seat across from his desk. "So we're all agreed that it was really the *Ares* the Darshik dragged all the way back to Xi'an?"

"Yes, Admiral," Celesta spoke up. "Several former crewmen, including Ensign Accari, positively identified her from the damage she took that prevented her from coming back home."

"If Wolfe had properly scuttled the ship *like he was supposed to* we wouldn't have this problem,"

Marcum growled, rubbing at his receding hairline with the palms of his hand.

"I disagree, Admiral," Admiral Pitt said, walking into the office from a room off to the side that Celesta hadn't noticed before. "The location of Wolfe's derelict was highly classified and it was a system of no interest save for the Phage core mind that had been hiding there. We must assume that the Darshik found the *Ares* due to some connection to the Phage. That's likely going to be an important fact later."

"Thanks for stealing my thunder, Pitt," Marcum snapped. "Okay ... yes, we know the Darshik have a connection with the Phage, but not the one you're probably thinking. Do those in this office with the proper security clearance remember the message Wolfe got at the end of the Battle of Nuovo Patria?"

"Something about a test being concluded," Celesta said, trying to remember the exact phrasing.

"Our Vruahn friends had told us this was unprecedented, but that wasn't necessarily true," Marcum continued. "While I doubt Colonel Blake, or the copy of him, lied to us, we know that his area of operation was very limited ... we've also learned that the Phage were everywhere, and when I say that I mean *everywhere.* We were so damn lucky that it's almost comical. Many species far more advanced than us fell before them."

"What do you mean '*We've also learned*' ... learned from where?" Pitt asked.

"The Ushin were also selected to be purged by the Phage," Marcum said. "They almost succeeded, but the Phage had to pull resources to deal with a new threat that ended up being a bigger pain in the ass than they thought."

"Us," Celesta said.

"Us," Marcum nodded. "The fight we put up during that war caused the Phage to temporarily abandon the Ushin, likely with the intent of crushing us in a blitz and then moving back to finish them. Thanks to Wolfe and Blake getting to the core mind that never happened.

"So ... that brings me to another interesting, highly classified bit of information. We didn't stumble across the Ushin, they came to us. They've known about us since we started pushing our borders out, but our environmental preferences are so different we weren't going to be competing for the same habitable planets, so they ignored us. The remaining Ushin know that we killed the Phage off for good and they want to repay us in some way, so they tracked our automated survey drones and waited for a crewed mission to show up to one of their planets."

"What can they offer?" Pitt asked, leaning forward.

"No idea," Marcum shrugged. "We have petabytes of data from the first contact team, and I can't make heads or tails of any of it. They appear to be much more technologically advanced than us, but from what I can tell they don't have shit for weaponry. Talking to the ambassador's team, I get the impression two-way communication between us is still very clunky and it'll be some time before high-level concepts can be discussed."

"Fair enough." Pitt leaned back on the couch. "So who are the Darshik?"

"They're the other side of the coin," Marcum said, flipping through some notes on his tile. "Ah, there we go. Okay, so the Darshik controlled six or ten star systems—you see what I mean about communication being tough—that butted up against what the Ushin recognized as their outer boundary. The Phage found them and began sterilizing their worlds before, inexplicably, they stopped. Two planets were spared: their homeworld and a second habitable colony world in the same system. This is where it gets a little muddy, but apparently the Phage issued the same 'test' and the results were different, thus the species was spared.

"The damage to the Darshik collective psyche, however, didn't fare so well. They became isolationists and then they began a sort of quasi-worship of the Phage, apparently convinced the fuckers were actually *protecting* them, if you can believe that."

"And then along comes humanity and kills their idol?" Celesta guessed.

"We're not sure of the timeline but that's our assumption," Marcum nodded. "It raises some disturbing questions, however. Like how did they know where the core mind was located, and how did they know where we were located?"

"Vruahn help?" Ensign Accari spoke up, looking stricken as he realized how inappropriate it was for him to speak without being prompted first.

"We don't think so, Ensign." Marcum showed no sign of annoyance at having a junior officer interrupt his stream of consciousness. "One of the things we were able to glean from the Ushin is that the Darshik weren't just left alone after the initial Phage assault; it seems they had continued contact with them, or it ... I still have trouble considering the Phage a singular entity."

"This makes more and more sense," Pitt nodded. "The Phage wasn't omnipotent. What better way to get the lay of local space and have defensible fallback locations than to find a willing partner? If the 'test' was to find a species with the traits it wanted in order to use them, then it explains why Blake had never heard of it. The Vruahn may have but they kept all the Colonel Blakes under tight control, so it's not something they'd likely pass on to him ... them."

Celesta almost smiled at his correction. Like most people who had interacted with Colonel Robert Blake during the war, she had trouble coming to terms with the fact that he was a manufactured copy of an ancient Earth explorer, one of many that the Vruahn had used to try and tame their runaway creation: the Phage. Before coming clean about having created such a devastating lifeform, the Vruahn had been cloning humans to fight the Phage in an attempt to mitigate the harm it was causing. Once it became obvious that holding action wasn't going to be enough, they stepped up their support of the human-led war.

"Captain Wolfe told me the core mind didn't die quickly." Celesta was talking before her brain could stop her mouth. "If there was a Phage unit in contact with the Darshik at the time of its death, it's possible that it passed on our location to them in its final moments. What if it did that with ten other species, a hundred?"

"Whoa!" Marcum almost shouted and raised both hands. "Let's throttle back here, Senior Captain ... we'll leave the wild speculation to the eggheads and we'll do what we do: deal with the immediate military threat. Lieutenant Emerson, write that down as an action item anyway," he said to his aide, a shapely young officer that was standing conspicuously close to Ensign Accari. "We don't have to chase that rabbit down the hole ourselves, but we'll pass on anything of interest."

"I think it's probably nothing," Celesta said, rethinking her comment. "Because if it is then the 'warning' we received makes no sense. What are we interfering with?"

"They're aliens, Captain," Pitt said. "It's a damn miracle they can talk to us at all, as our recent interactions with the Ushin prove. Let's not throw away a solid theory based on the wording of a message transmitted by another species."

"Did all this intel come from the Ushin?" Celesta asked.

"Most of it," Marcum said evasively. "We've been developing other channels of information in parallel. But for now I think that about wraps this up ... everyone but Captain Wright is dismissed. Don't leave the station, though. We have a lot to do before we respond to the attacks on our ships and people. Get out of here. That includes you, Admiral Pitt."

Once everyone had filed out and the door clanged shut again, Marcum leaned back in his seat.

"Now to discuss what I called you in here for in the first place," he said.

Celesta had fully expected this. Her abysmal performance in the Xi'an System had to be addressed. She fully expected to be knocked back down a rank from senior captain and it was entirely likely she'd lose the *Icarus*.

"I want you on a *Dreadnought*," Marcum said.

"Am I to serve aboard the *Amsterdam*, Admiral?"

"What? No, I'm not replacing Captain Everett nor am I demoting you, Celesta," Marcum said. "Yes, you could have performed better as taskforce commander, but you could also have done a hell of a lot worse. We'll debrief you fully on that later, but the important thing is that you've again showed that killer instinct I remember and love so well from the war. I want to put you on the bridge of a boomer and the *New York* is in need of a competent CO if we're heading back into a fight."

"I'm not sure what to say, Admiral." Celesta was stunned. Commanding a battleship was what every warship captain aspired to whether they admitted it or not. The *New York* was one of the new *Dreadnought*-class ships that were of the same generation as her own *Starwolf*-class destroyer. Her face twitched as she momentarily thought of her ship.

"What would happen to the *Icarus*?"

"It will be captained by an officer of appropriate rank and experience," Marcum said coolly. "I know she's your first command, Celesta, but that ship belongs to the Terran Federation. It'll be up to CENTCOM as to whose ass goes in the seat; more specifically it'll be up to me. While I'm open to suggestions, I don't want to give the impression that you have any sway once you're out of Ninth Squadron."

"That's not what I meant, sir," Celesta said hurriedly. "What I meant to say was is this a mandatory transfer?"

"You're .... you're actually thinking of turning down a top-of-the-line battleship?" Marcum's mouth was hanging open. "What is it that makes you destroyer captains all batshit crazy? Or was it simply the proximity to Wolfe for too long that scrambled your good sense?" He sucked in a breath and let it out slowly.

"The *New York* is still inbound," he said quietly. "Please take a couple days to think it over and we'll talk again."

"Thank you, Admiral," Celesta said uncomfortably, rising as she realized that had been a dismissal. "I really am honored you think—"

"Just keep this in mind," Marcum cut her off. "I place people where they can do the Fleet the most good, and by extension where they can do the Federation the most good, and by further extension where they can do humanity the most good. Your loyalty to your ship and crew is commendable, but as a Starfleet officer you have a higher duty. Dismissed, Senior Captain."

Chapter 7

Celesta had to constantly keep referring to the updated map on her comlink as she walked the corridors of the immense station. New Sierra was quite a bit larger than even Jericho Station had been due to the fact it had been built for heavy construction and large-scale production rather than maintenance and administration. CENTCOM had hastily converted the shipyard to its new headquarters, a move Celesta still didn't understand. The ability to quickly field new starships seemed far more important than housing the administrative arm of the Fleet. For that matter, why did they even need to be in orbit at all? Housing and headquartering them on the planet's surface seemed much more practical. She sighed as she walked. The war had taught them many hard lessons, but apparently they still had a long way to go.

She'd been walking down to the docking arm complex to meet the *New York* when she was docked, but her chirping comlink kept distracting her. It was a repeating text-only message from an unknown address asking that she make her way to crew processing as quickly as possible. All official Fleet communications were specifically formatted so she assumed the messages were either a glitch or something else. Either way, she ignored them. The next anonymous message, however, she couldn't ignore.

Damnit Wright... you'd have made a shitty intel officer. Get down to crew processing and wait there. I need to speak with you immediately.

She began to have suspicions about who was playing games with the com system, so when she was almost to the arching entry that led to the crew processing section she was surprised when it was Agent Uba who intercepted her.

"You certainly took your time, Captain." He grabbed her by the elbow and forcefully led her down a side corridor, looking about as he did to see if he was being noticed. He was wearing a Marine uniform that Celesta assumed was meant to allow him to blend in since the Terran Marine Corp was providing security on New Sierra for the time being.

"You promoted yourself to major?" Celesta asked.

"Actually I'm a full colonel, so call it a demotion," Uba said without a trace of humor. "Majors are not only ubiquitous but are largely ignored or actively avoided. A colonel, on the other hand, is too memorable."

"What's this about?" Celesta asked, yanking her arm out of the agent's hand as they marched down the service corridor.

"Someone needs to speak with you off the record," Uba said. "Through there." He was pointing at an unmarked door identical to the other half-dozen or so that dotted the corridor. Celesta, not for a moment thinking she was in any danger, walked up and opened the door, stepping into what looked like a recently vacated equipment closet given the amount of wiring dangling from the overhead tracks.

"You have some aversion to answering your messages?"

"Pike," Celesta said flatly as way of greeting the impeccably dressed man standing in front of her. "Or is it Lynch?"

"Pike wearing Lynch's clothes right now," Pike said. "I understand you've just been given command of the *New York*. I suppose congratulations are in order."

"I haven't accepted yet," Celesta said. "I get the feeling the appointment may be more about politics than my ability to command."

"Of course it's about politics," Pike said. "Any decision about who is commanding a battleship is always political. Marcum wants her current CO gone. Actually, he'd like the moron prosecuted, but he'll settle for drummed out of the chair in disgrace. The details why aren't important. He also thinks he can push you through as the replacement, a war hero whom he has a personal working relationship with ... the newly formed Parliament wouldn't even pause to sign off on the posting."

"Parliament?"

"I think they've changed the names of the old institutions just for the sake of change," Pike shrugged. "If you walk around down there it's the same old people playing the same old games. There's actually a strange sort of comfort from it."

"So why all the skulking about?" Celesta asked, wanting to get to the point despite the fact she was happy to have any chance to see Pike at all. The pair weren't exactly romantically involved, but there was a mutual interest that had blossomed during their time together when it seemed the agent was always popping up where the ship she served aboard happened to be. But, both were far too driven with their work to make any sort of time for a relationship.

"Aston Lynch was asked by the President-elect to come up and meet with a few CENTCOM officials to begin the transition of civilian oversight from the old Confederacy to the new and improved Federation," Pike said. "And no, I'm not actually performing the duties of a real aide ... I needed to speak with Marcum alone and his time is as regimented now as Wellington's, not to mention all the eyes that report on his movements.

"Anyway, when you were in there with him and Pitt, was the term *Prometheus* brought up at all?"

"No, it wasn't," Celesta shook her head. "What is it?"

"In addition to being a mythological figure out of Earth's very ancient past, it's the codename of a project that's being run so black that I can't even figure out who the principals are or where it is," Pike said.

"Why are you asking me?" Celesta said. "I spend all my time on the bridge of a starship on patrol, not sitting in oversight meetings about Fleet projects."

"Marcum knows what it is and we think he's being fed information out of that project that pertains to the situation with the Ushin and the Darshik," Pike said, his tone deadly serious. "This coincides with rumors of secret shipyards putting out a new generation of starship far more advanced than anything flying currently *and* the disappearance of your old boss."

"What do you mean 'disappearance?'" Celesta asked. "Jackson Wolfe is back on Earth ... I just talked to Jillian a few months ago."

"You may have talked to her, but she wasn't on Earth at the time." Pike shook his head. "Jillian and the children also packed up and moved to Arcadia while the provisional government was setting up before New Sierra was selected as the capital. She was heading up the training program for a new branch of service last I heard, but Jackson isn't there with her. It could all just be marital troubles, but it's a bit too convenient for my liking."

"This feels like you're chasing ghosts," Celesta scoffed. "Have you even been back to The Ark recently?" She was referring to a once-ultra secret planet that had recently been renamed 'Arcadia,' in some sort of not-so-subtle tribute to the lost planet of Haven. Personally she thought the name was ridiculous as well as being just a lazy phonetic extrapolation.

"I just returned," Pike said. "And you're probably right, but just the name *Prometheus* leads me to believe that someone involved is likely from Earth. That's just not a name that crops up in the enclaves and those who have heard of it are clueless about the reference."

"So what do you need from me that requires this sort of cloak and dagger routine?"

"I just wanted to know if you've heard of this program from Marcum. Even if you won't tell me the specifics I just need some direction to begin digging," Pike said. "I also wanted to know if the communications you had with your old CO were at all ... odd."

"I can tell you with complete transparency that I have not heard that name before you uttered it, and I've had no strange interactions with Captain Wolfe," she said. "In fact, we haven't spoken since his retirement was official. I'd heard that he and Jillian had married and had twins, but they were on Earth and the *Icarus* was on the Confederacy-ESA border patrolling."

"I see," Pike said. "I suppose it was too much to hope for that you had heard of the program and would willingly divulge classified information to me. Well ... now that business is out of the way, it seems a shame to waste this private closet since we're both here—"

"You never change." Celesta tried to inject a tone of disgust into her voice but failed, breaking into a laugh at the end. "As much fun as your offer sounds, Agent Pike, I have to be going. The tugs will have the

New York on her final approach as we speak and I'd like to at least lay eyes on her before I tell Marcum whether I accept or not."

"Make your choice carefully, Captain," Pike said seriously. "While it's within your right to refuse a transfer, if you piss off Marcum too badly you may find yourself in command of nothing."

"Thank you for the concern," Celesta said coldly as she opened the door and walked out. She was irritated not at Pike, but at herself for not realizing that command of the *Icarus* was not a given. If she turned down Marcum it might not be too much longer before he pulled her off the destroyer's bridge and put her in one of the infamous billets saved for officers who needed to be warehoused until they either served out their time and retired or simply resigned. With the prospect of a new fight on the horizon with another unknown alien species she couldn't afford to be so selfish, Fleet needed as many commanders with combat experience as it could get.

As she left the lower administrative decks she thought back to Pike's suspicions that Wolfe had something to do with this hypothetical "Prometheus" project. The agent was many things, but being prone to flights of fancy was not one of them. She knew that if he was fishing for information she might have then he had already put many of the pieces together himself, even if he wasn't sharing. If Wolfe was involved in it, why? Pike had made it sound like it was more of a research initiative and Wolfe, for as good as he was at operations and tactics, didn't have much experience or ambition in that arena.

With great effort, she pushed the entire mess from the front of her mind. She had no way to get in touch with her former captain, and even if she did she wasn't about to approach him about a project that was so clandestine the new President didn't even know about it. There was nothing to do about it and she had much more pressing matters to concentrate on. The last thought that flitted through her mind on the subject was how it was strange that after nearly half a decade of no news or contact the legacy of Jackson Wolfe was once again thrust into the limelight. From the final destruction of the *Ares* to his name being associated with a black project that sounded like it could also be illegal, and with the prospect of a new war looming in the background ... Celesta rarely ignored her instincts and at that moment they were telling her that her mentor was not going to be able to enjoy the quiet life of a retired Fleet officer that much longer.

****

Meeting the *New York* at the dock had been a disaster. Celesta had been given priority when she'd been spotted and, under mild protest, had been moved from the gallery to near the gangway. She spotted Captain Lee, the officer she recognized as having commanded the heavy missile cruiser, *Brooklands*, during the Phage War and gave him a friendly wave. The cold, almost hostile look she received in return shocked her as Lee gave her a perfunctory nod before pressing past her and into the waiting delegation from New America that had been standing ready to welcome the ship home.

"Don't take it personally, Captain," the *New York*'s XO said as she approached. Celesta remembered her face but couldn't recall her name or place where they'd met before. "Captain Lee is a good CO and I think he was under the assumption he was going to be named as the permanent replacement for NY's big chair."

"And he resents some politically connected usurper stealing his seat," Celesta finished. "Well, Commander, you may inform Lee he can rest a bit easier knowing that I won't be the one replacing him ... but someone will be." And with that she made her decision. She would do whatever she had to do to remain on the bridge of the *Icarus* even if someone else was brought in to take overall command of Ninth Squadron.

With the numbered fleets organizing back to their original states, mostly, she had no desire to leave Black Fleet and be assigned to Fourth Fleet, especially given the fragile political state the newly minted Federation found itself in while, against all odds, finding itself immediately on the brink of war. Now the real trick would be to find a way to get Admiral Marcum to see things her way. Deciding that sooner would be better than later, she pulled out her comlink and tried contacting Marcum's office to make an appointment for a face-to-face.

Surprisingly, she was told that the admiral would not have time to see her in the foreseeable future and that all planned briefings for the next few days had been cancelled. She checked her messages and saw that she had received no new orders either telling her to remain aboard the New Sierra Platform or to report to the *New York* for orientation. She'd always enjoyed a direct line to the top levels of CENTCOM given her status after the Phage War, so she had to assume that she wasn't the only one being given the runaround.

Her suspicions were somewhat confirmed when Admiral Pitt's staff also informed her that the flag officer would be unavailable for the next few days. Just as she was about to try and see if one of the multiple comlink codes she had for Pike would go through, she had an incoming request from Accari.

"Go ahead, Ensign," she said.

"*Ma'am, I just received word from the Icarus ... an Ushin formation has appeared in the system,*" her OPS officer said. "*From what Commander Barrett was able to gather, they weren't invited. He told me that CENTCOM has been locking down communications to and from the other ships in orbit trying to keep a lid on it.*"

"Where are you?" Celesta was moving against the rush of people all coming down to get a look at the *Dreadnought*-class ship.

"*In billeting,*" Accari said. "*I can no longer raise the Icarus from my personal comlink either.*"

"Stand by until I send word, but be ready to move," Celesta said. "Don't draw any attention to yourself, though. Just put on the uniform of the day, and when I tell you, move your ass with all due haste to *where* I tell you. Wright out." She flipped through a couple of menus before selecting a code she thought looked most promising and tried to open a channel.

"*You reconsider my closet offer, Captain? I'm a little pressed for time at the moment but I could—*"

"I need to get back to my ship," Celesta said.

"*Ah, look, Celesta ... there have been some—*"

"I know what's happening and I know they're locking down the station. I want you to find a way to put me on the *Icarus*," she pressed.

"*Couldn't you ask for a simpler favor?*" Pike asked plaintively and it sounded like he was trying to keep his voice muffled. She could barely make out other voices in the background, most shouting excitedly.

"Damnit, Pike! If you—"

"*Lower your voice!*" Pike hissed. "*I'm not even supposed to be here right now. Listen … get down to Maintenance Dock Delta-Delta-Four and go to auxiliary airlock hatch six-oh-two.*"

"Delta-Delta-Four, six-oh-two," Celesta repeated back.

"*Enter alpha-nine-one-seven into the keypad to get into the airlock,*" Pike continued. "*I'm sending a scan code to your comlink; just hold the display up to the hatch once you're in the airlock.*"

"Is this to what I think it is?" Celesta asked. "I'm assuming it won't just let me take off even if I knew how."

"*I'm sending it instructions now,*" Pike said. "*It'll take you to the Icarus and then make its way back here for me. This one is a bit different than the gen-one. You really only have to tell it what to do; there's not much in the way of actual controls. Look, I can't talk right now … just follow my instructions and tell it what you want. It really is that easy.*" The channel went dead and Celesta wasted no time forwarding the information to Accari before pulling up the map of the station again to figure out where the hell the maintenance docks were.

Thankfully, they were just two lift rides away; down eleven decks and about half a kilometer of walking and she was there. She was shocked that Accari was already waiting there, looking slightly winded.

"You made good time, Ensign," she said.

"Yes, ma'am," Accari breathed. "There's a cargo lift that runs the entire span of the platform, from the maintenance docks all the way to the com center at the top. I asked another ensign that worked in Logistics if I could use it."

"A word of advice, Ensign Accari," Celesta said as she keyed in the code to open the airlock's inner hatch. "An admiral's aide is not the type of person you want holding a personal vendetta ... unless you like assignments to the listening posts they're putting up all along the ESA border systems." Accari looked like he was going to protest, thought better of it, and then just nodded.

"Understood, ma'am," he said simply. "Although the ensign in Logistics approached me—"

"That was not an invitation to discuss your love life, Ensign," Celesta said sharply, rolling her eyes as the hatch opened with a sharp *pop*. "Now get in before someone sees us."

"Yes, ma'am," Accari said again, this time his cheeks flaming red. Celesta just shook her head as she stepped into the small chamber and resealed the airlock door after her.

Chapter 8

"Is this what I think it is?" Accari asked as he walked around the smallish main area of the ship.

"Yes," Celesta said distractedly. "You're standing in the main cabin of a Tsuyo Corporation Broadhead II, one of only three known to be in existence." The original Broadheads were small, stealthy ships that the Tsuyo Corp had made available to certain governmental agencies as well as a few well-placed and extraordinarily wealthy civilian clients. It had packed a lot of speed, sensor capability and a modest arsenal in a miniscule package. Agent Pike had been assigned one of those original ships and Celesta had heard a rumor that his had logged more flight hours than any of the other Broadhead hulls combined by over a factor of ten.

Now, apparently, his connections with the new incoming President gave him access to Tsuyo's latest and greatest, and Celesta had to admit, she was impressed. She slid into the luxurious pilot's seat and gave the minimalist instrument panel the onceover. The ship had accepted the scan code Pike had provided and an animated icon floated across one of the displays, letting her know it was ready to accept commands.

"Activate interface," Celesta commanded. Instantly the terminals winked on and began shuffling pertinent information around the enormous, one-piece curved glass display. She reached out and began shuffling the individual readouts to where she wanted them.

"Find the *TCS Icarus*," she said. "She'll be in orbit near DeLonges."

"*TFS Icarus located*," the ship responded in a pleasant baritone, correcting her on the fact the destroyer was now a Terran *Federation* Ship and the Confederacy no longer owned her. Celesta had half expected the voice to be young and female knowing Pike the way she did.

"Can you bypass the system-wide com lockdown and get me a direct channel to the bridge?"

"*Affirmative. Shall I initiate ship-to-ship channel now?*"

"If you please," Celesta said politely.

"*This is the Terran Federation Warship, Icarus. Please identify yourself and state your intentions.*" Lieutenant Ellison's voice came over the speakers after a bit of a lag.

"This is Captain Wright, please patch me through to Commander Barrett," Celesta said, waiting for the fifteen-minute com lag again.

"Good thing the orbits put the two at their closest point," Accari said as he sat in the other chair on the small bridge. "Otherwise the com lag would be nearly an hour."

"Indeed," Celesta agreed.

"*This is Barrett, Captain,*" Barrett's voice came back. "*We're currently in a holding orbit over DeLonges in formation with ten other ships, only two of them Fleet warships. The Icarus is FMC and we've even been replenished in flight: fuel, propellant, and replacement missiles were flown in from Bespitd Depot. Ready to receive orders, ma'am.*"

Celesta smiled. Instead of wasting time with idle back and forth with such a long com lag, Barrett had supplied her with their position, ship status, and that they were ready if she needed them. Once again she patted herself on the back for insisting that the former tactical officer be promoted and assigned as her XO.

"Very good, Commander," Celesta said as her hands danced over the display. "I'm sending you a set of coordinates that will put you beyond the orbit of the fourth planet. Take the *Icarus* there, hold position and go silent. Anti-collision beacon only, no Fleet transponder codes for now. I'm on my way to you. Wright out."

"We're flying this thing out there, ma'am?" Accari asked.

"We're certainly not sitting in this cramped ship for our own amusement, Ensign," Celesta said. "Ship, calculate a flight plan to the coordinates I just sent over the ship-to-ship channel and prepare us for departure."

"*Flight plan calculated and ready to execute,*" the ship said. "*Powerplant online, main engines online, navigation sensors online. When do you wish to depart?*"

"Immediately," Celesta said, wishing every piece of Tsuyo tech was so agreeable. "Then prepare to dock with a *Starwolf*-class destroyer when we reach our destination."

"*Understood,*" the ship· said. "*Beginning decoupling procedure. New Sierra security has locked down all departures. Would you like to bypass normal security protocols?*"

"Affirmative," Celesta said, hoping that everyone was indeed too busy to look too closely at where she might have disappeared to.

"*Stand by,*" the ship said. "*Security bypass successful. Decoupling and engaging main drive on new course.*"

There were some bumps and bangs that reverberated through the small ship as it disengaged the mooring locks holding it to the station. Celesta watched as they drifted downward relative to the enormous platform on small puffs of gas from the attitude jets. Once they'd drifted down enough to clear the other docking complex that had been dead ahead and a small antenna cluster off their port side there was a smooth, deep hum and the ship surged away from the New Sierra Platform.

"I'll be damned," she said. "Reactionless drive ... and one that actually works."

****

"*Icarus*, arriving," the computer intoned over the shipwide intercom when Celesta stepped through the hatchway of the auxiliary starboard airlock followed by Ensign Accari.

"Is Agent Pike with you, ma'am?" Commander Barrett asked after Celesta had returned his offered salute.

"No, he was nice enough to let me borrow his ship though since they locked down New Sierra," Celesta said. "Are we secure here?"

"Yes, ma'am."

"Then let's go to CIC and you're going to show me what's been going on in this system while I was stuck playing politics," she said, marching away so quickly her two officers had to rush to catch up. "Not you, Ensign," she said over her shoulder. "Go to the bridge and keep an eye out at OPS. We'll have an overview brief for the bridge crew later."

"Aye aye, ma'am," Accari said, peeling away and heading for the lifts.

When Celesta walked into the CIC, which was actually called the Combat Operations Center but oddly referred to by the different acronym, she was pleased that it was a hive of activity and her crew was well on top of the new situation.

"Captain on deck!" a senior chief bellowed when he looked up from where he was looking over a spacer first class's terminal.

"As you were!" Celesta barked before the others could extricate themselves from behind their stations.

"Officer of the watch! Front and center," Barrett spoke as he walked into the dimly lit room.

"Lieutenant Commander Washburn, CIC Operations Officer, sir," a tall, graceful officer with ebony skin said as she came around from behind the enormous tabletop holographic display. Celesta smiled briefly at the memory of Captain Wolfe, who had helped finalize the design for the *Starwolf*-class ships, digging in firmly and refusing to allow holographic displays to be installed. But unlike her predecessor, who had thought them an unnecessary and distracting gimmick, Celesta was delighted by the detail the holographic displays could provide in three dimensions and promptly had them installed in all the Ninth Squadron ships when she'd been promoted.

"Double watch, Lieutenant Commander?" Barrett asked with a slight smile.

"I wasn't comfortable leaving with the captain absent and alien ships coming uninvited into a Terran system, sir," Washburn said. Celesta nodded her approval and gestured to the display.

"Can you catch me up on what's been happening?"

"Yes, ma'am," Washburn nodded and walked back to where she'd been manipulating the display.

"At 1724 ship's time we received word from the boundary patrols that five unknown contacts had transitioned in deep within the system and had then disappeared. At 1732, this call came out on the unsecure intrasystem channel—" She reached over and pressed an icon on her display.

"*We greet our Terrans friends and severely apologize for this breach of protocol,*" the modulated voice came over the speaker, once again giving Celesta a chill down her spine. "*There is a large emergency and we must make accelerate our negotiations. We will hold position until we receive word.*"

"—and once it was over our com system was overridden by CENTCOM and we've only been able to receive general navigation data and instructions direct from New Sierra to hold fast," Washburn said.

"That's why we were so surprised when you were able to break through and order us out of orbit," Barrett said. "We'd been trying to get in touch with you or Ensign Accari, and then when that didn't work began sending requests directly to New Sierra Platform to have them at least forward you a message."

"What are our new friends doing?" Celesta asked.

"From what we can tell out here, just sitting there, ma'am," Washburn continued her briefing. "They've activated a position beacon and we can detect com traffic to and from their formation, but the encryption isn't something our com section is able to crack, at least they don't have the actual decryption routines. I wasn't going to order them to try and forcefully break it without your permission."

"Let's leave that alone for now," Celesta said. "Where are we in relation to their formation?"

"They're parked in a heliocentric trailing orbit behind the sixth planet ... here," Washburn said as the display winked out and then came back up with a representation of the DeLonges System, complete with ranging data. "We're here"—a green spot winked on deeper in the system from the flashing red dot of the alien formation—"just over two point six billion kilometers away. Their ships are also emitting a bright, rotating laser strobe that we assume is meant to broadcast their position in conjunction with the RF beacon. We're tracking them with the *Icarus's* optical sensors as well as the passive detection grid."

"And so far no Fleet ships have moved out to meet them?" Celesta asked.

"No, ma'am," Washburn said. "At least none that we can detect with our passive sensors."

Celesta drummed her fingers on the edge of the tabletop display, lost in thought for a moment. "Commander Barrett, call the bridge and go dark," she said after a moment. "I want the *Icarus* under strict EMSEC protocols, no light pollution, no RF emissions."

"Aye, ma'am," Barrett said and stepped away from the table while pulling his comlink.

"Do you think they're really friendly, Captain?" Washburn said.

"They claim to be, Lieutenant Commander," Celesta said, resisting the urge to shrug helplessly. "But we know the Darshik sure as hell aren't and I would bet a year's pay that this unexpected visit has something to do with them. What I'm more worried about is how the

Ushin just happen to show up so deep in Terran controlled space, exactly at the new capital world just as the new government is being ratified."

"They had to have tracked the *Amsterdam* and *John Arden* back from the meeting point," Barrett said as he walked back up to the table. "Which means they have active trackers they attached to the hulls that are capable of superluminal transmissions or they have a way to track ships while in warp."

"We know those are at least theoretically possible," Celesta said. "The Vruahn were able to track us in warp *and* they had superluminal coms. The Darshik didn't strike me as that advanced but I know less than nothing about the Ushin other than what CENTCOM has decided I need to know to do my job."

"I wonder how much they know," Barrett mused aloud. Celesta resisted the urge to mention what Marcum had divulged along with what Pike had asked her about a certain black project he was trying to track down.

"All idle speculation right now," she said. "XO, you remain here for a bit and coordinate the flow of data up to the bridge. Lieutenant Commander Washburn, excellent job managing CIC while I was absent. Please call up a relief so that you can get some rest while we're all just staring at each other across billions of kilometers … if it gets any more interesting than that, I'll need you fresh and ready."

"Aye, ma'am," Washburn sounded relieved that she would be able to go and get some rest.

"I'll be on the bridge," Celesta continued. "We'll maintain split watches for now and maintain our current state of readiness. We won't go any higher until the Ushin move, we get word from CENTCOM, or the Darshik make a surprise appearance."

"You think that's coming, Captain?" Barrett asked.

"Something chased the Ushin all the way to the DeLonges System, Commander." This time she did shrug. "I doubt it was overwhelming desire to talk to humans again."

****

"OPS, status," Celesta said as she walked onto the bridge.

"No change in the Ushin formation," Accari said. "Ship is still on heightened alert and FMC. We're also tracking the *Amsterdam*'s navigation beacon as it moves out to meet the alien formation."

"We're still on com lockdown?"

"Partially, ma'am," Ellison said. "The local area channels have been opened up and Fleet is instructing us to limit all radio calls to essential navigation traffic only. All ships are still being told to hold their current positions ... no direct inquiries to us as to why we left orbit over DeLonges yet."

"Very good." Celesta sat down in her chair and logged into the terminal by pressing her thumb on the screen for a biometric reading. She had to go through two more security checks before accessing her private server and retrieving a set of codes Pike had given her directly following the Phage War. At first she thought he was trying to gain her favor as he had openly professed his interest in her, but she then learned that he often would pass on the same type of information to Jackson Wolfe if he thought it would be useful.

She then accessed the *Icarus'* com array from her terminal and punched in a specific frequency, one that wasn't normally used in Fleet com protocols. The expected data stream was there, so she applied the CIS decryption codes to it and the stream resolved into a continuous broadcast that her terminal couldn't decipher.

"OPS, I'm routing a data stream to your station," she said. "Run it through the grav-detection network's subroutines and then pipe the results to the main display."

"Aye, ma'am." Accari sounded confused but went to work as soon as Celesta included his terminal in the subnetwork she'd created to isolate the highly classified broadcast.

Near the end of the Phage War the researchers at Tsuyo Corp had begun to crack open the vault and release some of the technology they'd been working on, one of which was a detection grid that used six satellites deployed from a starship to detect gravimetric waves and allow them to detect the presence of a Phage combat unit without having to paint it with an active radar signal. It cut the detection time at least by half since all they had to do was wait for the signal from the detection grid as opposed to transmitting a high power radar signal, waiting for the returns, and then waiting further as the computers processed it all.

The downside was that the grid, while accurate, had a relatively small range of detection due to the need for each satellite to be connected to the others via a laser. After the loss of Haven it was decided that the DeLonges System had to be protected at all costs and the system was implemented on a grand scale, hundreds of individual detection grids set up to cover all the spots that the tracking stations weren't, basically anywhere there wasn't a jump point. The data was all sent directly to a discreet new addition to the com drone platform where the information was processed and then rebroadcast as an encrypted data stream. With the former Warsaw Alliance and Asianic Union planets breaking off it was decided to keep the system's existence classified for the time being.

"I had to make some adjustments, but the feed from the interferometer network you sent me is now live, ma'am," Accari gestured to the main display where gravimetric anomalies were being displayed and cataloged. "We aren't able to access the database they're using to identify known signatures so everything will be coming up as an unknown ... I'll begin filling in what we know from the contacts we know from either passive sensors or nav beacons."

"Good work, Ensign," Celesta nodded. "Tactical! While OPS is busy filling in the blanks, I want you watching that feed for any newcomers, specifically someone that appears deep in the system and didn't come from any known jump point. Alert me the instant you have anything."

"Aye, ma'am," the lieutenant, junior grade said from the tactical station. Celesta made a mental note to ask where Lieutenant Commander Adler was since it was still in the middle of first watch. As her crew busied themselves with her orders, she pulled up all the ship's logs for the time she was on the New Sierra Platform and began reading through all the entries Commander Barrett had submitted. It didn't take her long to see that not only had Barrett performed well in her absence but the crew had been steadily increasing the readiness of the ship, not just sitting idle in orbit. After reading one of the last entries regarding the reintegration of the reactionless drive system she debated back and forth in her head for a moment before issuing her next order.

"OPS, inform Engineering we'll be switching over to the RDS," she said. "Helm, secure main engines from flight mode but do not purge the plasma chambers, just lower the pressure to twenty percent above minimum."

"Securing main engines, aye," the helmswoman said. "Purging the plasma overcharge once the RDS comes up green, Captain."

Celesta felt a twinge of nerves as she watched her ship switch over to the new prototype drive system, but she had complete faith in Commander Graham and his team. If they said they had a way to mitigate the risk from employing the RDS then she would take that as absolute truth.

Now all she had to look forward to was the most despised and inevitable part of space warfare: the interminable waiting.

Chapter 9

"Have you located the *Icarus* yet?" Admiral Marcum asked as he paced the bridge like a caged animal. He'd tried to locate Celesta Wright when the Ushin showed up, intent on having her with him on the bridge of the *Amsterdam* to observe Captain Everett and advise him at the unexpected appearance of their new ... friends ... though he supposed that friendship was tenuous at best.

He wasn't sure what pissed him off more: the fact he couldn't find her or the fact he was actually surprised when he'd been told the *Icarus* was last spotted moving out of orbit and thrusting hard towards the outer system. Marcum wasn't sure how she'd gotten off New Sierra during the lockdown, but he was certain that little shit, Pike, was instrumental in helping. When he'd confronted the damn spook the man had the gall to stay in character as Wellington's aide and act like he had no idea what he was talking about, sneering at the admiral in front of the entire staff as he did so. Marcum made a vow to make the weasel pay dearly for that when he had the opportunity.

"No, Admiral," one of the sensor operators on the big battleship said, almost fearfully. "She's running dark and the—"

"Just keep at it, son," Marcum growled before walking up beside Captain Everett and lowering his voice to just above a whisper. "You're comfortable bringing her out here with all the damage?"

"As I said, Admiral, we're the only ship that it makes sense to send out," Everett said. "The *New York* would have likely taken nearly two days to get back underway. We'll be okay, sir. She's still got most of her teeth and an intrasystem skirmish won't tax our remaining main engine."

"Let's hope it doesn't come to that." Marcum shook his head. "What in the hell are they doing here?"

"If I were to guess, sir, I'd say that this could only have something to do with the attack during our initial negotiations, not to mention the ambush of our taskforce in the Xi'an System," Everett said. "I noticed their translations are getting easier to understand."

"That should help the ambassador," Marcum muttered. "The most important diplomatic event in the last four centuries and they send an idiot I wouldn't trust to negotiate my next divorce settlement."

"I, uh—"

"Forget I said anything," Marcum said.

"Of course, Admiral," Everett said with a nod. One of the main reasons Marcum liked Captain Everett was that, in addition to proving to be an extremely capable captain, he was someone who knew how to keep his mouth shut. Marcum was often blowing off steam and saying things that should not be uttered by flag officers about elected politicians or the Commander in Chief while in the presence of a subordinate officer, but in all the time the *Amsterdam* had been flying his flag not a single one of those comments had been spit back out by the rumor mill. The fact Everett could be trusted to allow his boss to vent without fearing the shipboard gossip kicked him up quite a few notches in Marcum's esteem.

Captain Wright, however, was another matter. Despite the fact he liked her personally, her tendency to follow in her former commander's footsteps and buck the chain of command was something he would not tolerate.

He had put up with Wolfe all those years because he had been red meat for the bleeding hearts in the Senate and had been put in a place he couldn't really do any damage: the bridge of an obsolete starship that served as little more than a courier and was crewed by troublemakers and rejects. But, it had been one of the few successes of the Earth Commissioning Program the politicians could wave around and Wolfe himself had been largely ignored by CENTCOM and Fleet Operations until the damn Phage happened to show up in the middle of his patrol route.

Once that happened all Wolfe's unsavory habits became a constant nuisance. He would habitually disobey direct orders, take Fleet property and personnel wherever he wanted, whenever he wanted on missions that made sense to nobody but him, and the damnable hell of it all was that because he was part lucky, part good, and had killed so many Phage, the civilian oversight of Starfleet would have drummed him out had he even suggested that Wolfe was not only *not* a hero but should be prosecuted.

Captain Celesta Wright, Wolfe's former executive officer, seemed to have picked up some of his less-admirable qualities but, like her boss, she was almost untouchable due to her actions near the end of the war. Almost. His blood burned at how casually she had ignored his orders and taken a ship, that had also been ordered to stay put, off to any damn place she pleased and now they had no idea where the *Icarus* was. For all he knew she'd warped out of the system and was flying off for a vacation. When this was over he'd make sure she never commanded so much as a transfer shuttle for her remaining days in Starfleet.

"Enjoy this last little jaunt, Wright," he said quietly to himself. "I'll yank you off the bridge of that ship so fast your head will spin."

"Sir?"

"It's nothing, Captain," Marcum said to Everett. "I'll get out of your way up here. Let me know if something comes up."

"Of course, Admiral," Everett said, almost managing to not look relieved the flag officer was leaving his bridge.

****

"We're approaching our holding point, boss," Pike said, leaning back in his seat. "I'm also getting an update that the evacuation of the Senate—sorry, *Parliament*—is proceeding in an orderly fashion. The four Fourth Fleet cruisers are standing by and the shuttles should be landing momentarily."

"Pike," Wellington said in a pained voice, "I don't have an enormous ego, but do you really think it's appropriate to call the President of the United Terran Federation *boss?*"

"I thought it was just the Terran Federation." Pike ignored the question, not wanting to get into a discussion about Wellington's ego. "When did we get united?"

"Just fly the damn ship." Wellington was rubbing the bridge of his nose. "When will we be able to break into the *Amsterdam*'s secure link?"

"I can do that anytime," Pike said. "But this does beg the question, why did you send Ambassador Cole back out here when you, as President, are in the system?"

"It's about propriety," President Augustus Wellington said, slouching in the copilot seat and wearing a suit that Pike knew likely cost more than half a year's salary for him. "They have arrived in our system uninvited and unwelcomed ... a small delegation with a handful of ships and likely led by some unimportant Ushin diplomatic corps lackey, or whatever they call them. It would be inappropriate for the Terran President to come out personally to meet them."

"I think I get—"

"And to answer your other sarcastic question," Wellington rolled right over top of Pike's comment, "we're now the *United* Terran Federation because we want to present a unified front to the Eastern Star Alliance. They've now cut off all official channels of communication and have sent notice that Fed ships are no longer guaranteed safe passage through their territory."

"I hadn't realized it'd gone that far," Pike said quietly. "Shall I break into the *Amsterdam*'s secure com array and begin recording?"

"If you please," Wellington nodded.

Pike reached over and pressed the icon flashing on the large, curved display that would execute a script that would allow the Broadhead II's intrusion avionics to force their way into the *Amsterdam*'s secure com array.

"You make that look so easy," Wellington said idly.

"To be honest, the job is getting a little boring," Pike admitted as the system reached out and negotiated through a secret "back door" into the battleship's com system. "Tsuyo has built in so many failsafes that I don't do much more than run automated sequences to get intel. It's coming up now ... looks like Cole is speaking directly to the Ushin delegation."

****

"While we're always happy to see our Ushin friends, you must understand that your appearance in this star system has caused this process some ... complications," Ambassador Cole said. He was sitting in a dedicated room that was completely isolated save for the direct connections to the secure com array.

"*Our sincerest apologies, Ambassador, but events have unfolded in such a way that we feel an acceleration in our negotiations is necessary,*" the disembodied voice came in over the speakers. Cole couldn't help but notice that the Ushin real-time translation matrix had evolved rapidly to be just about perfect. Actually, the improvement was more than a little suspicious when compared to the open channel broadcasts, but he put it out of his mind. He was also grateful that the audio from their actual vocalizations was not being transmitted. Their image was distressing enough but their voices caused an irrational spike in his anxiety levels. But he was a lifelong bureaucrat and a trained diplomat so he could hide his stress and fear in order to get the job done.

"Please elaborate, if you will, Ambassador," he said. Cole had no idea if that was the proper title or not, but it was the one they used so he assumed the translation would work the other way. The more complete translation matrix was aboard his ship, the *John Arden*, but the *Amsterdam*'s more powerful computers were picking up the slack nicely and adapting to what it saw on the Ushin side.

"*The Darshik attacks on our respective delegations, your ships in one of your own star systems, and our cargo fleet is a common concern we share,*" the Ushin ambassador stated. "*As was briefly talked about in our opening talks, we have no martial force capable of repelling the Darshik's most recent aggression. Our defensive screens are obsolete and in poor repair. We know that your mighty navy was not only victorious over the Phage, but your warships can defeat Darshik vessels in single combat."*

"You seek protection?" Cole asked simply.

"*We seek an alliance,*" the Ushin corrected. "*One that will be mutually beneficial to the both of us. To demonstrate our commitment to this we are transmitting a series of stellar coordinates ... they are for two planets not far from your own boundaries that are perfectly suited for Terran colonization. In exchange for you extending your fleet's sphere of influence, we will make available all of our survey data that pertains to systems of use to your species.*"

"Just so I have something to approach my government about ... how many habitable planets are we talking about?" Cole asked, his eyes narrowing slightly and his breathing increasing a tick. Planets that were already habitable were highly prized and exceedingly rare. In fact, there had only been two discovered in all the years after humanity's initial push out from the Solar System when they had found dozens of planets all in the same relative stellar neighborhood. A group of new worlds would be a valuable prize to the Terran Federation, but would it be worth going to war over?

"*According to the preliminary results of our query there are twenty-six planets within practical distance of your territory that we would be willing to relinquish control of,*" the Ushin ambassador pressed, and Cole couldn't help but wonder if the alien had been able to read his involuntary response at the mention of new habitable worlds.

"Not an insignificant number," Cole nodded slowly, regaining control over his reactions even though his heart was beating heavy in his chest. *Twenty-six new planets?!* "But please understand, Ambassador, that we've just come out of a costly war that has not only

122

strained our resources but has weighed heavily on the spirit of our people," Cole continued. "I can offer no guarantees that my government will be willing to provide what you're asking for."

"*Of course you will need to consult with your peoples' government,*" the Ushin said. "*Bear in mind, the offer of surveyed and available worlds is not all we offer. While your prowess in the art of war far exceeds our own, we have technological advancements that we would be willing to share for the mutual benefit of all.*"

"I would suggest that we now—" Cole broke off as the video and sound disappeared, leaving him staring at a blank, silent terminal. "What the hell?" Before he could move over to ask the technician outside what happened, alarms began blaring through the ship.

"Oh, shit."

Chapter 10

"Target all enemy ships! Prioritize all targets and put two shrikes on each," Captain Everett was barking. "Helm! Get us underway, all ahead one-half, bear as she goes."

"Ahead one-half, aye!" the helmsman called.

"Shrikes are not responding, Captain," the tactical officer called out. "Munitions teams are being deployed to the launch tubes to check the connections."

"What range weapons do we have?" Everett asked calmly.

"We only had the Shrikes, sir. They were emptying the magazines before we—"

"Coms!" Everett cut off the excuse. "Sound the general alert through the system ... we are under attack. Suspected force of the same type of ship that attacked the Xi'an System ... unknown numbers, unknown strengths. Get any ship that has working standoff weapons out here ASAP! Tactical! Bring all available laser batteries up and begin full power active scans with the targeting radars."

"Captain! Two more of the Ushin ships have been destroyed," his OPS officer reported. "They have one left and it's pushing down ... towards us! They're moving down into the system."

"Are they being pursued?"

"Yes, sir!"

"They're going to try and put us between them and the Darshik," Everett said quietly.

"Returns on the enemy ships coming in, Captain," the tactical officer reported. "Eleven ships total, three coming down towards us and the others look to be taking a position outside the orbit of Deveroux." He was referencing the sixth planet in the system, an odd rocky world that had been flung out of the inner system some billions of years prior and had taken up a stable orbit in the outer system.

"They're not just holding out there," Admiral Marcum said, speaking for the first time since arriving on the bridge after general quarters had been sounded. "They're going after the depot."

"Shit!" Everett swore. "Coms! Send a message directly to Bespitd Station and tell them to get in the lifeboats and get the hell out of there."

"Good call," Marcum nodded, still speaking quietly. "They can't do anything out there, better get them as far away as possible while they have the chance." Bespitd Station was a Fleet munitions depot, specifically storing Shrike and Hornet missiles. It was simply a waypoint that ships would stop at on the way out of the system, have the specialized shuttles ferry over their loadout, and then accelerate to transition velocity and hit the Columbiana jump point or come about and circle the system for the other departure vectors.

The thought was to keep the bulk of the dangerous munitions off New Sierra Platform and away from both the populated planets in the system. It had a minimal maintenance crew and, like the com drone platform, was just something that was always in the background and not given much thought. It also had zero defensive capabilities. Fourth Fleet had built the station and had not given a single thought to the fact that someone might actually attack the DeLonges System. Everett knew there was no defending the station for those aboard it so he didn't bother trying, instead giving them the order to get into the boats and shove off. Maybe they'd outrun the destruction coming if the Darshik opened fire on the depot.

"This isn't good, sir," Everett muttered. "We're flying in with only close range weapons, the rest of the fleet is so far down the well it'll take them the better part of two days to get out here, and we're likely about to lose a sizable chunk of missiles we'd probably like to put into Darshik hulls."

"And we're still in better shape than when the Phage first came knocking," Marcum said. "I wouldn't—"

"We must protect that last Ushin ship!"

Marcum and Everett turned and looked at the same time to see a wild-eyed Ambassador Cole running onto the bridge with the Marine sentry in hot pursuit.

"Our first priority will be to—"

"You don't understand, Admiral!" Cole shook his head. "They need us far more than we need them ... and they're willing to pay dearly for that. This could change the balance of power in this region of space, but if the entire contingent is wiped out it may all be for naught."

Marcum's nostrils flared as he tried to control his temper, enraged that a diplomat barged onto the bridge of his flagship during combat operations and started barking orders. But the admiral—the CENTCOM Chief of Staff, no less—was as much a political animal as the ambassador was.

"You're certain of this?" Marcum demanded harshly. "This is worth the risk to human lives?"

"I have a recording of the conversation." Cole's head bobbed up and down. "The Ushin will still honor it even though their ambassador has apparently been killed."

"Captain?" Marcum said.

"You're in luck, Ambassador," Everett said, looking at the diplomat in disgust. "The Ushin ship is coming down the well towards us, heading for the planets and orbital platforms. My primary job is to keep the Darshik from reaching those Terran assets and it looks like I'll be able to protect your Ushin friends as a bonus."

"We've picked up a massive explosion on optics, sir," the OPS officer called out. "Initial analysis is that Bespitd Station was just taken out."

"Did our transmission have enough time to make it out there?" Everett asked.

"No, sir," the com officer said somberly.

"So the remaining ships out of the eleven will be on their way down as well, and they can do those intrasystem hops," Everett shook his head. "Ambassador, I would transmit any information you have that your replacement will need down to New Sierra now."

"First Haven, now New Sierra," one of the sensor operators muttered to herself. "Fucking aliens."

Everett opened his mouth to admonish his spacer, but realized that he completely agreed with her.

****

"Confirmed, ma'am," Accari reported. "The Bespitd munitions depot has been destroyed.

Amsterdam is showing eleven targets through the link, but they're having trouble tracking them."

"And the Ushin ships?" Celesta asked.

"One left, looks like it's trying to get down below the *Amsterdam* while the Darshik ships are pursuing."

"How long until we can launch our Shrikes?" Celesta asked.

"Twenty-nine minutes, ma'am," Lieutenant Commander Adler reported from Tactical. Celesta did the math in her head and could only marvel at the sheer speed the RDS was capable of ... when it was working. As soon as the detection grid had let them know that the Darshik had appeared in the new capital system she'd immediately ordered the *Icarus* onto an intercept course at full acceleration. They'd been on the other side of the system and were flying along a heliocentric course around to the engagement, as opposed to flying down close to the primary star and back up on a more direct route, and they would still beat the rest of the fleet there by over thirty hours.

They were relying on the *Amsterdam*'s tactical telemetry coming over the Link to steer them in the rough area of the engagement, and Celesta would order her active sensors on at the last minute, not wanting to give away the element of surprise. Since there had only been two engagements up to this point they had no way to determine how the Darshik ships detected other objects in space, but from her own staff's post-mission analysis it seemed they had similar limitations as Terran ships in that if the target wasn't decently close or actively transmitting it became exponentially more difficult to spot. With the RDS pushing the *Icarus* along they had the added benefit of no thermal plume from the plasma thrust main engines lighting up their path.

"Transmission coming in, ma'am," Ellison said. "All channels—I think it may be from the enemy fleet."

"Put it through," Celesta tensed up.

"*Warning was given. Now you will burn with them.*"

"End transmission, Captain," Ellison said. "No repeat ... just that."

"That sounded—"

"Enlightening, actually," Celesta cut off Commander Barrett. "We now can be almost certain this has to do with our recent association with the Ushin."

"Does that help us in the immediate situation, ma'am?" Barrett asked.

"It does now," Celesta said crisply. "We're the pointy end of the spear everyone ... we do not make policy nor are we paid to consider the philosophical ramifications of armed conflict. Tactical, remove the safeties from the Shrikes and prepare all forward tubes to fire, full spread, and stand by on close-range weapons."

"Shall I charge the capacitor banks for the auto-mag, ma'am?" Adler asked.

"Yes," Celesta said after a moment of thought. "And have the magazine loaded with high-explosive penetrator rounds."

"Aye, ma'am."

Accari had taken the liberty of putting a series of countdown timers on the main display; one had just gone to red, showing that they were within ten minutes of being able to launch their standoff weapons. Another was blue, letting her know she was still over forty minutes from what would be considered the "engagement area" based on the number of ships involved and the capability of the *Icarus* to maneuver within that area of space. It was a deceptive term since an engagement area could still cover half a million kilometers, but with the RDS that was now a much smaller pocket to fight within than it was with the plasma engines. She could now order the ship to decelerate or come about very quickly as opposed to a flyby that required them to target and fire at speed and within a brief window.

"Active sensors," Celesta said calmly. "All targeting and ranging radars active, point defense lidar and radar as well."

"Aye aye, ma'am, all active sensors now online," Adler said. "We shouldn't have too long before we get returns."

Sure enough, their range had closed so much that within the next five minutes the threat board began to populate with targets and friendlies, or "friendly," since the *Amsterdam* was the only Terran ship in the vicinity.

"Coms, let the *Amsterdam* know we're inbound and will be launching our first salvo at the trailing Darshik units coming down from the remains of the Bespitd munitions depot," Celesta ordered. "Ask Captain Everett if he has any other requests of us on this first pass."

"Aye, ma'am," Ellison said and pulled his headset back up.

"Active target tracks confirmed, ma'am!" Adler reported a bit too loudly for Celesta's taste. "Shrikes are locked on and ready. We have eight missiles ready to fly, how do you want them deployed?"

"One missile each," Celesta said. "Target the trailing ship and come down the line from there. Let me know when the missiles are updated." In her first engagement the Darshik hadn't shown any capability to intercept or block their missiles, so she didn't want to waste too many of her heavy hitters when she didn't have to, especially with the ammo dump having just been blown up. "Make sure the Hornets are also getting active tracking updates," she said as an afterthought.

"Shrikes are ready, ma'am," Adler said.

"Fire first salvo!" Celesta ordered: "Helm! Full reverse, cut our relative velocity by seventy percent."

"Missiles one through eight are away," Adler said. "Tubes reloaded and all birds are tracking clean."

"All engines reverse, aye!" the helmsman called out right before there was a sharp *bang* that reverberated through the hull and the lights flickered.

"Report!" Celesta said when her crew just looked at each other for a moment, apparently dumbfounded.

"RDS has failed, ma'am!" the helmsman called out. "We're ballistic. Engaging MPD mains now."

Celesta sat pensively as the deck rumbled gently from the main engines building thrust and coming up to full operating range.

"Main engines answer full reverse, ma'am," the helmsman said. "We won't be able to cut our velocity enough before we overshoot the engagement."

Celesta pulled up the data from the helm and nav station and saw that her pilot was right: the RDS had pushed the *Icarus* to such a high velocity that she couldn't slow down enough even with the powerful main engines burning full reverse. Since the MPDs were capable of equal amounts of forward or reverse thrust it wouldn't accomplish anything to spin the ship for a braking maneuver.

"OPS!" she barked.

"Talking to Engineering now, ma'am," Accari assured her. "They're resetting the RDS pod power interface as we speak."

"At least we know Commander Graham's power interrupt works," Barrett said. "Otherwise we'd be ballistic *and* powerless drifting right into the line of fire."

"Tactical, do we have a shot with the auto-mag?" Celesta asked, ignoring her XO.

"Negative, Captain," Adler said. "Our velocity is too high, we're too close, and the Darshik ships are maneuvering too erratic—"a loud squawking from her terminal stopped her for a moment—"two of our missiles have been destroyed by an unknown enemy countermeasure."

"Track the others," Celesta said. "Helm! Engines to zero thrust and bring us about ... we're going to overfly the engagement no matter what, let's at least get her pointed back in the right direction. Coms, inform the *Amsterdam* of our ... predicament ... and tell them we'll be back as soon as we can."

"Aye, ma'am," Ellison said. He looked like he was about to say more but the tactical officer cut him off.

"Four missiles have struck home! Two targets destroyed, two adrift," Adler said. "I've lost contact with the remaining two Shrikes."

"And we're too fast and close to launch the second wave." Celesta slammed her fist down on her armrest. "Damn!" Her shout made everyone jump and look over.

"Two Darshik ships have moved in close to the *Amsterdam*, Captain," Accari said. "Training long range optics on it now, they may be trying to grapple on and—whoa!" On the main display one of the Darshik ships, dwarfed by the mass of the *Amsterdam*, evaporated as the battleship actually thrusted laterally towards the target and opened up with all her starboard laser batteries. The concentrated fire shredded the smaller ship. "Target is destroyed, ma'am."

"They won't approach another Terran battleship that confidently again," Celesta said. "OPS! Where the hell is my RDS?"

****

"Target vaporized, sir!"

"Helm! Engines to no-thrust and bring us about," Captain Everett said sharply. "Put her nose back the way we came and rotate Y-axis ninety degrees to starboard. Tactical, that other ship is still coming in … you know what to do."

"Aye aye, sir!" his tactical officer said. "Starboard batteries charged and ready to fire … ranging now … nineteen seconds until they're close enough."

"Let them have it at maximum range," Everett said. "Their hulls can't take the heat, and if they're still coming close I have a feeling they're after more than a handshake. They are *not* to take this ship. Understood?"

"Yes, sir!" came a ragged chorus from the bridge crew that wasn't fully immersed in their task.

"OPS, status on the *Icarus*?" Everett asked.

"Captain Wright says her RDS pod has failed and they can't decelerate on the mains enough to be of any use," the OPS officer said, reading the status one of the com officers had sent her. "The *Icarus* is overshooting our position and will be back as soon as they get the RDS reset and operational or when the mains can bring them about."

"Firing!" the tactical officer called. "Multiple hull breaches ... adjusting fire ... target is coming apart, Captain!"

"Helm! Bring us back to our original course and orientation, engines ahead one-half," Everett called out, his hands shaking from the excitement of battle.

"Coming about," the helmsman said. "All engines ahead one-half, aye."

"Tactical, clear our area!"

"Why was Wright running her RDS and main plasma engines at the same time?" Marcum asked quietly. "I thought the systems weren't able to be engaged simultaneously."

"I'll ask her when this is over, Admiral," Everett said, failing to keep the irritation out of his voice.

"Of course, Captain," Marcum said after his face turned a few different shades of red, and he swallowed his retort with visible effort.

"We have two targets loitering out of range dead ahead," the tactical officer reported. "The remaining five ships have disappeared."

"Disappeared?" Everett asked in disbelief. "How did they just—" He broke off and looked at Marcum in horror.

"Get the *Icarus* on an open channel now!" the admiral shouted at one of the com officers. "Broadcast it to the fleet."

"Go ahead, sir," the officer said.

****

"*Icarus, this is Captain Everett on the Amsterdam,*" the voice came over the bridge speakers. "*We have five unaccounted-for targets left. I believe they may have executed one of the intrasystem jumps they used against your taskforce to bypass our defensive perimeter and continue pursuing the last Ushin ship.*"

"We concur, Captain," Celesta said. She was standing behind Lieutenant Commander Adler and looking at the target tracks, having already come to the same conclusion before the call came in from the flagship. "If you're able to handle your two stragglers, we're about to switch back over to our RDS and we're already carrying a lot of velocity; we might be able to catch them."

"*My thoughts exactly, Captain,*" Everett said. "*This goes for any other Fleet warships in the system ... you are cleared to engage the enemy. If it isn't Ushin or Terran, open fire and don't let them approach close enough to grapple on. Watch the overlapping fire. Amsterdam out.*"

"Shit," Barrett growled. "With everyone running weapons free at random vectors this system just turned into a shooting gallery."

"Uh, Commander, the channel to the *Amsterdam* is still open," Ellison said. "It's just switched back to private ship-to-ship instead of on the Fleetwide channel."

"*You disapprove of our tactics, Commander Barrett?*" the unmistakable voice of Admiral Marcum came over the speakers. Barrett gave Ellison a look that could have melted hull plating.

135

"We're all just trying to figure out how to approach this with the least amount of collateral damage, Admiral," Celesta answered before Barrett could.

"What's the Icarus' status, Captain?"

"The RDS pod flaked out ... again ... when we tried to decel into the engagement," she answered. "We had too much—"

"Yes, I heard all that," Marcum interrupted. *"I'm just curious how you're running both of your main propulsion systems simultaneously."*

"My chief engineer has developed a power interface that allows us to use the RDS while keeping the MPDs primed and ready, Admiral," Celesta said. "Before that it was blowing power junctions out and creating an unacceptable hazard to my ship."

"I see," Marcum said. *"Do you think you can get it back up in time to catch those five ships? I won't go into detail, Captain, but it is utterly vital that Ushin ship survives. With the New York still in berth you're the only ship that can get there in time. Can you do it?"*

Celesta looked around the bridge for non-verbal status updates from a few of her crew before answering.

"Yes, Admiral. We can do it."

Chapter 11

"RDS responding normally to commands, ma'am," the helmsman reported not even ten minutes after the conversation with Admiral Marcum.

"Very good," Celesta said. "Nav! Set course for the middle of the Darshik formation. Tactical, you're going to have to not only track the enemy ships but be aware of incoming fire from the Terran ships down near New Sierra's orbit. OPS, you help her with that."

"Course entered in and ready, Captain," the nav station operator said.

"Come onto new course, all ahead flank."

"RDS ahead flank, aye," the helmsman said. "MPD main engines to zero thrust, plasma chambers still at operational levels."

"Good, good," Celesta said, grunting slightly against the acceleration of the reactionless drive as it overwhelmed their artificial gravity and inertial compensators. "Let's keep them there for now since the RDS pod is a bit temperamental."

She could only marvel at the power of the new drive as she watched the *Icarus* race past her old maximum real-space velocity on the main display and get there in a matter of minutes. Commander Graham had told her that he could remove the governors on the system and the drive could reach its top relative speed almost instantaneously, but it would kill all the crew and likely destroy the ship in the process. She allowed herself a moment of nostalgic regret as, even while flying into an engagement where they were badly outnumbered, she could see the end of an era approaching. The old plasma-burning starships were slow and ungainly for the most part, but they required a high degree of skill and coordination to fly, something Fleet spacers took great pride in. Even the retrofitted *Starwolf*-class ship with a drive pod bolted on under the aft almost flew itself. She had to assume the next generation of Terran ships would be even more capable and just as sterile, almost able to be operated by anybody.

"Updating Shrike target packages, ma'am," Lieutenant Commander Adler said. "Do you still want one per?"

"Fire two missiles per target," Celesta said, checking the master armament status window on her terminal to see how many of the specialized munitions were left. "Have the crews reload all eight forward tubes; we'll snap fire a second volley if it looks like it's needed."

"Aye, ma'am," Adler said.

"Thirteen minutes until we're in weapons range," Accari reported. "Ushin ship has made it within the New Sierra defensive boundary; Darshik ships are slowing slightly."

"Coms! Get on the Fleetwide and warn them that these Darshik ships might try to jump in behind their picket line," Celesta said. "Are there any Black Fleet ships down there?"

"Two missile cruisers," Accari said. "The *Solstice Wind* and the *Zephyr*, both Fourth Squadron."

"Coms, order those two ships up off the line to flank the Ushin ship," Celesta said. "Tell them if my authority isn't good enough then they can take it on faith I speak for CENTCOM Chief of Staff at the moment."

"Aye, ma'am," Ellison said distractedly. The destroyer only had a single com officer, and although the com section in the CIC did manage a lot of the more mundane traffic it was still a lot for one person when it came to fast-developing operations that needed a lot of coordination.

"Ma'am, we're within firing range," Adler said.

"Hold your fire." Celesta was looking at the threat board. The Darshik ships were still pursuing the Ushin down the system, but their forward velocity made it unlikely that their missiles would reach them in time before they hit the hastily assembled defensive perimeter. But the *Icarus* was quickly coming upon them and seemed to have a definite edge in real-space speed.

"Ma'am?"

"I said hold your fire!" Celesta said sharply. If she fired her Shrikes at maximum range they would leave the tubes, but their delta-V would be insignificant compared to the still-accelerating destroyer. "We're going to hand-deliver these," she said with a smile. "Helm, use your own judgment but I want you to drive this ship right into the middle of that enemy formation, all available power."

"Aye, ma'am!" the helmsman said and reached for the manual controls. Like all starship pilots her helm operators were highly competent ship drivers, but in the modern Fleet they rarely did much more than enter course corrections into the computer and verify everything was responding as it should.

The *Icarus* shuddered slightly as the perhaps over-exuberant helmsman ran the RDS up past flank and bumped into the emergency power settings. Celesta let him go. This would either work or it wouldn't. If the drive shit the bed ... again ... at the critical moment they would simply scream past the engagement and have to maneuver back around on conventional propulsion. Again.

She watched the range closely, the real-time and estimated positions on the display converging as they closed and lag time in their radar returns lessened. So far it looked like the Darshik were wholly focused on the Ushin ship and were largely ignoring her mad rush even though her ship was broadcasting with active sensors and coms. The enemy was arrayed in a loose phalanx and the *Icarus* was bearing down on the lead ship. Perfect.

"Tactical, target two Shrikes each on the four flankers," she said. "Get ready to snap fire and then be ready with the forward laser batteries for the last one."

"Target tracks are locked and ready, ma'am."

Celesta just nodded as she watched the *Icarus* actually pass the outer ships, then the next in line, as she closed up on the tail of the leading enemy ship. Now that they were so close, relatively speaking, she saw her ship was travelling much, much faster than the Darshik.

"Fire!" she barked when she felt she was at optimal range. "Helm! Full stop!"

"Missiles away! Tubes reloading," Adler said, grunting as the RDS reversed fields and the ship was being rapidly hauled to a stop in space. Celesta had to lean back and plant her feet in the carpet to keep from sliding out of her seat as the helmsman expertly ran the power up and back to keep a steady decel without creating a dangerous situation for the crew. The ship had almost come to a complete stop relative to New Sierra when the thing Celesta had been half-expecting happened.

"RDS offline!" the helmsman called, eliciting groans of disgust from the rest of the bridge crew. "MPDs coming up now."

"Two targets destroyed, one disabled, one undamaged," Adler reported after ten tense minutes of watching the helmsman get the plasma engines configured for flight. "Lead ship has stopped and the outermost ship to the right is turning in. I think we have their attention, ma'am."

"Helm, bring her to starboard forty degrees." Celesta's eyes never left the tactical display. They were all close enough now that the radar data was real-time. "Ahead full."

"Ahead full, aye," the helmsman reported.

"We saved the Ushin ship but we may be screwed." Commander Barrett pointed to the accelerating Darshik ships. "Our plasma engines can't match that rate of acceleration. They'll catch us."

"Yes, but the Ushin *and* New Sierra were saved," Celesta said. "We can't—"

"Flanking ship has just been destroyed!" Adler called. "Missile hit from one of ours."

"Coms channel request coming in for us—"

"Put it through, Lieutenant Ellison," Celesta interrupted.

"Captain Wright, this is Captain Lee aboard the *New York*," the familiar voice said. "We have your last target in sight and are closing the range now. Your aft will be cleared momentarily."

"Captain Lee, I owe you a drink when this is over," Celesta said with relief. She would do her duty, but it didn't mean she was necessarily happy with having to be the sacrificial lamb to accomplish a mission objective. "Happy hunting."

****

"One ship escaped, sir," Pike said as his own instruments corroborated what he was being told over the Link. "The *New York* took out the lead Darshik ship in the formation, but the last flanker the *Icarus* missed was able to skirt around and disappeared off radar."

Wellington stirred in the copilot seat as if prodded. He'd actually managed to fall asleep in the middle of a battle, albeit as an observer. Augustus Wellington was not a young man nor a particularly healthy man, a lifetime of excess catching up with him as his skin sagged and his midsection swelled. Pike wasn't the man's caretaker, and he did understand the wisdom of making the powerful lifelong politician the new President to keep the other enclaves in line until the Federation—sorry, the *United* Federation—had its feet under it, but he wondered if the man was up to the job. Being President was basically signing up to have your life shortened by fifteen years from stress, and he wasn't sure Wellington had fifteen left to give.

"I'm assuming we have no way to track the enemy ship that escaped," Wellington stated, not actually asking a question. "We need to act fast on this. Did the bulk of Parliament make it out of the system?"

"No, sir," Pike said. "The four cruisers made it away from New Sierra but they're days away from their jump point."

"Recall them." Wellington hefted himself out of the seat. "Then get us back to the planet and have Admiral Marcum in my office the moment he can physically make that happen. Would it be faster to just pick him up on the way?"

"That ... wouldn't be advisable, sir," Pike said carefully, thinking about the ramifications of blowing his cover.

"Whatever," Wellington waved him off. "Just make all that happen. I'm going to try and get some sleep before we land ... something that will certainly be in short supply once we start this off."

"I'm almost afraid to ask, Mr. President," Pike said, "but start what off, exactly?"

"Isn't it obvious, Mr. Lynch?" Wellington smiled humorously. "We're going back to war, and far before we're ready."

Pike began entering the necessary commands to the fleet under his credentials that identified him as speaking for the President himself, a hard, cold lump forming in his stomach as he did. As an intelligence operative, and one that covered far more territory than most, he knew that Wellington's quip was a vast understatement. The Federation had lost forty-eight percent of its territory to the splintered Eastern Star Alliance. That was half its planets, people, ships, and manufacturing capabilities. The Darshik were a defeatable, if inscrutable enemy that a full strength Starfleet might stand a chance of turning away, at least based on the strength they'd shown so far in the opening skirmishes. But Starfleet now consisted of the First, Fourth, and a severely battered and weary Black Fleet, officially designated the Seventh.

The ships were tired, the people were worn thin, and Pike had grave misgivings as to what might happen if the newly formed Federation decided their first official act was to send the Fleet back into the breach. He hoped when the history of man was written that the centuries of peace prior to the arrival of the Phage weren't an anomaly as Captain Wolfe had often insisted, but the more they spread out the more they were finding that the galaxy wasn't the quiet, friendly neighborhood it at first appeared to be.

Chapter 12

"I came as fast as I could, Mr. President," Marcum huffed as he marched into the temporary office of the Chief Executive with as much dignity as he could muster. "The *Amsterdam* had to come full about and she's missing one of her main engines."

"Grab a drink of water and a seat, Admiral," Wellington waved him to where three other men were sitting in large, overstuffed recliners. "We have a lot to discuss and not enough time to do it in.

"You'll all note that Ambassador Cole is conspicuously missing during this meeting. He's currently en route to his own starship where he will escort the remaining Ushin ship away from New Sierra and DeLonges and hopefully finalize what could be a very lucrative treaty deal for the Federation. I've vested him with enough authority to conclude the deal quickly, but he knows what his limits are. He assures me the Ushin on the remaining ship are also able to speak for their people ... something about rank being non-existent in their culture or some bullshit. What I need from you gentlemen, as the more influential members of your respective enclaves, is to make sure any treaty we bring out of these negotiations is ratified quickly so that CENTCOM may act upon it. As you've no doubt guessed it will involve the use of military force."

"I think you'll find that your hands will be full simply convincing us first, Mr. President," James Nelson from Britannia said in a clipped accent that identified him as being from the capital world. "I find it hard to believe that it is in the best interests of the United Terran Federation to become militarily involved in a dispute between the Ushin and the Darshik."

"That's fair enough, ah ... Mr. Nelson," Wellington seemed to flounder as the legislative members were no longer called senators. "Putting aside the three attacks on Terran ships, two in sovereign Terran space for a moment, let's go over some facts that I think you might not be fully aware of.

"When the Asianic Union and Warsaw Alliance broke off, they took a sizable chunk of the New European Commonwealth with them. For all intents and purposes call it the entire enclave, since the planets still loyal to the old Confederacy are astronomically located such that we would have to fly through ESA systems to reach them, which they are no longer allowing. Latest intelligence before the blackout indicated they were actually mining some of the more strategic jump points ... that's an unprecedented move in our history as a spacefaring people."

"We're all well aware of this, Mr. President. If there—"

"What isn't widely known," Wellington went on, steamrolling over the interruption without even raising his voice, "is that the Third, Fifth, and Eighth Fleets were largely left intact after the Phage War. That means that despite our technological superiority, the numbers favor them. And it gets better ... Admiral?"

"Practically speaking, all of our fissile material came from the New European Commonwealth." Admiral Marcum stood, having already been warned by the President that he would be required to provide technical background during the meeting. "Specifically, two planets that are controlled by the ESA."

"Is this really a problem?" Nelson asked skeptically. "We still have over sixteen star systems, some with multiple habitable planets. Statistically some of those systems must have the material we need."

Marcum shook his head slowly as if exhausted at having to explain something simple to someone so dense. "The material isn't the issue," he said. "We can get Uranium-235 almost anywhere ... but the processing facilities to produce it in useable quantities are on those two planets. We need the enriched product they produce for our fission-fusion warheads. Thankfully, starship reactors are much more simple and don't require such an exotic fuel or we'd be in an even worse place, but at our current rate of consumption we'll lose our ability to produce Shrike warheads within the next year. In case anybody was wondering, the Shrike has become Fleet's primary ship-to-ship weapon."

"And the Bespitd munitions depot was just destroyed." Former Senator Illoka from New America nodded his head in understanding. "Other than scaring us, why is this important?"

"Because the Ushin, as part of our tentative treaty agreement, have offered us technology that will allow us to no longer need fissionable material from the ESA worlds, at least not for weapons production," Wellington said. "We'll get into those details later, but the more significant offer from them is up to twenty-six new, human-habitable planets within practical range of our territory."

This announcement set off a flurry of loud, shocked responses as each member of the new Parliament tried to wrap their head around the implications of so many new planets ready for colonization.

"As you can see, gentleman, this is quite an offer," Wellington said, finally moving to sit behind the wood desk that dominated the room. "But it's not without some drawbacks, both philosophical and practical. First to the practical, if you wouldn't mind, Admiral."

"Realistically, we would struggle to fend off a serious offensive on our own territory," Marcum began. "That means that any military assets that are sent to help the Ushin leave us just that much more vulnerable. There has been a strong effort since the Phage War to implement planetary and system-wide defenses, but so far only the more wealthy systems have managed to get anything in place. We're working to mitigate that, but there's currently nothing in place so we're completely dependent on a depleted Starfleet. So ... from a purely practical standpoint we can deploy the Fleet to help the Ushin or hold them back and protect our own systems."

"This raises another problem," Nelson said, his eyes never leaving Marcum's. "I've seen the numbers ... Fleet doesn't have enough ships to protect *all* Fed planets."

"No, it doesn't," Wellington cut in. "No matter what's decided here, hard choices will need to be made about what systems are critical and which will need to fend for themselves. So now that we know what's at stake, here's where the logic gets a bit mushy. In the last ten years we've gone from knowing about one other species from humans in the galaxy to four new ones, each seeming to be much further up the technological ladder than we are."

"Is there a point to this, Mr. President?" Illoka asked. "With all due respect, sir, we all know we're here to be sold on something. Let's hurry along to the point and then we can get down to the nitty gritty of the matter."

"Very well," Wellington said. "We need allies. From what we've been exposed to it's unrealistic to think that we can remain isolated and keep to ourselves. We're too spread out, our ships are too slow, and we're extremely vulnerable after the Phage War. The Ushin are offering territory, planets, and technology in exchange for military intervention. With the new Articles of Federation we've all just signed I have the authority to deploy CENTCOM assets in emergency situations, but I don't think this would count as one. For the Fleet to be involved in the Ushin/Darshik conflict I would need a resolution from the Parliament. Let's also not forget that we've been attacked as well."

"What you're essentially asking us is if we're willing sacrifice people and ships defending one alien species from another, but not out of some misguided altruism," Nelson said, standing up to indicate he wanted the floor. "While this is not something we've had to deal with in the last few centuries, it's not without precedent. Most of Earth's history in the post-industrial age was defined by the application of military force. The Americans in particular had a very aggressive interventionist doctrine towards the end of their run, and even the reformed North American Union liked to apply pressure with its Navy. This sort of action is always presented to the public as being something other than what it really is: using force to protect something someone has that we want, or to take it from someone else who won't share. Am I right so far?"

"Yes," Wellington said, his eyes narrowed with suspicion, but he made no move to stop Nelson.

"The Ushin are willing to pay dearly for our help," Nelson continued. "Over two dozen habitable worlds and access to their superior technology ... I don't see how we can say no. You all heard the reality we're faced with: Without help the Federation won't last long, and the ESA will be able to pluck even more worlds from our control, one by one. This is not something I do lightly, Wellington ... but I'll take your proposal to the floor and push it through."

****

Pike shut the feed off and leaned back. He'd discreetly planted a listening device on Wellington when he'd brought the President back to New Sierra. It was something he regularly did, and without much guilt, since he worked for Wellington directly and the man was woefully inadequate when it came to briefing his personal intel operative after such a meeting. Pike had learned early on that it was much more efficient to just listen in and get the entire picture so he was ready when Wellington inevitably came to him with some outlandish request afterward.

What he had just listened to, however, disturbed him greatly ... but should it? The PMs and the President had basically just colluded to drag humanity into another war for what amounted to payment by the Ushin. Despite having a military organization that was hundreds of years old, the concept of war was largely lost on this generation of humans. The Phage War was a flailing, knee-jerk reaction to being attacked, but what Wellington was proposing was an offensive based on false pretense in order to gain the resources the Ushin were willing to part with. Was he being naive in thinking this was something they should not be considering? He certainly didn't think of himself as much of an idealist, not given the things he'd seen and done in his lifetime, so what was it about this in particular that made it so repugnant?

Taking the scale factor away he had to concede that this was no different than some of the things he'd done as an agent in the CIS. Were any of his political assassinations really so different than sending a few squadrons of starships to hit the Darshik? When you boiled away the distracting details of each there wasn't really any distinction between his killing of a single person to encourage a certain political outcome than there was in killing Darshiks for the Ushin.

"What the hell," he muttered and began bringing the Broadhead's primary flight systems back online. Pike had what was kindly called a "flexible morality" and it was one of the main reasons he was found to be psychologically suited for work as an agent.

He directed his stealthy ship into a steep climb that would take it out of the low orbit it had been loitering in and break connection with the device he'd put on Wellington. It was one of the better bits of tech he'd gotten from CIS before the fall of Haven; the tiny transmitter would actually dissolve away the next time the shirt was laundered and his boss would be none the wiser. As he felt the throb of the Broadhead's reactionless drive he wondered what, if anything, he should do with the ill-gotten information. Normally when he pulled one of these counter-intelligence stunts with his boss it was as a sort of checks and balance and he never trafficked information that couldn't have been found through legitimate means had someone just known to look.

This was different, and he couldn't easily explain away potential actions he might take that would be rightly considered treason were he found out. The documents he'd leaked to the media regarding Jackson Wolfe notwithstanding, he had no desire to be branded a traitor and he really had no moral high ground to plant his flag on save for a vague uneasiness about senior politicians manipulating the government for gain. But was there really anything wrong going on here? The Fleet flies out to help a species that is asking to be protected and is offered a haul of planets in return. Alliances have been struck for weaker reasoning and other than the "politics as usual" aspect of it Pike wasn't so certain Wellington and Marcum were in the wrong.

No ... for now he'd just keep the recording to himself and do as he was ordered. Wellington hadn't been able to get a straight answer out of his CENTCOM Chief of Staff regarding Project Prometheus, so while they'd been hooked into the *Amsterdam's* com system via the Tsuyo provided backdoor Pike had also cast a wide net through any of Marcum's files he could find. As soon as he'd dropped off the President at the New Sierra

Platform his new orders were to start hunting for whatever this project was.

"Gonna be another long, lonely trip," he groused as the Broadhead zipped away from the planet and towards the Columbiana jump point.

Chapter 13

"Captain Wright is on the com, Admiral." Marcum's aide stuck her head in his office.

"Thank you, Lieutenant Emerson," Marcum said. "I'll take it in here."

"Senior Captain Wright reporting as ordered, Admiral." Celesta's face appeared on the monitor.

"Are you alone in your office, Captain?" Marcum said, fighting to keep his voice neutral.

"Yes, sir."

"I don't think I need to tell you how badly you've pissed me off this time, Wright ... suffice it to say that at my earliest convenience you will be removed from the bridge of that ship," Marcum started, still struggling to keep his tone measured and professional.

"Unfortunately for me, that day isn't today. I've reviewed Commander Barrett's service record and I just don't think he's ready to assume command, nor can I afford to have the *Icarus'* efficiency go down the shitter by swapping in a new command staff on the brink of a major offensive. I need Ninth Squadron and your ship at their best." Marcum stopped and just stared at his captain. She was staring back at him impassively, not offering any explanations or excuses.

"Needless to say, I don't think you'll need to worry about me forcing you onto the bridge of the *New York*. What it is about you Black Fleet officers that makes you think you know best is beyond me ... but I'm about to do some long-overdue house cleaning once this—"

"Admiral, if this is supposed to be some sort of pep talk before a major military operation I fail to understand how this in any way is helpful to either you or me," Celesta said, managing to look bored by the whole thing.

"Oh, I'm sorry ... am I holding you up, Captain?" Some of the anger Marcum was feeling began to slip past his façade.

"No, sir, you're not," Celesta said calmly. "But you've indicated that we have an operation upcoming and I'd prefer to focus on that. I'm not denying that I disobeyed orders and ordered my ship out of orbit as well as leaving the station while it was on lockdown. We could argue the finer points of that, but I get the distinct feeling that it wouldn't be a productive conversation, at least not right now."

"Very well, Captain." Marcum swallowed down his retort. How was she able to so easily get under his skin? He knew it was beginning to look like he had a personal axe to grind with regards to Wright and that put her at an advantage.

"Barring any surprises during tomorrow's full session of the new Parliament, it will be announced that we've agreed to terms and will be entering into a limited protection treaty with the Ushin. We're expecting a full brief package from Ambassador Cole's staff in the next few hours, and as soon as we're authorized we'll be sending the first intelligence assets to begin verifying everything we're told.

"Due to a variety of reasons, not the least of which being the attacks on Terran ships and systems, we will want to move very quickly to take back the initiative. The Ninth Squadron will be deploying with the advanced formations to establish beachheads in the Ushin systems we'll be expected to clear of Darshik ships."

"Do we have any sort of intelligence on Darshik strength levels in these systems, sir?" Celesta asked. "We're only marginally more familiar with them than we were with the Phage when it attacked, and I'd prefer not to have a repeat of how that turned out."

"Nor I, Captain." Marcum leaned back in his seat. "We're in a wait and see position until Cole's team gets the briefing scrubbed and sent up to us. Communicating with the Ushin is still ponderous and, at times, inaccurate so it's slow going."

"And yet we're rushing in to—"

"You and I don't make policy, Captain," Marcum cut her off. "And we'll not be discussing it now. The reason for this meeting, besides wanting to look you in the eye before I decided whether or not to have you relieved of command, is to tell you I want you to begin organizing all Black Fleet assets in this system any way you see fit to facilitate a quick deployment. You'll be the first ships out to the initial rally point and then your destroyers will be flying ahead of the convoy when we make the final push. My aide will be transmitting your official orders that will give you the authority you need. Any questions?"

"Many, many questions, sir," Celesta said. "But it will wait. We'll begin redeploying all Seventh Fleet ships as soon as our orders come in."

"Then that will be all, Captain."

"Aye aye, sir."

****

Celesta killed the channel and stared at the screen for a long moment, noticing the details of CENTCOM's new crest for the first time as it replaced the image of Admiral Marcum's scowling face. She really didn't think what she'd done had been so severe as to warrant the Chief of Staff's reaction. In her mind, she'd taken bold, decisive action when everyone else seemed to flounder and had pulled their asses out of the fire by getting her ship to where it could do the most good. Instead, it looked like it had sunk her career. She also caught a whiff of an underlying anger directed towards her. Celesta had always thought Marcum was one of her more ardent supporters despite Wolfe's warning not to trust him. How she went from being considered for the command of a battleship to being told her days in Starfleet were numbered was a mystery to her, but like her mentor had said over and over: Marcum's rank of admiral became an honorific when he became CENTCOM Chief of Staff. Now he was a politician before he was an officer.

"Commander Barrett and Ensign Accari, please report to my office," Celesta said conversationally and waited for the computer to beep softly to let her know it understood and had paged the two officers. When the knock came at the hatch a moment later, she let the two in and motioned for them to take a seat.

"Is there a problem, Captain?" Barrett asked, obviously concerned.

"More than one, but let's get to them in order," she said as she began pulling up the sensor feeds and putting them on the four large monitors that were arrayed along one bulkhead. "We've been tasked with prepping the local Black Fleet assets for redeployment to an as yet undisclosed staging point. We should have orders coming up momentarily that will give me the authority to order them onto new courses."

"We're leaving, ma'am?" Accari asked. "Right after this system was attacked?"

"We're preparing for a counterattack," Celesta corrected. "I'll explain all that in due time. I think the faster we get out of this system the better, however, so let's take a look at our orders and get to work."

Her orders from CENTCOM ended up being as vague as she expected them to be, but they did empower her with enough command authority to get the other Seventh Fleet captains underway and steaming up to where she wanted them. Since most of the Black Fleet ships were orbiting DeLonges she sent an immediate transmission to Orbital Control to have them all moved up to a high holding orbit and ordered them up to escape velocity. It would take the better part of the day for them to untangle themselves from the random formations they had moved into to get up and away from the planet.

Celesta had no doubt her Fourth Fleet counterpart had received similar orders and she wanted to get her ships moving first. After she'd sent Accari up to the bridge to handle getting her orders to the fourteen ships in orbit around DeLonges, she messaged Lieutenant Ellison directly to have him order the two Black Fleet assault cruisers in orbit over New Sierra to form up on the *Icarus*.

"I think the sixth planet will make the most sense to form up around," Celesta said, having changed one of the monitors to a real-time depiction of the DeLonges System with a top-down view. "We'll still be far enough down the well to give the older ships plenty of room to accelerate to transition velocity, but we'll be out of the mess down here."

"So we're really doing this," Barrett said. "We're going to war over the attack in the Xi'an System."

"It would appear so," Celesta said slowly. "You feel we shouldn't?"

"I feel like I would like to know more about the Darshik, and from a source independent from the Ushin," Barrett said. "While most people have no idea what the Phage actually was, we do. The Vruahn could have been straight with us the moment they knew Xi'an had been attacked the first time, but they withheld support and information until after millions were dead."

"And you think the Ushin are similarly duplicitous?"

"Maybe." Barrett shrugged. "I do think we're being spoon fed information in order to reach the conclusion they want us to. I'm also not so certain I believe that a race of beings with advanced starships and colonies on other planets somehow can't build an effective weapon and deploy it. The Vruahn were also pacifists but were able to build powerful warships, the Phage itself, and even cloned humans to do their fighting."

"Unfortunately, Commander, we're all drawing our conclusions based on the limited information we each have," Celesta said, ignoring the last part of his comments as they raised an unpleasant reality. "And that isn't much, given that CENTCOM and the civilian oversight is being very tight-lipped."

"How do you reconcile with that, Captain?" Barrett pressed her.

"I simplify it for myself," she said, turning to him. "I took an oath when I joined Starfleet and accepted my commission. If I'm told that to protect humanity we need to fly back in harm's way, then that's what we'll do. I may question the wisdom of it, but if the time comes when I find I can no longer perform my duty in good faith I'll resign my commission and return home. But what I won't do is openly defy the orders of those who are appointed over me."

Barrett said nothing and Celesta couldn't help but wonder if her professed faith in the chain of command was a result of her previous meeting with Admiral Marcum.

The admiral's biting, angry remarks had completely blindsided Celesta, as she thought she had enjoyed his trust and genuinely felt she was doing what was expected of her. She was from a world where trust was earned and not so fickly revoked, and the higher she rose in the ranks of Starfleet and the closer she got to that gray demarcation line that blurred the boundary between military and politics the more she realized things weren't so cut and dried. It didn't bother her so much that Marcum had used her and her ship's legend to further his own agendas, as she was beginning to suspect was the case, but she was annoyed that despite the repeated warnings from someone who had been there she'd still allowed herself to be caught off-guard when it turned on her.

"How long until those two cruisers get up here?" she asked Barrett. He blinked a few times at the sudden change of subject before recovering.

"Fourteen hours, ma'am," he said. "Give or take an hour. They're parked down in a holding orbit stationary relative to the Platform, actually trailing along behind it. Once they're cleared they'll have to push away into traffic and move through three transfer orbits to get up to us."

"Send them new orders to just meet us over the sixth planet with everyone else." Celesta stood and logged off her terminal. "I want the *Icarus* away from New Sierra as quickly as possible."

"Aye, ma'am."

****

"This has to be some sort of record," Admiral Marcum commented as he read over the summary sheet of the resolution that had just been passed in the Parliament. "Nearly unanimous too."

"Always a few holdouts," President Wellington said as he sat carefully in his seat. "Don't worry, it's all in there. How are things on your end?"

"Wright and Everett are organizing the taskforce." Marcum laid the document down on the table in front of him. "The *Amsterdam* is in no shape to fly so I'll be transferring over to the—"

"You'll be handing command of this mission over to Fleet Admiral Pitt, or another suitable flag officer, and you'll be transferring your stuff down here to your office … the place where you're supposed to be when I need you," Wellington said. "You're the CENTCOM Chief of Staff, the liaison between Fleet and my office. You are *not* supposed to be standing on the bridge of a starship interfering with your people. From what I've seen recently you're far too close to the operations side."

"Mr. President, if I may—"

"This is not a negotiation, Marcum!" Wellington said loudly. "Either get with the program or get busy with your resignation. I need you doing the job your position requires. You're fairly useless to me if every time I need an answer from you I have to wait four weeks for a com drone to find you."

"Yes, Mr. President," Marcum said neutrally, knowing this was an argument he wasn't going to win. "I'll assign someone as soon as I get to my office. I can't afford to have Pitt gone for that long."

"That's fine," Wellington said. "Just make sure it's someone who can work well with Captain Wright since she'll be executing the initial push. Which ship is taking the *Amsterdam*'s place? This is just idle curiosity, mind you ... I'm not micromanaging Fleet operations."

"It'll have to be the *New York*," Marcum sighed. "She's the only *Dreadnought*-class ship that's FMC. The *Amsterdam* is out and the others are at the Tsuyo-Barclays Shipyards over Arcadia getting the RDS refit."

"Get your people spun up and get those ships out of the DeLonges System as fast as you can," Wellington said. "We have legislative approval on this so let's not sit on it. The Ushin are holding up their side of things so far, at least according to the diplomatic team, so as soon as Fleet Planning decides this is an acceptable risk given the size of the taskforce we're fielding I want them underway."

"Yes, Mr. President," Marcum stood. "Will there be anything else, sir?"

"Yes," Wellington said slowly, his eyes going cold. "I've been making some discreet inquiries and have so far been getting nowhere, so now it's time to get it from the horse's mouth, as the saying goes. Have a seat, Admiral. You're not going anywhere until I get a complete rundown on what the hell Prometheus is and don't spare any of the details."

"It's an artificial intelligence research project," Marcum shrugged, trying to control his reactions. "We have it isolated for its protection and that of our own networks, not to mention the damn ESA sniffing around. We're using it to wargame through various training scenarios ... it's nothing of particular import. Was there some reason you're asking about that project specifically, sir?" He knew that sprinkling in just enough truth would help him cover his own ass later should

Wellington ever find out what was really going on in the Arcadia System.

"I don't like having to hunt for answers, Admiral," Wellington said, turning his back in what was an obvious dismissal.

****

"The drone just made dock, Cap—Mr. Wolfe! There are com packets for you, both personal and project related."

"We're colleagues, Danilo. Jackson is fine." Jackson Wolfe looked up from his tile as his assistant came in. He felt bad for the young man given the isolation that Project Prometheus demanded of its staff, but the Cube had spoken to him and he knew that if he hadn't gotten him off New Sierra quickly some overzealous spook would have had the poor bastard "stored" somewhere so that he couldn't spread around what he'd seen.

"Technically, you still outrank everyone here," Danilo said.

"That's just for the bean counters." Jackson stroked at the three months of beard growth. "My rank is just an equivalency, I'm no more a brigadier general than I am still a starship captain. We're all just researchers. So ... why has the delivery drone's appearance made you so excited?"

"There was replacement coffee aboard." Danilo smiled.

"That is good news," Jackson stood. "Times were indeed becoming desperate as I found myself going through all the assorted teas looking for something with enough caffeine to justify drinking something that tastes like lawn clippings. Have Stevens and Marcos unpack commissary provisions first … I'm sure the rest of the equipment can wait."

"Yes, sir." Danilo straightened and walked out of the room. Jackson just shook his head, thankful the young man had at least stopped actually trying to salute him. The problem was that a lot of the rest of the staff of Project Prometheus wasn't any better. There were ex-Fleet and even a few former Marines, all who had served during the Phage War, that recognized him immediately when they'd established the new facility. For months the hushed whispers when he walked by and even some snapping to attention when he walked into a room had prompted him to take steps. The customs and courtesies were familiar, as were the surroundings, but Jackson wanted his people relaxed and focused on the task at hand. He also didn't want any misconceptions, by either his staff or himself, that he was still the "Captain."

He got up from his desk and left his cramped office. Despite there being many other, larger rooms available, there was a definite comfort level in his current accommodations. He walked down the passageway, intent on being one of the first to tear into the month's new coffee shipment when a loud alarm blared and red lights flashed in the corridor.

"Administrator Wolfe to the port, aft airlock … Administrator Wolfe to the port, aft airlock." The voice over the intercom belonged to the facility's computer. "Security teams to the port, aft airlock … security teams to the port, aft airlock."

That last part got Jackson hustling. Project Prometheus had been housed in a deep-space facility, disguised in order to keep those a bit too curious away. The issue with a good disguise is that having overt security tended to spoil it, but not having it meant you ran the risk of unwanted visitors being able to get up close before noticing them. It appeared they had just such an incident.

"Report!" Jackson barked as he strode across the antechamber that was connected to the auxiliary airlock, shouldering through armed security contractors as he did.

"Unknown ship has just made hard dock," the team lead said. "No transponder signatures and we didn't pick it up on thermals until it was so close it was able to connect to the collar with a flexible gangway."

"We have visuals up?" Jackson asked.

"Yes, sir," the contractor said. "Stand by." He slung his weapon and entered some commands into the terminal beside the airlock hatch, routing the external optical feed so that Jackson could see what kind of ship had just latched onto his lab without permission. When the sensor trained down from above and he could see a top profile of the ship, he ground his teeth in anger. He should have expected this sooner or later.

"Please send this message via the inductive link in the docking collar: 'What the fuck are you doing here, Pike?'"

"Verbatim, sir?" the contractor asked, his hands pausing over the terminal.

"If you please." Jackson nodded once. It was another minute before a reply came back.

"It says, 'President Wellington has asked me to come find you.'"

"*President* Wellington?" Jackson muttered. "Go ahead and cycle the lock, Stanford. Keep an eye on this guy until I give you the all clear. He's a bit goofy but very dangerous."

Stanford entered in the security code that would allow Pike to externally command the airlock cycle and stepped back, raising his weapon halfway as he did. It wasn't even another full minute before the red lights ringing the airlock hatch began flashing amber and then a solid green as the pressure was equalized and the hatch locks were released.

"Fancy meeting you here," Pike said as he strolled into the antechamber, completely ignoring the half-dozen infantry carbines aimed in his general direction. "Project Prometheus, I assume? Or have you completely lost your mind and this is now where you've taken up residence in your retirement ... keep in mind the beard is actually making me think it's the latter."

"Pike," Jackson said slowly, "you really shouldn't be here. Careful security measures are in place and all of this was approved at the highest levels of CENTCOM and under blanket immunity within the Senate."

"That's one of the issues." Pike looked around, still ignoring the security team. "There is no more Senate, no more Confederacy either. "We're now the *United* Terran Federation and your immunity may not have survived the restructuring. President Augustus Wellington would be most grateful if you could give his humble servant a brief explanation of what it is you're doing here." Pike's statement started the security personnel muttering amongst themselves before Jackson raised his hand.

"It looks like much has happened and we've been somewhat ... isolated," Jackson said. "Stand down, everybody. I'll take responsibility for this one. Stanford, cancel the alert and let everyone know we have a plus one aboard."

"Yes, sir."

"This way, Agent Pike," Jackson said and led his friend out of the airlock area and back towards his office. "So how did you find us?"

"It damn sure wasn't easy," Pike said, keeping pace. "So who should go first? It's obvious you've been *way* out of the loop on current events and it seems I'm slipping that something this elaborate could be put in motion without me getting much information on it."

"Why don't you go first and catch me up," Jackson said; he'd much rather be breaking into the new coffee than talking to Pike. If he was here, it meant that the whole project was in danger of being exposed. There was still so much left to do before information could be allowed to leak out to the political class. The trick would be convincing Pike to go back to Wellington and claim he couldn't find anything else out about Prometheus and hope the Senator—make that *President*—did what he usually did and move on at the next distraction.

****

"That's all very ... surprising," Jackson said after Pike had finished with his ninety-minute marathon recitation of events up to when he'd left the DeLonges System. "I knew about the attack in the Xi'an System and the Ushin first contact, but I wasn't aware that it had progressed to the point that New Sierra was under attack."

"That's about the long and short of it." Pike shrugged. "We're getting ready to mount a counteroffensive with your former protégé leading up the first wave."

"Wright has destroyed more alien ships in combat than any other Fleet captain," Jackson said. "She seems the obvious choice. So how did you find us?"

"I took a chance that you wouldn't be far from your wife." Pike smiled. "I knew she was here on Arcadia developing the new crew training program for the ships Orbital Command is getting, or whatever the hell they're calling themselves this week, so I parked in the system for the last six days and monitored all the com traffic and outbound flights. Given the secrecy of the project and the assumption that you were the principal I made the leap of logic that you would prefer a facility that wasn't planetbound. So when I followed that resupply drone out here I knew I was in the right place … there was no way it was random chance that the drone flew up and docked to one of the two remaining *Raptor*-class destroyer hulls left."

"I knew that choice was going to come back to haunt me," Jackson said with a half-smile. "But, the *Pontiac* was still completely intact since New Sierra Shipyard had never gotten around to decommissioning her once the Phage War kicked off in earnest. The powerplant is more than adequate for what we need and I know how to keep her running with a minimal crew."

"Is she fully functional?" Pike asked, surprised.

"More or less," Jackson said. "We had the missiles taken out of the magazines but everything else is as it was when she was parked out in the boneyard." The pair fell into an uncomfortable silence for a moment, each knowing what had to come next.

"What the hell are you doing out here, Wolfe?" Pike asked. "If it makes you feel any better, I really am operating under direct authority of the President."

"It does, marginally," Jackson said. "I'd have felt better if Marcum had given his blessing as well, but since this project would technically be operating under the new CENTCOM charter it looks like the admiral has been trumped. It'll be easier if I show you."

Jackson knew that the secret was exposed even if he didn't show Pike what it was they were working on aboard the *Pontiac*. The spook now knew what ship they'd set up shop on, and even if he repositioned her the old destroyer couldn't be hidden forever, at least not within practical range of the project's logistical support. So he would roll the dice and hope the agent came to the conclusion that, for the time being, Prometheus was better kept a strict secret, even from the new Federation President.

"Is that what I think it is?" Pike asked flatly as they walked through the hatch into the forward cargo hold.

"It is," Jackson confirmed. "It's the stasis chamber the Vruahn gave us. Cube, this is Agent Pike ... go ahead and say hello."

"Hello, Agent Pike," a voice said, unmistakably coming from the stasis chamber. "I have heard of you. It is a pleasure to make your acquaintance."

"You taught it to talk!" Pike nearly shouted.

"I didn't teach it anything," Jackson shook his head. "It ... woke up ... for lack of a better term. It's self-aware. An unforeseen accident that popped up in a hastily designed system."

"There aren't any Phage bits still in it are there?" Pike whispered.

"No," Jackson said firmly. "There was some talk of preserving the organ we had in there, but in the end the piece was incinerated and this machine put into storage. Then it started asking for help."

"I think you'd better start at the beginning," Pike said, following Jackson up to the cube that was surrounded by equipment and technicians.

Chapter 14

The Phage was essentially a biological weapon, an entity that had been designed by a species called the Vruahn to act as their guardians, allowing them to give up martial pursuits and focus their energies on purely scientific endeavors. But their creation became sentient and, eventually, insane. It repurposed its original mission to one that saw it try to eradicate all competing life from the galaxy.

While humans had discovered the existence of a "core mind" and had launched an expedition to find it they had also struck an uneasy alliance with the Vruahn to try and corral their creation. One of the items exchanged in the partnership was a stasis chamber, the Cube sitting in the *Pontiac*'s cargo hold, that could fool a formation of Phage combat units that a human ship was actually one of them when it was loaded with a transponder from one of the Phage heavy units. The transponder was actually a biological organ and needed to be carefully protected and hooked to a support system to keep working.

Before the plan to use the Cube could be fully executed, however, Jackson Wolfe, commanding the *Ares* at the time, had located the core mind and destroyed it with a fast-acting neurotoxin. But Jackson had moved the Cube to the *Icarus* prior to hunting down the core mind and, before the *Ares* could complete her mission, Celesta Wright had used the device to fly right within one of the largest Phage formations ever recorded during the entire war and singlehandedly destroy over four hundred combat units.

"So I get that the Cube's sentience is likely an aberration created by the Vruahn programming, but as anything other than a scientific oddity, what good is it?" Pike asked before turning to the Cube. "No offense."

"None taken, Agent Pike," the Cube said. "To answer your question, my processing power is greater than all of your planetbound supercomputers ... combined."

"It's right," Jackson said. "It employs some sort of quantum processing that allows such a small computer to pack a large punch. In addition to being able to power through any computing task we set before it the Cube was also plugged into the Vruahn aggregate computational network before they severed the connection, likely believing it was lost on the *Ares* before one of their ships brought us back home.

"The sheer scope of its knowledge is staggering. We've not only been able to prove out our own scientific theories in record time but we're now moving into areas of theoretical physics that were well beyond our understanding. The *Pontiac* is now home to over two hundred of humanity's best scientists, researchers, and engineers ... all working with the Cube on projects of practical application and others that are purely theoretical."

"And all the secrecy is because—"

"Because, just like you, judging by the look on your face, there are many who would be exceedingly uncomfortable with trusting a Vruahn computer," Jackson said. "Not to mention something that used to hold part of a Phage Super Alpha. We can't afford to let the whims of politics shut this down. I've seen the reports, Pike ... *two* more alien species popping up in less than a decade and the Cube has told us of two more in equally close proximity beyond that."

"Son of a bitch," Pike swore, a look of understanding dawning on his face. "It was you. Is you.

Prometheus is where Marcum has been getting all of his inside information on the Ushin and Darshik." Jackson just nodded.

"We were the first people he consulted when the Ushin scout ship intercepted the survey team," he said. "We've been a failsafe. The Cube is able to confirm some, but not all, of what the Ushin tell us as well as provide analysis of the Darshik from a point of view we lack."

"Is there any special insight you'd like to provide before we send the Fleet in to hit the Darshik at the request of the Ushin?" Pike asked sarcastically.

"We're prepping an intel brief now, actually," Jackson said slowly. "Who do you think you're talking to? Do you think I would do anything to put Fleet personnel in harm's way if there was something I could do to prevent it?"

"I really don't know what to make of this right now." Pike just shook his head. "I can follow the logic as to why this has been kept secret, but it's a lot to process. So what have you put together from this project that falls on the practical side?"

"You know the training program Jillian is helping develop for the new Orbital Authority ships? That's just a cover story; the ships the new branch will be getting are just going to be smaller, stripped-down versions of the *Starwolf*-class design." Jackson turned to lead Pike away from where the technicians were trying to work.

"What her team is doing is setting up a streamlined program to train up crews quickly on a whole new generation of Terran starship. Integrated reactionless drives, anti-matter weapons and sensors far ahead of what we have now … five new classes of ship, each needing crews that are trained to their higher performance envelopes."

"Where are these ships?" Pike asked hopefully.

"The first keels are being laid at a secret facility run by Barclays Ironworks," Jackson said after a long pause.

"Holy shit," Pike said softly. "You've cut Tsuyo Corp out of the loop completely on this?"

"For right now all system designs stay under the strict control of this project office," Jackson said. "I wasn't privy to the decision-making on that one, but I don't necessarily disagree with it."

Tsuyo Corporation had been *the* provider of military hardware to the Terran Confederacy since there was such a thing. The company was so old it had originated on Earth and had actually been involved in the project that developed the first functional warp drive. As such, their power was immense, both politically and militarily. Few decisions were made within the old Senate without their approval or at least input, and they ran such a tight ship that there was little anybody could do about it, at least not if they still wanted access to Tsuyo tech.

They were so guarded that even on CENTCOM starships there were systems that were forbidden to be accessed by Fleet engineers. The company was so large and influential that before the Phage War had turned Terran politics on its head the board of directors had actually been colonizing its own planets with the intent of making Tsuyo Corp a sovereign power. Given their stranglehold on technology and manufacturing it was entirely plausible that they could have pulled it off without much of a fight.

With that in mind and once it became apparent that Prometheus would produce useable outputs quickly, the project oversight had decided that maybe it would be better if someone besides Tsuyo was given the contract to begin manufacturing the prototypes. Barclays Ironworks, a commercial ship builder in the Britannia enclave, had been quietly approached about running a secret shipyard for the new generation of starships. Despite their partnership with Tsuyo, the smaller firm had leapt at the opportunity and agreed at once.

"You're not going to give me the location of this new shipyard, are you?" Pike asked.

"That depends on what sort of agreement we can come to." Jackson shrugged.

"What do you want?" Pike asked, almost afraid of what the older man would say.

****

As the Broadhead pushed away from the *Pontiac,* Pike was overcome with a moment of nostalgia as he saw the big *Raptor*-class destroyer swallowed back up by the black as the floodlights shut back off. He sat for a moment as the ship came about on its new course, remembering the same man, but a different, although identical ship. Or was it the same man? Jackson Wolfe, the legendary starship captain that defeated the Phage practically singlehandedly, a man who despised politics in any form, now looked and sounded like any other government bureaucrat. To be fair his project was a lot more important and useful than ninety-nine-point-nine percent of the paper pushers out there, but he was still just a project administrator now … filing reports while the scientists and engineers did the heavy lifting. That bothered Pike more than anything else he'd seen on the *Pontiac*.

When you stripped away all the specialized training and all the toys, he was a soldier. He followed orders, mostly, and wasn't prone to fits of introspection or existential thinking, but the Cube bothered him. He'd spent five days on the *Pontiac*, talking to the Cube, talking to the staff, and trying to formulate a conclusion that made sense. Jackson had asked him not to divulge the details of the project to Wellington, but that wasn't something Pike felt he could decide. No matter what the eggheads had told him the Cube was still a piece of Vruahn tech that had interfaced directly with the Phage and had now blossomed into a fully sentient intelligence by random chance. Hell, he wasn't even sure if he believed that basic premise.

Jackson had surprised him again by refusing to give him the exact location of Barclays' new shipyard, and although he had provided detailed specs for each new class of ship he had unwittingly forced Pike's hand in relation to his first request. The agent would now have to use his credentials as Aston Lynch to bring pressure to bear upon the Britannic government to cough up the yard location and it was unlikely he'd be able to do that without Wellington's approval. To get that he was going to have to tell his boss everything about Project Prometheus and trust him to do what he thought was best.

"Damn you, Wolfe," Pike said aloud. "Computer, set course back to New Sierra and execute ... max performance."

"Acknowledged."

By the time the second generation Broadhead transitioned out of the Arcadia System, Pike was already sound asleep in his seat. The computer analyzed his breathing and reclined the seat back until his labored snoring subsided, then it dimmed the lights and shut down the curved control panel. The adaptive software had become accustomed to the agent falling asleep on the flight deck and had developed a set of responses to make its sole occupant more comfortable.

****

"Secure connection established, ma'am," Ellison said.

"That will be all, Lieutenant," Celesta said. "Please wait outside."

"Yes, ma'am."

Celesta leaned back in her seat and waited for the preliminary command level briefing to begin. She'd opted to attend the video conference in her office and had her com officer come in and set up the necessary decryption routines so that she could display it on the monitor bank mounted on one bulkhead. The *Icarus* had been flying circles around Juwel, one of the few remaining planets from the New European Commonwealth that was still controlled by the Federation. They'd arrived a full three weeks earlier and had been waiting for the rest of the taskforce to trickle in as well as the new theater commander. It had been rumored that Admiral Marcum would not be flying his flag on the *New York* as everyone had assumed.

She was of two minds about this since Marcum was by far the most experienced flag officer still serving in CENTCOM, but he was also Chief of Staff and it was highly unorthodox that he should be personally commanding missions. Celesta freely admitted to herself that the admiral's sudden shift towards her played no small part in her relief that he wouldn't be directing the action. The Phage War had forced them all into roles they weren't used to playing, but she strongly felt it was time for Starfleet and CENTCOM to get back to the business of being a professional military organization and that meant sticking to doctrine and adhering to policy.

"Please stand by," a voice intoned over the link, startling Celesta. A moment later the video monitors came on and the crest of the *TFS New York* was displayed before it also faded and was replaced by the feed of Fleet Admiral Wilton standing behind an unadorned lectern, flanked by the flags of the United Terran Federation on the right and Starfleet on the left. Celesta knew of Wilton, of course, but had never met the man nor served under him in any capacity. What surprised her more than anything was that Marcum had sent a Black Fleet admiral out to run the operation and not one of his friends from Fourth Fleet HQ.

"Let's get this started," Wilton said without preamble or any sort of greeting. "We have a lot to do and we're already behind the curve. I see that ... yes, we're all linked in, it looks like. This briefing is going to be a one-way flow of information. I've disabled your ability to transmit onto this channel so feel free to clear your throat, cough, or sing the old Confederacy's anthem, but whatever you're doing you damn well better be paying attention. There will be a lot of information coming at you and you'll be responsible for knowing it. This briefing is classified Top Secret, special instruction two.

"Now then ... this mission will be a counteroffensive to free two Ushin-controlled systems from Darshik influence. One system is heavily defended by the enemy, the other appears to just have a light rearguard. Since all of our intelligence is coming from our new allies we'll be forced to recon ourselves before committing our forces. Trust but verify, as they say. We have four CIS Prowlers currently on their way to both systems to gather intel. I hope to get com drones from each team within the next few days, but no guarantee on that.

"If you'll look at the accompanying imagery you'll see that the heavily fortified system is defended by someone who knows what the hell they're doing. Only the second planet is habitable, and the bulk of their forces are concentrated between the orbits of the second and third planets with outlying patrols flying random patterns in the outer system. As you'd expect

176

from someone who has dug in, they have a slew of active sensor monitoring stations also scanning the outer system."

Celesta knew that often commanders without much experience tried to hold an entire system and not give an inch of ground to an attacking force, but that was virtually impossible. By the time you get to the outer planets of a typical star system you're talking about a patrol distance of nearly five billion kilometers, and that's just along the ecliptic plane. The number of ships it would take just to provide an overlapping sensor grid, and the logistical infrastructure required to support them, would bankrupt both New America and Britannia within half a year, and that was assuming they even had that many ships to begin with.

The more effective strategy was to sprinkle the outer system with listening buoys and randomized patrols while concentrating the bulk of your force in a place you could more easily defend. If you knew where the enemy would likely appear, like Terran system jump points, all the better. What she was seeing in the scaled diagram of the defended system wasn't exactly proof the enemy commander had a lot of combat experience, but it was an indicator. More importantly, their defensive formations provided important clues as to the capabilities of their ships. If Celesta was defending the DeLonges System with a squadron of the Vruahn fast attack boats she had seen during the war, with their real-time sensors and prodigious speed, she'd just park over the planet she was protecting and dare anyone to come in.

"Assuming the Prowlers don't come back with contradictory information on our provided intel, the Ninth Squadron will be the first in. Senior Captain Wright will move her three ships into formation here"—a blue chevron indicating the Ninth appeared on the diagram— "and begin a bit of a distraction to allow us time to move in our ships for the opening shot.

"Captain Wright, you'll be broadcasting a message provided to us by the Ushin declaring that the Darshik are no longer welcome in that system and demanding they withdraw immediately. I want you blaring active sensors so that you not only see any incoming but you provide a point of focus while I sneak in the heavy missile cruisers. You'll be on your own for a bit, but your *Starwolf*-class ships should be just as fast as anything fielded by the Darshik. Just be aware of their intrasystem jumps and know that you're free to take whatever actions you deem necessary in order to keep your people and machines safe while performing your mission, up to and including opening fire at any threatening gestures by the enemy."

Celesta had more than a few questions, but she knew this was just a preliminary overview and the *Icarus* would be getting much more detailed orders afterward that she could go through and then ask questions or lodge complaints. She had confidence that her ships could keep up with the Darshik warships in real-space, it was the aforementioned intrasystem jumps that had her worried. If she had more information on how they navigated them or the requirements needed that would allow her to use the system's "terrain" to her advantage it would be a big help.

She was now only half-listening as Wilton was giving each major grouping a breakdown of what would be expected of them. Truth be told, she was elated with her squadron's role in the upcoming offensive. It would only be *Starwolf*-class ships in her formation so there would be no holding back for slower, older ships. She also liked that they were being turned loose as a bit of a wildcard and not given the usual role of escorting the lumbering heavies down the well, a mission that basically made them targets.

Celesta pulled her tile over to her and, with an eye to the rest of the briefing, she began to sketch out how she wanted to array her ships. There were only so many strategies you could employ with three destroyers, but each also carried a complement of ten Jacobson drones that could be used to create a little more confusion. The Jacobsons were the most advanced unmanned spacecraft the *Starwolf*-class destroyer could carry. They could be loaded with mission-specific modules to tailor it to the role it was being asked to perform. While she was messing with different deployment strategies she also pulled up the mission module loadout they carried and began going through that. Depending on how long Admiral Wilton expected them to fly through the system alone kicking up dust there were some interesting things she could do that would likely confuse the hell out of the Darshik commanders. It would at least be something they hadn't seen from Terran ships before.

Chapter 15

"Director Wolfe?"

"It's just Jackson." The answer came back with just a dusting of irritation. "What can I do for you?"

"An unscheduled delivery just made dock," the orderly said. "There was a data card in it addressed to you with no origin marker."

Jackson wordlessly held out his hand, not taking his eyes off his terminal monitor. The orderly put the package in his hand and turned to walk back out through the hatch.

"Thank you," Jackson said politely and set the packet on his desk. He assumed it was from his wife, Jillian Wolfe, formerly Jillian Davis. She was younger than him by a margin that raised some eyebrows, but not enough to make him seem like a lecherous old man. The fact he looked younger than his forty-nine years helped out a bit. She had been the OPS officer on his first command, the *TCS Blue Jacket,* and then had followed him over to the *Ares.* After serving with distinction as his executive officer once Celesta Wright had been given the *Icarus,* she had resigned her commission when he had retired after the war.

He had begun to suspect that she had a harmless infatuation with him and was thus unprepared to learn just how deep her feelings went. At first he had been afraid that the intensity would wane once they were civilians, but, if anything, losing the distraction of the commander/subordinate dynamic to their relationship had made them equals in every aspect of their life and brought them closer together. In short order after his return to Earth they had started a family and were the proud parents of healthy, beautiful twins, a boy and a girl.

Jillian was such a stabilizing force in his life that he wasn't surprised when she'd simply begun packing when he came home and proposed that they re-enter service as contractors with the Prometheus Project. What did surprise him was that she had no desire to go back to work for him. She used her own connections to secure a position on Arcadia and before they'd even arrived at their new home she was scheduled for orientation at her new job. In a move that surprised Jackson even further, she'd also submitted the paperwork to change her last name from Davis to Wolfe, a practice that, while still common on Earth, was almost non-existent in most of the enclaves. She explained it as a purely business tactic: the name Davis was common and she had no particular attachment to it, but Wolfe opened doors and commanded a modicum of respect just by its association to Jackson's exploits.

"Hopefully the children are okay," Jackson said as he popped open the courier package and shook the data card into his hand, frowning as he did. The handwriting wasn't Jillian's, but he did recognize whose it was and it wasn't likely welcome news. He slipped the card into the slot and let his terminal read the contents.

"Hey, Captain." Pike's face popped up on the screen. "You can relax, nothing horrible has happened since last we talked. Just flying around aimlessly looking for a secret shipyard ... thanks for that, by the way. The reason I conned one of your planetside handlers into doing this for me is that I had a bit of an idea.

"Contained on this data card are all the post-action reports from every interaction we've had with the Darshik. There are the obvious conclusions made by our analysts, but the petabytes of raw data from the Prowlers could take years to go through. There's likely nothing there, but I figured your pet Vruahn AI might be able to chew through it quickly enough to make it useful.

"You didn't hear it from me, but the Fleet has mobilized the largest taskforce since the last battle of the Phage War and will be hitting the Darshik in two Ushin systems to push them back per the terms of the treaty. Although I shouldn't, I'll keep you up to date on what's happening ... it's just the kind of guy I am. Pike out."

Jackson rolled his eyes and selected the after-action summary of Celesta's first encounter in the Xi'an System. His frown deepened as he read what an Agent Uba had reported. It looked like she might have rushed down into the system with a bit too much reckless abandon, even if she had been correct that it had been an AU or ESA ploy. She'd accorded herself well after the initial shock wore off, but he thought she had learned a bit more caution from her time serving under him. He hoped she wasn't becoming too enamored with her own reputation to the point that she felt untouchable.

After having to grit his teeth and watch the *Ares* be destroyed completely in the Xi'an System, he concentrated on the overview of the Darshik ships and tactics. He was thoroughly unimpressed save for the "lance" they employed that looked to be some sort of directed plasma weapon and those tricky intrasystem "hops." After going toe-to-toe with the Phage, this enemy looked to be more of an even match for the Terran fleet's capabilities despite the fact they'd knocked Starfleet back on its heels a bit. The rest of the analysis looked like fairly standard fare and especially dry reading so he skipped it. Instead he pulled out a blank data card and began transferring the raw data from the encounters onto it, redacting any information that he thought might cause a bias.

"Danilo, get in here," he said into the intercom as his terminal beeped to tell him the process was done.

"Yes?" Danilo asked as he appeared in the hatchway.

"Take this down to the research team dealing with adaptive modeling and tell them I want it run through the Cube at their earliest convenience," Jackson said, handing him the data card. "Tell them I want it to try and see if a predictive tactical model can be derived with the limited amount of information given."

"Is this real-world data?"

"Yes, but don't tell them that," Jackson said. "I want an unbiased result."

"I'll get right on it." Danilo turned and hustled out of the office.

As his assistant left, Jackson had to remind himself that he was a project administrator now, not a Fleet officer. He would pump the data through his system and give the results back to the person who had requested it ... he wouldn't add his own comments or concerns, nor would he make any recommendations. All of that was someone else's job now. Despite his own internal admonishments, he couldn't refocus on what he had been doing before Pike's packet showed up, and his right leg bounced up and down with a nervous energy as his thoughts kept drifting back to the Fleet gearing up for its first major engagement since he'd retired.

****

If Celesta thought her crew was getting impatient waiting for the rest of the taskforce to show up, it was nothing compared to waiting for the go-order. All the ships had been replenished, orders disseminated, and tactics agreed upon. The only thing left to do was get the operation started. She had just started her watch on the bridge and had barely settled into her chair when Lieutenant Ellison called to her.

"Captain Lee from the *New York* is sending a personal channel request for you, Captain," her com officer said. "Would you like it at your station, ma'am?"

"Send it to my office." Celesta stood back up. "Ensign Accari, you have the bridge."

"I have the bridge, aye," Accari said distractedly from the OPS station. Celesta backtracked to her office and logged back into her terminal just as the channel request icon lit up.

"Captain Lee," she nodded when the video resolved. The *New York* was flying six thousand kilometers astern of the *Icarus* so the video quality was flawless with zero lag. "What can I do for you?"

"Captain Wright," Lee said. "I've received unofficial word that Admiral Wilton will be ordering a movement soon. But ... that's not why I wanted to talk to you before we got underway."

"Oh?" Celesta asked carefully.

"I wanted to apologize, ma'am, for my behavior when you met us at the dock on the Platform." Lee seemed to squirm in his seat. "Regardless of what scuttlebutt I'd picked up about being replaced, I had no call for such unprofessional behavior. I've been an admirer of yours since the Battle of Nuovo Patria."

"No apologies needed for dirty looks, Captain." Celesta had to try hard not to smile. "If only that were the worst thing that was hurled my way from other officers. I know you were given the *New York* as a provisionary spot during CENTCOM's restructuring, but if you're a captain that's worth a damn you'll want a chance to fight for your seat. The *Brooklands* was a major player in the war ... I think you've earned a right to prove yourself."

Lee opened his mouth to say something and then just nodded his head. "Thank you, Captain," he said after a momentary pause. "I just wanted to clear the air before we broke orbit. Thank you. *New York* out." The channel closed and Celesta leaned back to contemplate the odd exchange.

Captain Lee had been the CO of the *TCS Brooklands* during the war, a Seventh Fleet heavy missile cruiser. He'd been involved in many battles and had performed his task with a sort of calm efficiency, but when CENTCOM had tried to put him on the bridge of the *Icarus* when her first CO was relieved for cause Captain Wolfe had declared Lee unfit for destroyer duty. Instead, he'd pushed hard to have his XO, Commander Wright, named as the interim CO of the *Icarus* and, in the spirit of expediency, CENTCOM gave ground.

It was only natural that when Lee found himself on the bridge of a battleship that he would harbor resentment when, once again, it looked like Celesta Wright was going to swoop in and take it regardless that it was always meant to be a temporary posting. She didn't doubt that Lee would do his job to the best of his ability aboard the *New York*. What did worry her was that the lingering doubt of being told he wasn't cut out to be a destroyer captain due to a lack of boldness or decisiveness might lead him to overcompensate, to make rash decisions that put the mission and his ship at risk.

With a mental shrug she forced the issue from her mind. Her responsibility was to her mission, the *Icarus*, and Ninth Squadron. In that order. She didn't have the luxury of worrying about what was happening on the bridge of a Fourth Fleet battleship that wasn't even going to be in her formation once the operation started. Captain Lee was left in place on the ship by Admiral Pitt and she'd have to trust that he knew what he was doing.

"All hands to duty stations, all hands to duty stations," Ensign Accari's voice came over the intercom. "Prepare for ship's movement." A moment later her office intercom pinged, as did her com link.

"Captain Wright, please report to the bridge."

"Finally." Celesta stood and smoothed out her utility top.

They had received their official move order and since the Ninth was to jump in first, and were the fastest ships in the fleet, Celesta was given clearance to climb up to departure altitude first and come onto course for the jump point. She elected to fly the course on her main engines, not wanting to risk the RDS flaking out and not needing it since the other two ships, the *Atlas* and the *Hyperion*, didn't have the drive refit.

Once the formation had swung around Juwel and reached escape velocity the three destroyers peeled off onto their new course and away from the rest of the taskforce.

"Confirming new course, ma'am," the chief at Nav said. "We're where we need to be."

"Very well." Celesta stood up. "Helm! All ahead full. OPS, inform Engineering to prepare the warp drive for deployment."

"Ahead full, aye," the helmsman said, the deck vibrating as the main engines were run up to full power. They were still weeks away from any actual fighting, but the crew was razor-sharp as the ship was now on her way to meet the enemy. Most were still stinging from the slap they'd received in the Xi'an System and were looking forward to moving on the Darshik with a full battlegroup in tow.

"*Icarus* is at transition velocity, ma'am," Ensign Accari called out.

"Thank you, Ensign," Celesta said calmly, but made no call to the helm to throttle the engines back. The *Icarus* was topped off with propellant and having more velocity than needed when initiating a warp transition was never a bad thing. She watched as her ship raced up to .15c before calling for a throttle back.

"Helm, zero thrust," she ordered. "Utilize engine power as needed to maintain current velocity."

"Engines answering zero thrust, aye," the helmsman said. "Steady as she goes, on course for combat jump point Tango."

"Mr. Accari?" Celesta asked.

"Jump point is twenty-nine hours away at current velocity," Accari said, correctly guessing which information his captain wanted.

"Commander Barrett, at jump minus ten hours I want the warp drive deployed and a full system test done," Celesta said to her XO. "Between now and then I want readiness drills by all departments *including* Engineering. Maintain normal watch schedules for now, but I want the nervous energy on this ship put to good use."

"Aye aye, ma'am," Barrett said crisply.

"Carry on," Celesta said, walking off the bridge and pointing to Barrett to let him know he had the watch. Her crew was still the same combat-hardened group they were before they met the Darshik in the Xi'an System, but the incident had stung them as the whole affair could only be called a loss for the Terran team despite the *Icarus* destroying two enemy ships. She intended to make sure they didn't have a lot of time to

187

reflect on that during the long warp flight, and there was no point in waiting for the time it would take to traverse the Juwel System to start.

She was looking forward to redeeming herself after Xi'an, but she carried a healthy respect for her enemy into the fray. Their ability to jump around within a system and transport whole starships away wasn't something to be taken lightly, but she'd be damned if she tiptoed onto their turf and skulked around the edges, afraid to be noticed. It was high time these assholes learned just who in the hell they were messing with.

Chapter 16

"Transition complete, verify position," Accari called out.

"Position verified!" the nav specialist called out. "We're less than five hundred kilometers from our target jump point, just inside the heliopause of Tango System."

"OPS, stow the warp drive and inform Engineering I want the RDS online immediately," Celesta ordered. "Helm, use our transition velocity and maneuvering thrusters to clear the area. I want the mains ready to take over for the RDS without pause, so have the plasma pressure at full operational level. Tactical!"

"Passive sensors already scanning, ma'am," Adler said. "Thermal imagers verify enemy presence down in the system. I'll update as the data resolves."

"Set condition 2SS," Celesta said, adjusting the readiness level of her ship. The crew had already been at general quarters before they'd transitioned in. "Coms, inform Flight OPS that we'll be launching our drones as soon as we have confirmation the *Atlas* and *Hyperion* have arrived."

"Aye, ma'am," Ellison said.

"Transition flash!" Adler said.

"That's the *Hyperion*," Ellison said. "They pinged us with a com laser the instant they arrived."

"Captain Walton is quick on the draw," Barrett said as he watched his terminal.

After the initial excitement there was nothing else to do until the *Atlas* showed up but watch the passive sensors to make sure a Darshik patrol didn't stumble across them.

"Settle down, everyone," Celesta said. "We can't do anything until the rest of the formation shows up." Maddeningly, it was another nine hours before the *Atlas* popped into the system. Celesta did the math in her head and realized the next formation in the taskforce was still another twenty-one hours away at the earliest. She was just about to have her first watch stand down for a four-hour break before beginning the operation to make sure they were fresh, but the Darshik apparently had other plans.

"Contact!" Adler exclaimed again, drawing an annoyed look from Barrett. Celesta also would have preferred a more measured, calm demeanor from her tactical officer.

"What do you have, Lieutenant Commander?" Barrett asked in exasperation after Adler failed to elaborate on what she'd seen on the sensor display.

"Unknown thermal contact moving on a crossing course ahead of us." Adler composed herself. "Putting it on the main. Computer estimates distance at just over four hundred thousand kilometers and increasing."

"Looks like one of the random patrols we're to be looking out for," Celesta said as the magnified and enhanced thermal picture depicted what looked like three starships running on their main engines coasting through the system. "They don't appear to be trying to hide, and they're not turning out to meet us."

"It looks like they're lined up in a single column; all their attack formations so far have been phalanx or stacked," Barrett said. "I agree, Captain, this looks like a patrol that missed our transition. I think we need to operate under the assumption they've spotted us and reported our position, however. I'd hate for them to slide by just for their buddies to jump in on top of us."

"I think we're going to modify the plan a bit." Celesta sat back down as she watched the range between her ships and the enemy increasing at a steady rate. "Helm, do I have engine power?"

"Yes, ma'am! RDS is active and ready."

"Tactical, bracket those ships and begin feeding telemetry to the Shrikes; one missile per target and stand by for my order to go active," Celesta said. "Look alive, people! We're going to jump on this target of opportunity and then we'll move back to our original plan. Coms! Send a message to our other ships via tight-beam laser that when they see our Link go active that's the signal to begin the operation as planned."

"Aye, ma'am."

"Nav, plot me a course that will put us right up behind those ships, maximum performance," Celesta said, her adrenaline starting to spike as things were about to go live.

"Course plotted on last known locations," the nav specialist said. "It's going to be a bit fluid since we'll be doing updated via the passive sensors and we're not—"

"I understand the risks," Celesta cut him off. "Helm, execute your new course and be ready to make instant adjustments. All ahead full."

"All engines ahead full, aye!" The *Icarus* surged forward on a wave of gravimetric distortion, quickly reeling in the ships that had already passed them and were heading back into the inner system.

"Let me have a running estimated range to target," Celesta ordered.

Lieutenant Commander Adler looked distressed and didn't answer right away.

"Tactical!"

"Targets are gone, Captain," Adler said after a moment. "They disappeared from passive sensors and now there's no trace of them on thermals ... that shouldn't be possible even if they did a full engine shutdown."

"They jumped away," Barrett said. "The question is, did they spot us, or was this part of a predetermined course?"

"Helm, zero thrust," Celesta ordered. "Steady as she goes, no braking maneuver ... just maintain your heading for now." She was just buying herself a few moments to think while not having her ship dead in space. She could either alter her course and start the mission as they'd originally planned, or she could use the superior speed and acceleration of the RDS to try and relocate the patrol and try to take it out prior to the main body of the fleet arriving. Three less ships was not insignificant, but there was also no guarantee her destroyer would be successful in taking out all three.

"Helm, come about onto your original course, ahead one-half," she said. "Coms! Inform Flight OPS that they're to begin deploying our Jacobson drones."

"Aye, Captain," Ellison said.

"Back to the original plan?" Barrett asked.

"We don't have the luxury of a hunting expedition right now," Celesta said. "The fleet isn't that far behind us, and we're going to need the drone data

192

sooner than later. OPS! Initiate the Link. Put all of our received drone data onto it once it starts coming in along with our own sensor data."

"Link active, ma'am," Accari said. "Flight OPS is reporting all drones have been launched and are inbound to the target area."

Celesta watched on the screen as all her expensive Jacobson drones began to fan out away from the ship as they flew at maximum acceleration down into the system. Once they were within the orbit of the sixth planet, all the drones would bring up their active sensors and begin to map out the enemy positions near the objective while also, hopefully, causing one hell of a distraction that would allow the three destroyers to move down to be of better use when the main body of the fleet arrived.

She thought back again to the three ships she'd lost track of, her instincts still wanting to hunt them down. Logic overruled her instincts, however, as she knew time wasn't on her side. There was no doubt in her mind there was a CIS asset somewhere out there observing everything, and she'd rather not have to explain to her superiors why she had been unable to prep the system for their arrival as had been her one and only task.

"Receiving Link updates from the *Atlas* and *Hyperion*," Accari said. "Adding their drone data to our threat board. Both ships are underway and moving into position."

Over the next four hours the crew watched as the projected tracks of the drones reached out from their three-ship formation. It would be another six hours at least before the tiny ships would fire up their active sensors and give them a much clearer picture of what they were dealing with further down the system. So far all they could really tell from the passive sensors was that there did indeed appear to be a substantial Darshik presence about where the Ushin had said it would be.

"First of the drones are going active," Accari reported, stifling a yawn as Celesta walked back onto the bridge after grabbing a quick meal in the wardroom. "We'll have a much clearer picture of the enemy numbers once they update on the Link."

"When are the first ships of the main body supposed to arrive?" Celesta asked as she sat down.

"Still another twelve hours away at the earliest if they departed on schedule," Accari said.

"Call up your relief, Mr. Accari," Celesta said. "You too, Lieutenant Commander Adler. I want first watch rotating out for five-hour breaks and I want everyone rested and ready when the rest of the fleet arrives. I don't expect we'll see any action until they do, but sleep in your uniforms anyway."

There was some grumbling but her crew didn't question her orders, and soon the relief watch officers began trickling onto the bridge to receive turnover and begin their own long, tense watch. Sitting in an enemy-controlled system while all was quiet was worse than a running battle. At least that's what most of the spacers said until they were actually *in* a running battle.

"Captain, I think you should take this chance to get some sleep," Barrett leaned over and whispered. "We'll need you fresh." Celesta opened her mouth to argue and then the weight of her exhaustion and the stress of sitting in an occupied system seemed to crush in from all sides. She turned to her XO and nodded once, standing to leave.

"XO, you have the bridge."

****

Celesta had only slept for a little over three hours, but she felt enormously refreshed as she strode back onto the bridge in a clean uniform and a mug of coffee grasped in her left hand.

"Report!"

"Drones have gone active and the data is just now coming over the Link," Ensign Accari said. She looked at him suspiciously, but the young officer did appear to be fresh and rested. It wouldn't be unusual for him to wait until she left the bridge and then just stay on duty.

"How does it look so far and are any of the enemy ships reacting to the active sensor net?" she asked, sitting down and logging into her terminal.

"There are a *lot* of targets flying in twelve distinct groupings, all flying along the orbit of the Ushin planet," Accari said. "There also seems to be no reaction to the drones' high-powered tactical radars. Not even so much as a directed scan."

"That's interesting," Celesta mused. "Keep me updated as we get better resolution on the makeup of those formations. Has there been any word from either the Ushin planet or their ships that were supposed to meet us here?"

"Negative, Captain," Accari shook his head. "The only thing making noise in this system right now is us."

Over the next ten hours the bridge crew was in constant contact with the CIC as the drone sensor network Celesta had employed began to gather more details about the enemy formations. They knew there were at least one hundred and nineteen ships, almost four and a half times the number of Terran ships that would be in the fight and more than twice as many as the Ushin had claimed would be in the system.

The high-resolution radar scans were picking out over sixty of the cruiser-class vessels they'd already tangled with, along with a more or less even distribution of what looked like smaller frigates and support craft. The emitted radiation scans of each formation were inconclusive given the range the drones were operating from, but she could see that over two-thirds of the enemy armada was showing signs of active weaponry. So why weren't they reacting to the drones? They knew from the previous engagements that the Darshik could detect their RF-based sensors, so why weren't any ships coming out to investigate?

"OPS, I want one of our Jacobsons reconfigured to try and slip in through the gaps of the Darshik formation. I want eyes on the Ushin planet," Celesta said. Something didn't smell right about the entire situation, but she couldn't put her finger on it. The hell of it was she had no idea if this new behavior she was seeing in the ships down in the system was at all normal. Their lack of knowledge about the Darshik, and in fact their new Ushin allies, was something that she felt was an avoidable and potentially dangerous oversight by CENTCOM. It was one thing to enter into a protection pact, but they'd committed most of their combat-ready forces without much due diligence that she could see and now they were already facing more than double the ships they had accounted for.

"Ready to upload the new parameters, ma'am," Accari said. "Flight OPS will send it in the next burst transmission. We just want to divert one drone?"

"Yes," Celesta nodded. "Just the one. It may not make it through, but I want to see what the state of the surface is."

"The closest Jacobson should be on its way down to the planet within the next forty minutes," Accari said. "We also have some handshake requests on the Link. Four distinct queries."

"Confirmed, Captain," Ellison said over his shoulder from the com station. "Leading elements from the rest of the taskforce are emerging from the jump point."

"The drones are already raising a hell of a racket down near their lines," Celesta said. "Let's keep our own emissions to a minimum; passive sensors only and directional burst transmissions when needed. If the Darshik move at the new arrivals, a few more ships broadcasting as a distraction won't make much of a difference. Lieutenant Ellison, please tell the new arrivals to pass along that we've seen at least three Darshik ships free-flying through the system but have lost track of them."

"Aye aye, ma'am."

Celesta discreetly popped a few stim tabs into her mouth and washed them down with a healthy swig of coffee. The ship's chief medical officer would lose her mind if she knew what the captain was doing, but Celesta instinctually knew that things were in motion that wouldn't allow her to leave the bridge for any length of time. It also meant that she would be required to stay for an extremely long watch since all the players were spread out across the system. The com delays alone were just over an hour between the *Icarus* and where the rest of the fleet was deploying.

"OPS, keep an eye on the Link feed," she said. "I want to know when the *New York* arrives and I want to know when the Ushin fleet gets here."

"Aye, ma'am," Accari said. "How many ships are the Ushin sending?"

"Unknown," Celesta said. "I wouldn't expect more than a token amount, and then I wouldn't expect them to actually do much. From what I understand about the treaty agreement we've signed onto, neither

CENTCOM nor the Ushin expect their fleet to do any real fighting."

"You'd think they'd be willing to put a bit more effort into liberating their own star system," Barrett grumbled while rubbing his bloodshot eyes.

"You'd think," Celesta nodded slowly.

Chapter 17

"Good morning, Director Wolfe." Jackson looked up in irritation, saw who it was, and just nodded as he continued eating his breakfast. Some people were simply incapable of using his given name apparently.

"What can I do for you?" he asked politely after swallowing.

"I was told you'd want this." The orderly handed him a sealed hardcopy envelope. "It was from that special analysis you had the Cube running that Danilo brought down."

"Ah! Thank you." Jackson placed the envelope beside his tray and continued eating, making no move to open it. The orderly took an awkward step back before turning and walking out, almost looking like he was retreating. Jackson shrugged and kept eating. Although the *Pontiac* had all her galleys in operation, and Jackson had taken to using the same quarters he'd occupied aboard her sister ship, the *Blue Jacket*, he'd been taking his morning and afternoon meals in the aft enlisted mess hall. Dinner he still took in the officers' mess up in the superstructure.

"He served aboard your old ship, that's why he's so nervous around you," Danilo Jovanović said as he sat his tray across from him. "If I'd known you were eating breakfast so late I would have hand-delivered those results."

"Do you remember which ship?" Jackson asked, thoroughly chagrinned that he didn't recognize one of his own spacers even if modern starships did house anywhere from five hundred to a few thousand people.

"Apparently he was aboard the *Blue Jacket* for a short time," Danilo said. "I think he might have actually been a Marine ... he talked about someone named Major Ortiz."

"That would now be Brigadier General Ortiz of the United Terran Federation Marine Corps," Jackson said. "Same person, though. I'll have to talk to him later as there were some interesting events on the old ship that I'd probably like to know if he was involved in. Was there anything interesting in the analysis?"

"Nothing I understood." Danilo began eating. "I only just glanced at it though."

Jackson opened the envelope and began reading through the cover sheet summary while his assistant and only real source of companionship aboard the ship ate in silence.

Jackson saw right away that it was extremely dry reading so it was likely he was looking at something the Cube itself had actually written. The machine still seemed to have a strange affinity for Jackson even after all the artificial intelligence specialists and behavioral scientists that spent time with it all day and all night, fussing over it and trying to understand it. They cringed when Jackson walked in the room and treated it like an unwelcome houseguest, barking requests at it. He still had bad memories of where the thing came from and who had sent it, and he wasn't entirely sure he trusted the story of how it came to be sentient, if it really even was. He'd seen a lot of interfaces on Arcadia that gave a more realistic simulation of intelligence than the Cube.

"This damn thing," Jackson muttered in frustration. "For being so intelligent it certainly seems to have a hard time with such simple requests. These conclusions make no sense."

"Dr. Allen thinks it does that on purpose so you'll have to go down to the cargo hold yourself and talk to it." Danilo said around a mouthful.

"Absurd," Jackson scoffed. "But it looks like I'll be taking a trip to the cargo hold to talk to the damn thing anyway."

Danilo just waved as he got up and deposited his tray in the recycling chute.

He felt slightly guilty at how short his temper was with the Cube, but it seemed like the project had run its course, at least as far as he was concerned. When it had asked for him specifically he'd been there to coax it through its "infancy" until it was able to comfortably communicate with anybody that tried to talk to it. Now, nearly five years later, he felt it was unnecessary for him to be stuck on the *Pontiac* and away from his wife and children. Even the novelty of being back aboard a *Raptor*-class ship had given way to frustration and anger as his children took their first steps and began talking, all while not really having any connection to him other than Jillian telling them he was their father. He'd petition Marcum again to be let off the project and, if that failed, he would take more drastic action and simply resign. The pay as an assimilated O-7 was nice, the civilian equivalent of a brigadier general, but he felt it was no longer worth the hardship.

The other factor was that the Cube was no longer producing results at the breakneck speed it had during the early years of the project. It had developed practical applications and techniques for much of what they only knew in theory, as well as reviewing and improving the designs of five new classes of Terran starships. Now it spent its days trying to convey concepts and theories to scientists, most of whom seemed unable to grasp even the base concepts. The application engineers fared no better as the Cube was now trying to describe technologies to them that they couldn't duplicate.

"I need to speak with it alone," Jackson announced as he strode across the rough textured deck of the cargo hold. "I won't be long. Thank you." There were some grumbles and hostile looks, but people had learned early on that the director was not a man who enjoyed having his orders questioned or ignored.

"Hello, Director Wolfe," the Cube said simply.

"You ran an analysis on all the information that was on that data card?" Jackson asked.

"Of course," it said. "That is what you asked, was it not?"

"Then how come I'm looking at the results of a single incident?" Jackson flipped through the report. "This is all just the raw data from one engagement ... looks like maybe Celesta's run-in at Xi'an. Where is the data for the Ushin ships that were destroyed in the DeLonges System?"

"I was afraid you would not understand the context," the Cube said in its condescending tone that made Jackson want to kick it. "Your own CIS did an admirably thorough job of the individual post-incident analyses. After a cursory check I saw nothing to be gained by repeating their work. Instead, I concentrated on finding correlation between all the separate engagements."

"Since they all involved Darshik cruiser-class warships I wouldn't think that'd be especially interesting," Jackson said.

"You would be incorrect in that assumption," the Cube said.

"Wait! You're certain about this?" Jackson asked, holding his hand up to silence the machine now that he knew what he was looking for in the report. It was all there, spelled out plain as day.

"I am as certain as I can be working with evidence I did not procure," it said. "Would you like me to further explain my conclusions?"

Jackson was already walking away and pulling his comlink out.

"Danilo, it's Wolfe," he said, looking back at the Cube one more time. "We need to send a priority message to New Sierra. Access the com drone platform and have one of the new point-to-point drones standing by. Use my personal access codes if you need to."

****

"Still no reaction from the enemy fleet," Adler said. Celesta just nodded and shifted uncomfortably in her seat. The stimulants she'd been popping were tearing her stomach up and she was struggling to find a seated position that helped.

"Something's wrong," Barrett shook his head. "We shouldn't be here with so little—"

"Stow that," Celesta almost hissed. Her entire bridge crew was becoming increasingly on edge as the Darshik flew their lazy patrol below them and the Terran fleet amassed up near the system boundary, just inside the heliopause as the cruisers flared out from the jump point.

The *New York* had finally made an appearance and Celesta had risked a burst transmission to Admiral Wilton requesting an orderly withdrawal until they could determine what the hell they were looking at, or at least wait until the Ushin arrived for additional confirmation.

He'd berated her for wanting to flee in the face of victory and in no uncertain terms told her he thought Admiral Marcum was right and the stress of commanding the Ninth might be too much for her.

She had ground her teeth as she read the message, but sent no reply. It apparently didn't matter that she had more combat experience than all of the flag officers combined when they smelled an easy victory and the chance to fly back home a hero.

"All the missile barges are deployed," Accari said. Celesta didn't bother admonishing his use of the derogatory term for the heavy missile cruisers. "The *New York* has just sent the final alert over the Link; first volley will be away in … eleven minutes ship's time." Celesta did the math and saw that the alert must have been sent over four hours ago given the com lag. It also meant that Wilton's warning was meant for the main body of the fleet and the Ninth Squadron destroyers would have to deal with the incoming fire after the missiles had already left the launchers.

"OPS, plot a projected arc for the incoming missiles and let me know when we'll need to activate our transponder to keep from being targeted," she said. "I want a five-hour buffer on that. Coms! Make sure the *Hyperion* and the *Atlas* get the same information."

"Aye, ma'am," Ellison said, his speech almost slurring. She looked around at her crew and made a decision based on what they were seeing from the Darshik so far and the fact their fleet's missiles wouldn't arrive for some time. She plugged the numbers in at her terminal and, assuming maximum performance of the Shrikes of seven hundred and fifty g's of acceleration with a maximum velocity of .17c, they were still looking at just over nineteen hours before the first wave arrived.

"XO, stand down first watch," she said. "That includes you and I. Have CIC send up a qualified bridge officer to take over. Listen up! I want all of you getting down to your quarters for six hours of uninterrupted sleep by way of the mess deck. Go ahead and take the opportunity to get cleaned up and changed and then I want you back on watch in eight hours."

"The backshops have been rotating people through in split-sixes, ma'am," Barrett said. Normally under general quarters everyone worked a twelve-hour shift to provide maximum overlap between the three watches, but with not enough work to go around most department heads preferred to divide that further into six-hour shifts to keep the boredom and fatigue at a minimum until the ship was actually in combat.

"Very well," Celesta nodded. "You have the bridge until the relief from CIC arrives."

"I have the bridge aye, Captain." Barrett nodded and stood, walking over to Lieutenant Ellison to assist in getting everyone moving to where they needed to be.

Celesta knew she'd need to take a "downer" to try and counteract the stims enough so that she could actually sleep. That alone was risky given how exposed they were, but the greater risk was having her on the bridge in command without her full faculties. She was already having trouble focusing and her brain seemed to be wrapped in a fog. If she could manage five or six hours of sleep after a full meal it would help tremendously.

She ate with machine-like efficiency, hardly tasting her food, and was lying in her rack, boots still on, within twenty minutes of leaving the bridge. As the sedatives began to gently coax her mind down from the artificial high of the stims and she felt her body relax, she was still dwelling on the tactical situation further down in the system. Admiral Wilton had already committed to the plan, but she felt like there was something more at play that they were missing. Moments later her brain finally unclenched from around that thought and she fell into a deep, dreamless sleep.

****

Celesta woke with a start, a momentary pang of panic hitting her as she looked around the dark room. But soon the usual hums and pops of her ship underway reached her ears and she heard no alarms so she forced herself to relax, looking at the glowing clock on the far wall. She'd actually managed to sleep for six and a half hours and felt fully charged and ready to go. Gauging that she had about twenty minutes before she needed to get up to the bridge, she pulled a clean uniform from a wall locker and went to her personal head to shower.

Once showered and changed, she took a moment to log into the terminal at the desk in her quarters to check the *Icarus's* vitals before leaving. She made a mental note to talk to her steward as she ran her hand across the top of the terminal monitor and came back with a healthy layer of dust mixed with the grime that was ever-present on a starship. It was all the aerosolized fine lubricants and coolants that worked their way through the air exchange ducts and were even deposited all the way up in officer country.

All the ship's major systems were in the green and she saw Commander Barrett had signed off on the last ship's log entry. She hoped he had just gotten on the bridge in time to sign the log and hadn't pulled one of his usual stunts, grabbing a twenty-minute power nap before sneaking back on duty after he'd been ordered to his quarters. With a final inspection of her black utilities she exited her quarters and made her way directly to the bridge.

"Report," she said calmly as first watch was coming back on duty and getting turnover from their counterparts.

"*Still* no reaction from the Darshik formations, Captain," Barrett said. "They have to be able to detect the incoming missiles at this point with their own sensors even if their range is as limited as our own. Our transponder went active on schedule and Lieutenant Commander Washburn added our drone sensor network telemetry to the Link channel that's feeding updates to the incoming Shrikes."

"Brilliant." Celesta nodded her approval. "There was no issue with the integration? There are over two dozen drones out there."

"She had the CIC put all the data on a composite channel and the *Icarus* is broadcasting the data, ma'am," Barrett continued, reading his turnover off his tile.

"Make a note that if this works I want her credited with the idea," Celesta said. "Has there been any further word from our fleet?"

"Just the standard calls from the *New York* announcing the second and third Shrike volleys," Barrett said. "No new orders or warnings. We lost one drone but the cause is inconclusive. It could have been a mechanical failure or it may have gotten too close to a Darshik formation."

"That brings up an interesting theory, ma'am," Accari spoke up. He plunged ahead when all heads on the bridge turned to look at him, not just his captain. "What if all these Darshik ships are an automated defense screen? From what we know about the Ushin it wouldn't take much to keep them at bay; why waste the crews when you could put your damaged and obsolete ships around the planet with simple programming to shoot anything that came too close?"

"Interesting," Barrett nodded. "We could send another drone in—"

"Wait," Celesta held up a finger. "It wasn't the drone that we'd sent to get a look at the planet, was it?"

"Stand by, ma'am," Accari said, a flush creeping up his neck as the captain asked an obvious question he should have had the answer to. He pulled up his headset and began speaking animatedly, likely to someone down in Flight OPS. The crew down there would have picked the particular drone to receive the updated mission profile and someone likely forgot to update it in the log.

"Confirmed, Captain," he said after another moment. "The drone that was supposed to take a low-orbit pass of the planet was lost before it reached the Darshik defensive perimeter."

"That only raises further questions," Celesta said. "Keep the rest of our drones on the line providing targeting information to the incoming missiles. The first volley will give us our answers without wasting another Jacobson. What's the time to impact of the leading edge?"

"First missiles will impact in just under seven hours, ma'am," Lieutenant Commander Adler spoke up. "We're now receiving real-time telemetry from the weapons over the Link."

"Let's light her up," Celesta said loudly. "Tactical, bring all weapon systems to full readiness and stand by to go active sensors. OPS! Tell Engineering that we'll be maneuvering shortly. Helm, make sure the RDS is ready and that the plasma chambers on the mains are at full pressure."

There was a chorus of confirmations as the bridge crew began feeding instructions down to their respective departments to shift the *Icarus* from a stealthy profile to fully combat ready. Celesta watched her terminal as all the indicators greened up, each indicating a tactical system that was reported as fully ready.

"Tactical, full active sensors," she ordered once the activity subsided. "Begin high-power scans of our immediate—"

"Contact! Dead astern!" Adler shouted as the sensors went active. "Range is only one hundred kilometers!"

"Helm, ahead flank!" Celesta also shouted. "Tactical, snap fire Hornets, all aft tubes!"

"Aye—" Adler's confirmation was cut off as the ship bucked, the deck heaving upward, and the sound of a massive explosion somewhere in the ship could be heard and felt. Alarms blared and everyone seemed to be shouting at once.

"Hornets away!" Celesta heard Adler shout.

"RDS pod was hit with … something!" Accari called out. "Engineering isn't responding."

"Track the hornets! OPS, jettison the RDS pod," Celesta called as the first wisps of smoke could be seen coming in through the air handler vents. "Helm, all engines ahead emergency!"

"Main engines ahead emergency, aye!" the helmsman called. "Nav, please feed me course corrections and updates."

"You got it!" the chief at Nav called.

"Three Hornets have impacted the target!" Adler said. "They've slowed, but are still moving to pursue."

209

"RDS pod has successfully decoupled and has been jettisoned," Accari reported. "Still waiting on a status update from Engineering and Damage Control."

"Coms! Flash message to the rest of the fleet ... tell the rest of the Ninth to check their six," Celesta barked. "Helm! Come to port fifteen degrees by seven degrees declination and maintain acceleration. Tactical, fire at will ... whatever you've got!"

"Remaining Hornets away! Tubes reloading," Adler said as her hands danced over her station. "Helm, maintain current attitude ... I'm going to let them have it right in the face with the aft laser batteries."

"Holding course!"

"Ranging ... firing!"

On the aft-facing imagers the lasers shot out into space, refracting intermittently off the exhaust gas left by the passing Hornets. The batteries pulsed in a seeming random pattern as individual projectors fired and then shut down to cool before firing again. Celesta could see that the *Icarus* was venting atmosphere from the aft section, but her focus was on the boxy Darshik cruiser bearing down on her. The last two Hornets from the aft tubes were destroyed by the cruiser's point defense, but the heavy beams of the aft batteries were another story.

The image washed out momentarily as enormous amounts of thermal energy were released from the lasers hammering the enemy's hull at such a close range. The tactical computers detected the damage and redirected all the other projectors to that area. The prow of the cruiser mushroomed out and the metal sagged and sloughed away, blown clear by the explosive decompression every time the *Icarus's* guns breeched another compartment.

"Cease fire!" Celesta called. "Helm, come to port another ten degrees and keep the throttles to the stops. Tactical, two Hornets right into the damaged prow, if you please. Wait until we've opened the range up to ten thousand kilometers."

"Aye aye, ma'am," Adler said.

"OPS, get *someone* on the intercom and tell them I better get a status on my ship within the next few minutes," Celesta said as she watched the tactical display. The Darshik ship was still under power, but appeared to be flagging and was no longer turning to pursue.

"We're clear, ma'am," Adler announced. "Firing Hornets." Celesta watched, fascinated, as the weapons streaked out of her ship and, at such close range, seemed to impact the Darshik cruiser almost instantaneously. The gashed prow swallowed both missiles and then the hull rippled and undulated before rents appeared in the side and high-pressure gas pushed the ship into a tumble. A split second later the imagers washed out as the cruiser exploded with enough force that even with the safety buffer she'd put between them the *Icarus* was pelted with debris and the hull reverberated with more than a few hard bangs.

"Target destroyed!" Adler called. "Scanning for more."

"OPS, what's the status of the *Hyperion* and the *Atlas*? Check their Link broadcast," she said. "Nav, plot us up and away from the Darshik defensive perimeter and preferably away from the incoming missiles of our first volley. Put us back close to where we started. Helm, engines to zero thrust until you get your new course and then come about at half power."

"Engines to zero thrust, aye."

"Both our other ships also had Darshik shadows, ma'am," Accari said tensely. "The *Hyperion* is exchanging fire and maneuvering, the *Atlas* destroyed their target but took significant damage to their starboard main engine. The data is about forty-five minutes old."

"Coms, order the *Atlas* to pull up and out of the formation," Celesta said. "I can't use a destroyer limping around on one engine. Tell Captain Caruso to start steaming for the jump point back to the Juwel System."

"Aye, ma'am," Ellison said.

"Captain, damage control teams are reporting in and Commander Graham is also sending his report," Accari said. "CIC is confirming that we were hit with that energy lance, which they now think is some sort of short-range directed plasma beam. The RDS took the brunt of the hit but we have six hull breaches, two critical, and four crewmen seriously injured from radiation exposure. No other casualties."

"Were we able to fling the RDS pod clear?" Barrett asked.

"Yes, sir," Accari said. "The shearing charges all worked as they were supposed to, and two of the six solid boosters fired and pushed it off the hull. Engineering is reporting minimal damage to our power systems as it was taken out."

The pod had been designed to be blown clear of the ship should there be some emergency with it that threatened the *Icarus*. There were cutting charges attached to the eighteen massive bolts that held the pod fast to the hull along with the power cables. After that, six solid boosters that would push it out and away. Since the drive didn't really work by pushing directly on the ship's hull, it was able to be attached with just enough hardware to make sure it stayed in place during high-g maneuvers when it wasn't in use.

"Commander Barrett, please go inspect the damage personally and see to our people," Celesta said. "Tactical, keep the active sensors up. That son of a bitch was just sitting there behind us and waiting. We can't afford to let another sneak up. Reload all launcher tubes and auto-loaders and make sure your munitions crews are keeping up."

As the crew scrambled to follow her orders, Celesta had a moment to think about what it meant that Darshik cruisers had been sitting out there so close to her ships without striking. There was the abduction angle, but those weren't the class of ship that they'd seen grab the *Leighton* and disappear, and she couldn't help but shake the feeling that it had something to do with the seemingly oblivious Darshik flotilla orbiting down below them. What the hell were these bastards up to?

****

"Commander," Graham nodded to Barrett as the XO walked through the main hatchway to the Engineering area.

"How bad is it?" Barrett asked without preamble.

"Not nearly as bad as it could have been," Graham said, blowing out a breath through his lips. "That plasma lance hit the RDS pod, something that's made of six-inch-thick alloy hull plating. I think when the field generators blew they incorrectly assumed they'd hit something vital and shut their weapon down. Had the pod not been there it's feasible they would have cored this ship all the way to the reactor room with that thing. We'd have never known what hit us."

"They fired when we went to active sensors," Barrett said. "They were sitting back there for who knows how long until they knew they'd been spotted. All in all, I'd say we're lucky to be talking about this."

213

"It would appear so," Graham nodded. "Good thing the captain is fast on her feet. I don't think we could have taken another hit from that thing at close range. Oddly enough, the older ships are made of hull material so thick they could probably stand up to it for a bit, but these *Starwolf*-class hulls are just so damn thin. They shed off the heat better but once the ablative shielding is gone, that's it."

"You're not the first one to say that," Barrett smiled as he recalled his former CO's disdain for the class of ship named after him. "How are your people?"

"They'll be fine," Graham said. "Being treated for exposure so they're out for a few days, but nobody dead or missing. Come along this way and I'll show you the worst of it."

Barrett had seen battle damage on the last two ships he'd served aboard, both lost during humanity's battle with the Phage, so it wasn't the scope of the damage that surprised him, more the precision. The Phage had also used directed plasma weapons, but they lobbed it out in a burst that expended its energy over a wider area. A ship like the *Icarus*, specifically designed for that conflict, had heat-resistant ablative shielding over the outer hull that would absorb and dissipate most of that spent thermal energy.

The Darshik used the superheated gas in a much different way. Apparently they could use a type of electromagnetic focusing apparatus, not dissimilar to what their own main engine nozzles used to direct plasma, and channel the burst down a "tunnel" so that it was focused when it struck the target. Commander Graham showed him the readings they'd taken that proved the existence of the focusing fields and it explained the "energy lance" others had reported seeing when in close combat with Darshik ships.

Graham couldn't hazard a guess as to the maximum effective range of such a weapon, but he said it would likely be just over what the cruiser was sitting at when they struck. Barrett tended to agree with the chief engineer. They'd have wanted to be within the performance envelope of the weapon, but just enough to give them a safety margin. Too close and they would risk detection by the passive sensor array. The fact they were able to sneak up so close was alarming in and of itself.

"Punched right through her like a knife through butter." Barrett whistled as he ran a gloved hand over the exposed edge of one of the hull breaches.

"And that's just where indirect streams broke loose from containment upon impacting the RDS pod," Graham said over the radio. The pair were in soft maintenance EVA suits since the compartments that had been breached hadn't been repaired yet and were still exposed to vacuum. "It's a weapon that is easily defeated with distance, but if it hits us directly—" The engineer trailed off, not needing to further explain the danger. If the *Icarus* was hit again at close range with the plasma lance she couldn't survive.

"Thank you for taking the time to show me yourself, Commander," Barrett said. "I'll need to get back to the bridge and give the captain my report. Your people did a hell of a job."

"Thanks, XO." Graham waved him back towards the temporary airlock his crews had welded into the hatchway. "Let's hope that's the only close run-in we have with their cruisers."

Chapter 18

"First wave impacting the Darshik lines," Adler reported. The bridge was tensely silent as they waited for the results of the first volley.

"OPS, take over monitoring the incoming Shrikes," Celesta ordered. "Tactical, concentrate on our immediate area."

"Aye, ma'am."

"Two of our drones were taken out by Shrikes," Accari reported. "The others are tracking to the enemy formation. Initial returns from the other drones indicate we're destroying a *lot* of ships, ma'am. Still no response from the Darshik formations."

"So we used two very expensive Shrikes to take out two horrifically expensive Jacobsons. Fantastic," Barrett quipped. "This is a strange way to fight a battle."

"This was always how our fleet was designed to fight," Celesta said with a humorless smile. "The missile cruisers would array themselves out of range from the defending force and lob in missiles, trying to break down the defenses before moving the carriers and destroyers in to subdue the planet. The defenders would then use missiles to try and hit our missiles. It was a doctrine that lasted hundreds of years. Since we never had a war, we never had to adapt."

"Until the Phage," Barrett nodded.

"Until the Phage," Celesta agreed.

"The kill ratio is off the charts, Captain." Accari shook his head in disbelief. "Even counting the two Jacobsons as friendly fire, our first volley had an effective kill rate of ninety-three percent. Forty-six enemy ships destroyed or disabled."

"And they're not even moving to fill in the gaps from the lost ships?" Barrett asked.

"No, sir," Accari and Adler said in unison. The *Icarus* was sitting at relatively close range and the data coming over the Link from their scattered drone network had very little lag, so Celesta was able to see that the Darshik were just taking hits and not bothering to respond in any way ... not even to try to get out of the way of the next fifty Shrikes that were coming in, and the fifty behind that. Something felt very, very wrong about this.

"Ma'am, personal message from the *New York* coming in for you," Lieutenant Ellison said. "It's from Admiral Wilton."

"What classification?"

"No classification and it came over the general Fleet channel," Ellison said.

"Send it here." Celesta moved her terminal over and adjusted the speaker volume so that only she and her executive officer could hear it.

"Captain Wright, all of our Shrikes have been launched and I'm ordering the heavy missile cruisers back out of the system. They're currently accelerating to hit the Juwel jump point," Admiral Wilton said, his visage as stern and humorless as she remembered. "We've reviewed the logs of the attack on Ninth Squadron; you did well in turning what could have been a loss of three ships into a sound victory. I was also impressed with your sensor network you've deployed via the Jacobson drones. All things we'll discuss in debrief.

"We're currently covering the missile cruisers' withdrawal, but we'll soon be coming down to mop up whatever the Shrikes leave behind. It will be the *New York* and five Fourth Fleet destroyers, all *Intrepid*-class ships. Wilton out."

"Eight destroyers and one boomer against whatever is left," Barrett said. "He seems pretty confident that the Shrikes will make this a quick fight."

"I'm inclined to agree with him based on what we know," Celesta said. "The first part of this operation was supposed to be the hardest, and so far it's been shooting fish in a barrel."

The second and third waves of Shrikes hit as she'd expected and there were only six Darshik ships left flying once the drones rescanned the entire area. Celesta had a hard lump in her stomach. This was all wrong and her crew could sense it too. Faces looked worried and apprehensive as they went about their tasks.

"Coms, have Flight OPS send three of our drones to survey the surface of the Ushin world," Celesta said. "OPS, make sure to send the *New York* our final target assessment just to back up what they're seeing through the Link."

"Aye, ma'am," Accari said, unusually subdued.

Celesta made no move to take the *Icarus* down into orbit over the contested planet before seeing exactly what was going on down there. With the bizarre way the Darshik ships had just suicided, she believed they may have been more of a decoy and that the real nasty surprise was some sort of planetary weapon. If they had weapon installations on the surface that were similar to their shipboard plasma lances, with nearly unlimited power feeding them, she was certain they'd be able to swat ships out of the sky. With the *Icarus* now running on her MPD main engines there would be no way to avoid it.

It was another four and half hours before the first scans from the Jacobson drones came in from the planet. Flight OPS had smartly put them on an intercept trajectory at maximum burn, having them fly by for an initial scan and then enter into a high elliptical orbit and begin decelerating so they could come back around and slide into a low geosynchronous for a more thorough look.

"Ma'am, there's nothing there," Accari said, clearly confused. "No power sources, no heat sources, very few artificial constructs. The atmosphere isn't even the right composition for what we understand about Ushin-compatible worlds."

"Coms! Sound an emergency withdrawal on the Fleetwide channel!" Celesta was on her feet. "OPS, recall our drones. If they can get here, capture them; if not, blow them. Nav, get us a direct course to the Juwel jump point. Helm, all ahead flank when you get it."

"Captain?" Barrett asked.

"This is a trap," Celesta said with certainty.

"I don't understand how the Ushin would want to—"

"The *Hyperion* just dropped off the Link," Accari said.

"Incoming transmission, not on any of the taskforce channels," Ellison said.

"Play it," Celesta ordered.

"*Please surrender your ships and yourselves,*" an artificial, emotionless voice came over the speakers. "*This is what must happen. Further fighting only prolongs the suffering of all.*"

"That's it, ma'am," Ellison said. "It just repeats over and over."

"Who the hell was that?" Barrett asked.

"The Ushin," Celesta spat. "They set us up. Tactical, keep up full-power scans of the system. They know we're here already so there's no point in hiding." The deck shook as the helmsman pushed the throttles all the way up and the *Icarus* came onto her new course at maximum thrust.

"Ma'am?" Barrett asked.

"Think about it," Celesta said bitterly. "The Ushin had to be in on this. They get us to swarm into this system and take on their decoys in a glorious battle and then, when all of our munitions are depleted and we're all congratulating ourselves on such a rout, the Darshik show up and hammer us.

"The Terran Starfleet is now virtually eliminated and the Darshik didn't have to fly system to system within our territory picking us off. They didn't count on our antiquated tactics, however, and most of the fleet is already heading home and everybody left is fully loaded and ready."

"We bit on it hard," Barrett nodded. "They seemed to know just the right strings to pull to get humans moving in the right direction. Shit … we thought we were flying out here to be liberators."

"Incoming message from the *New York*, ma'am." Ellison saved Celesta from having to answer. "They're confirming four Ushin ships at the edge of the system, almost two-point-five billion kilometers from the Juwel jump point."

"That's something, at least," Celesta mused. "If they aren't guarding the jump point they may not have too much knowledge of our territory past the DeLonges System. Coms, has the rest of the taskforce confirmed our withdrawal?"

"Yes, ma'am," Accari answered for Ellison. "They've confirmed through the Link status and the *Hyperion* has just reappeared on the net. They're saying they had technical trouble due to the battle damage they took from the Darshik cruiser."

"Mr. Ellison, send a message to the *Atlas* and ask them how they're faring on one engine trying to get out of the system," Celesta ordered before turning to Barrett. "Even with their head start I'm worried they won't have enough time to get to the jump point before the Ushin spring the next surprise on us."

The bridge again fell into a tense silence as they all waited for the other shoe to drop, the deep rumble of the mains at full power drowning out half a dozen muted conversations. Celesta knew that their only move was to get to the jump point and get the hell back to Terran space. She'd been somewhat privy to the initial planning stages of the hastily thrown together operation and now she was beyond thankful that CENTCOM had scaled back their taskforce drastically. They'd moved into the system with twenty-four ships, confident that their opening salvoes would clear the way for the destroyers to get down into the trenches and finish the Darshik occupation fleet off.

All of that was out the airlock now as it was obvious that the Ushin were working with the Darshik on some level, or vice versa. She didn't know if one was coercing the other or if they'd always been working in concert, and she honestly didn't care. If she could get the Ninth Squadron back to Terran space safely then she would consider herself lucky. There had been at least three cruisers in the system that had positioned themselves to take out the Terran destroyers at some opportune time, and she guessed that it was when the broadcast message had reached them.

"The Fourth Fleet destroyers are almost to the jump point, ma'am," Accari said. "They'd not been accelerating long before you called for a general withdrawal. Projected data says that they'll transition out in six hours; we'll know another four and half hours after that with the com lag."

"Understood," Celesta said. "Have Engineering begin prepping the warp drive, but leave the emitters stowed for now."

"Aye, ma'am."

"Incoming message from Admiral Wilton again, ma'am," Ellison said. "This one is classified for your eyes only."

"I'll be in my office." Celesta stood. "XO has the bridge."

"I have the bridge, aye," Barrett said.

Ellison had the message waiting in her buffer by the time she'd sat at her desk and logged into the terminal. She was perched on the edge of her seat, completely uncomfortable with being off the bridge while there was so much happening that was unknown.

"Captain Wright ... it looks like we've been screwed by our new allies," Admiral Wilton began bluntly. "We came about as soon as we got your withdrawal order; apparently my own intel analysts aboard the *New York* weren't as quick to realize what such an easy victory meant.

"There are some things you need to know in case we don't make it out of this system. I have no doubt the Ushin and the Darshik see where we're heading and have some other nasty surprise waiting for us. This was passed on to me by Admiral Marcum himself, and if the *New York* doesn't make it I have to be sure someone is able to know the *real* reason we're out here ... and it sure as hell isn't some damn noble pursuit like throwing off the shackles of the oppressors. I have faith that out of any of us you'll be the one to get your ship safely home."

Over the next half an hour the admiral plainly laid out the deal the Federation had made with the Ushin. When he'd finished, and she realized what it was they were fighting for, she went through a whole range of emotions. At first she was indifferent; militaries had always been the muscle that backed up political decisions, and fighting to free someone while being guaranteed something in return wasn't exactly the worst thing a government had ever done.

But as she reflected further and realized how quickly they'd mobilized and how little they'd understood of their allies or enemies, the anger began to blossom deep in her chest. It was no new phenomena to be used by her superiors as a pawn in the games they played, hell, it was just such an occurrence that put her on the bridge of Captain Wolfe's destroyer. A bigoted fleet admiral wanted him gone simply because he was from Earth and she thought the young and upcoming Commander Wright of First Fleet would be just the person. The admiral had put her on the bridge of the *Blue Jacket* with the express intent of having her replace Wolfe in as humiliating a way as she could manage.

But this wasn't then. Back then humanity had enjoyed centuries without armed conflict, and Starfleet did little but move cargo and posture a bit when the enclaves became fussy. The Phage War changed all that and now that they knew there were real threats out there, threats that could wipe the human race from

223

existence, she was no longer able to accept that this was just how things were done. Somewhere in the halls of power of the brand-stinking-new *United* Terran Federation someone had decided that it was okay to send ships and spacers into harm's way for a handful of planets and the promise of new tech from allies they could barely communicate with.

She reflected back on her time aboard the *Blue Jacket* and for the first time she understood, *really* understood what it was that Captain Wolfe had gone through. He'd fought an uphill battle against not only an enemy nobody understood or even believed existed while simultaneously fighting his own chain of command. The symmetry of it all wasn't lost on her as she was now the one in the big chair with a whole crew of men and women looking to her to do the right thing.

"*Captain Wright to the bridge immediately*," the computer intoned over the intercom.

Her chair hadn't even fully rolled back against the bulkhead before she was already through the hatchway and racing back to the bridge.

"Captain, we've lost contact with the *Atlas,* and the *New York* has dropped off the Link," Barrett said as soon as she emerged on the bridge. "Fourth Fleet destroyers are still steaming to the jump point and the *Hyperion* is accelerating to transition velocity. We're the furthest down the well right now."

"How long until we hit the jump point?" Celesta asked.

"Just over fifteen hours," Accari said. "We're nearing Delta-V roll off now." He was referring to the slim area at the top of a ship's performance band right before its maximum subluminal speed in which increased engine output had a negligible effect on acceleration.

"Go ahead and—"

"Contact! Multiple targets appearing further out in the system," Adler called. "Populating the threat board."

Celesta watched as the tactical computer extrapolated all the sources of data being fed into it and put up where it thought the enemy ships were located as well as their own forces. Even with the display being an artifact, or best guess by the computer, the enemy strategy was clear. They'd appeared just past the orbit of the fifth planet and were going to deny them the use of the jump point. The Fourth Fleet ships were already well past, but she could see the *Hyperion* and her own ship were charging right into a dragnet. She also could see that the projected positions of the *New York* and *Atlas* intersected with the new enemy formations. This time she held out little hope that Captain Caruso would pop back up on the Link again. A *Starwolf*-class destroyer with battle damage and a single engine was little match for what looked like at least a dozen Darshik warships.

"Coms! Tell the *Hyperion* to initiate a short jump out of the system," Celesta ordered. "They're going to have to risk it. They won't make it through that spread of enemy ships. Nav, plot me a course that brings us around to hit jump point Epsilon without losing velocity. Helm, keep the hammer down."

"We're pushing *deeper* into Darshik territory?" Barrett asked as Celesta ordered them to come about and head for the second jump point the taskforce had intended to utilize to get to the second Ushin system that was supposedly occupied.

"They'll think we are, Commander," Celesta said sharply, not appreciating the challenging tone her XO had used. "We need to pull them back away from those *Intrepid*-class ships. If we can force them to chase us with their intrasystem jumps, we'll clear the way and then

225

we'll extend and escape the same as we did in Xi'an. Look alive, people! This is what we're paid for."

The *Hyperion* was just outside of the minimum safety distance from the primary star that would allow them to execute a "snap jump," a maneuver CENTCOM still didn't authorize but had been effectively demonstrated by both Celesta and Jackson Wolfe on multiple occasions. It was hard on the warp drive, but so was enemy weapons fire. Unfortunately, that option wasn't available to the *Icarus* or she'd have already ordered them gone. They were too close to the primary star and the gravitational effect was enough that Fleet R&S eggheads had warned them that it could cause a fatal instability between their warp drive's gravimetric distortion rings and string their individual molecules all across the system.

"Course plotted and locked in, Captain," the chief at Nav said.

"Very well," she said, still standing in the middle of the bridge. "Helm, execute course."

"Coming about, aye. All engines still ahead flank," the helmswoman said. "It's going to be a little bumpy until we complete our turn."

"It's a fair tradeoff, Specialist," Celesta said. "Running into a dozen plasma lances would be bumpier yet."

Chapter 19

"Pike! What the hell are you doing in here?" Marcum snarled as the CIS agent walked in like he owned the place.

"It's Aston Lynch," Pike said. "Actually, it's Mr. Lynch, Admiral, and I speak with the authority of the President."

"Listen here, *Lieutenant Colonel,* you and I both know that you're—"

"What you think you know is irrelevant." Pike sat down without being offered a seat. "Admiral, you better get used to the idea that Aston Lynch is not only a real, legal human being, but that he's been imbued with a certain amount of authority by President Augustus Wellington. As a part of the civilian oversight I have no particular awe of rank, even for the Chief of Staff and a Fleet Admiral."

"Wellington will not always be there to protect you, Lieutenant Colonel," Marcum said, refusing to use Pike's alias. "Now ... what can I do for you?"

"I'm just curious as to why you haven't made an appointment to fill Wellington in on the latest that's come out of Project Prometheus," Pike said, looking at his fingernails. "The point-to-point drone did arrive a full day ago, did it not?"

Marcum froze and looked like he was actually breathing a bit harder.

"What ... where did you hear that name? I have no idea—"

"Save it," Pike held up a hand. "I just came back from the *Pontiac* and had a nice tour with Director Jackson Wolfe ... even had a short conversation with the Cube."

"I should have you detained right now for even speaking about this out loud on this station," Marcum said slowly.

"And I should kill you where you sit for not informing the President about this project and then, to double down on stupid, sitting on information that is vital given that we have a full battlegroup steaming towards an engagement under false pretense." Pike leaned forward.

"I don't think this is the place for this discussion." Marcum swallowed.

"What the *fuck* were you thinking, Marcum?" Pike hissed, now very animated. "Keeping something like that a secret from the Chief Executive? You know Wellington, how well do you think you'll fare when he finds out about this? Oh ... and move your hand away from that security button or I *will* make good on my threat. Who do you think you're dealing with, Admiral? If your security detains me or kills me there's already a full brief automatically ready to be transmitted to Wellington's personal inbox.

"This is coming out whether you want it to or not. It's what you'd call inevitability. Now, here's how this can play out: You can go down to the planet with me and we'll present this data to the President together, or I'll have you arrested and I'll tell him myself. Either way he has to be involved. I was willing to let this slide when it was a semi-interesting science project, but now ships and people are at risk because of your inaction. That I won't tolerate."

"Why give me the first option at all?" Marcum asked, no longer pretending to be ignorant of Prometheus.

"Let's be clear: I don't like you. I think you're a slimy, back-stabbing, opportunistic piece of shit ... but that doesn't necessarily make you any different than anyone who would replace you," Pike said. "Something about flag officers with ambition and serious character defects goes hand-in-hand, it would seem. Don't think I haven't forgotten about you opening fire on the *Ares* when Wolfe discovered The Ark while we were in a fight for our lives out on the Frontier.

"But you are a realist and a master strategist. As much as it kills me to say this, removing you would harm the Fleet and it looks like that's something we can't afford right now. You and Wellington have managed to drag us into another war we're not ready for and you'll do more good here than in a prison cell."

Pike watched the conflict play across Marcum's face. He'd actually intended to walk in and have the team of NOVAs he had waiting outside come in and take the admiral into custody and march him back out to the Broadhead in restraints. But the more he thought it through, the more he realized the damage to the morale of Starfleet he'd cause just for a few moments of sweet revenge.

"When do you want to do this?" Marcum finally asked. "And who's going to lead the meeting?"

"Within the next two hours, and you can do the talking," Pike said. "Wolfe sent us both the same message, even though it was addressed to you, so we're on the same page."

"Wolfe," Marcum said as if the name caused him physical pain.

"Don't be too hard on the director, Admiral," Pike shrugged. "He's not a great follower of orders but I don't think we can deny his loyalty or his results. We'll take my ship down to the surface. I'll give you an hour to make yourself presentable." Without waiting for an answer, Pike stood and walked out of the office, closing the door behind him.

He could have handled that a *bit* more diplomatically, but given his original plan that was the best he could do. He hadn't been exaggerating about his feeling towards Marcum; he despised the man and had hoped the Senate would have put him out to pasture once the oversight committee caught wind of what he and the former President were up to on that secret planet, The Ark. But then the Senate dissolved and Marcum was spared the embarrassment of an early retirement only to not learn his lesson and continue playing little games while wolves were at the door and scratching. Unfortunately, this time he wasn't so sure they hadn't gone out looking for the wolves and then led them into the house.

"Is everything okay, sir?" Commander Amiri Essa asked. The NOVA team leader and his men were dressed in what Pike liked to call tactical chic ... casual civilian clothes that they still oddly managed to make look like a uniform.

Amiri Essa had been refusing promotions in order to remain with his people. The NOVA teams were CENTCOM's highly skilled Special Forces that nobody in their right mind wanted to tangle with. Essa had been instrumental in helping Pike and Jackson Wolfe during the end of the Phage War, and they'd all remained loose friends.

"We're good," Pike nodded. "The admiral has seen the light and will be accompanying me to the surface of his own volition."

"You need us to be on the ship for escort detail?" Essa asked.

"Amiri, I think I can handle one nearly senior citizen officer," Pike said in a pained voice.

"Just making the offer." Essa shrugged. "You agents are notoriously soft and you've been playing President's Secretary for the last few years."

"The day I need some sloped forehead, knuckle-dragging NOVAs for help with one old man will be the day I toss myself out an airlock," Pike shot back. Essa and his men just laughed at the good-natured back and forth.

"Take it easy, buddy," Essa said, walking past the agent.

"You too," Pike said. "What do they have you doing these days?"

"Classified," Essa said, turning to wink.

Pike just shook his head and waited for Marcum to emerge from his office, hopefully with a fresh shave and uniform, so they could go down and make a very uncomfortable report to what was likely to be a very pissed-off President Wellington.

****

"That makes four targets that have jumped in behind us, ma'am," Adler said.

"Can we detect any other Terran vessels in the system?" Celesta asked, her voice giving away just how exhausted she was.

"No, ma'am," Accari answered. "We've recovered four of our Jacobsons, destroyed the rest, and no other Terran ships appear to still be operating within the system."

"Shut down the Link," Celesta ordered. "Let's start going quiet. I want active sensors still, but shut down all the telemetry broadcasts, beacons, and transponders."

"Aye, ma'am," Accari said. The young officer had been on the bridge for almost all of the battle after the Darshik had sprung their ambush, but he showed no signs the stress or fatigue were getting to him. He was as crisp and precise as when he'd first come on duty, and Celesta was imminently thankful for that. Even though he was only an ensign everyone knew his service record, and even officers that outranked him tried to emulate him.

The *Icarus* was flying a shallow arc to get around the primary star, and now that they were relatively close to the Class G2 main sequence yellow dwarf it seemed the Darshik weren't able to keep trying to jump in to close the gap between them. Celesta had been operating under the premise that the intrasystem jumps were just a more accurate version of their own warp transitions and that the enemy would be hesitant to perform them down closer to the star. Her theory had so far been proven correct as the enemy had tried three different times to jump in close behind, one time forcing her to launch a salvo of Hornets to give them something to think about while they escaped.

While the small jumps were an enormous tactical advantage for the enemy, their ships didn't appear to be able to overtake the *Icarus* in real-space. That gave them some small window to take a breath and think, but Celesta knew that once they came out the other side of their arc and headed back up the well towards Epsilon jump point that the Darshik would be able to get ahead of them and lie in wait. Then all she would be able to do was try and dodge their plasma weapons while fighting her way up to a safe range from the star to transition.

"OPS, go ahead and prepare a com drone for immediate deployment," Celesta said. "Include the complete ship's log since transitioning into this system as well as the sensor and com records. When Flight OPS gives you the ready signal, get it moving back through the Juwel jump point."

"You think they're setting a trap up ahead of us?" Barrett asked.

"It's their only course of action," she said, nodding. "They can't keep up with their subluminal drives so they have to try and coordinate their forces with intrasystem jumps and have them in place when we come around the star. They'll have plenty of warning and we won't be able to deviate too much if we want to hit the jump point before being swarmed."

"It's unfortunate we got ourselves trapped so far down in the system," Barrett said. "It's going to be another thirteen hours before we begin to put distance on the primary star again; perhaps we should rotate the bridge crew out for a short rest before we make the final push to try and leave the system."

"Make it happen, XO."

"Go get some sleep, Captain," Barrett said quietly. "I relieve you."

"You have the bridge, Mr. Barrett," Celesta said before walking out the hatchway. She'd come to trust Barrett's judgement in such matters and if he was firmly telling her she needed to get some rest, she needed to get some rest. He took his responsibility to the ship and crew very seriously and he would not sit by while a stubborn captain endangered the vessel or the mission because she was too prideful to ask for a relief watch.

In almost every measurable metric Commander Barrett was a more effective executive officer than she herself had been while serving under Jackson Wolfe. He wasn't ready for command yet, but when he was he would be a force to be reckoned with. Now all she had to do was keep him alive long enough so that he could realize his full potential.

Chapter 20

"Lieutenant Commander," Celesta nodded to the relief watch as she walked back onto the bridge after a fitful sleep that didn't last nearly as long as she would have liked. "Please report."

"All quiet, Captain," Lieutenant Commander Washburn said as she gracefully unlimbered her tall frame from the command chair. "We've been actively tracking all targets. Three made intrasystem jumps and have been reacquired on radar along our plotted course. They are currently out of weapons range. Two targets are still pursuing us but are slowly losing ground."

"They're just there to keep us honest," Celesta said. "Keep us from doubling back again and going silent to try and sneak our way out. Have there been any further attempts at communication from them or the Ushin?"

"No, ma'am," Washburn said. "The com has been silent the entire watch. Medical called up and asked me to inform you that all crewmembers injured during the initial engagement have all been cleared to return to duty."

"Thank you, Lieutenant Commander," Celesta said. "Sign out on the log and then consider yourself relieved. Will you be going off duty?"

"No, ma'am." Washburn signed her final ship's log entry and signed out of the terminal. "I'm in the middle of my shift. I will be returning to CIC."

Celesta didn't answer as she walked the bridge, looking over all the individual stations and checking over the tactical threat board that was constantly updating on the main display. The data was hours old, but it was obvious that the Darshik intended a fairly basic deployment that would array their ships out along an arc perpendicular to her current course. They had no way to know that she wanted to get to the space directly behind them, so they weren't committing fully just yet, hanging back and keeping enough distance to react to any moves she made.

The major disadvantage the Darshik had was they seemed to heavily favor that plasma lance. When it hit a Terran ship the results were inevitable as their hulls couldn't withstand that sort of abuse, but it was also extremely limited in range. More importantly, her laser cannons could begin cutting through their hull much sooner than their plasma could do to hers, but when you factored in six ships ahead of them the equation became much more convoluted.

Without the RDS the *Icarus* was fairly close in subluminal performance to what they'd seen from the Darshik cruisers with a slight edge in acceleration and speed. The enemy's intrasystem jumps were unpredictable and a major strategic advantage for them, but she'd began to understand the limitations of the maneuver and was able to somewhat counteract that. The major problem she had was that past the Epsilon jump point her plan was based on nothing. CIS had verified the path to the second supposed Ushin system was clear, but they'd done next to zero reconnaissance of the system itself, CENTCOM not wanting to risk losing the element of surprise and still trusting the Ushin intel.

No matter how she looked at it, they were going to have to run the blockade and push through to the only logical exit point left to them. Trying to circle the system again and hit their original jump point was not an option. The longer she gave the Darshik to plan and organize against her, the less likely it would be for the *Icarus* to make it out of the system in one piece.

"Tactical, have your backshop run a full test on the armament," she said, turning away from the main display. "One system at a time, and make sure the munitions shop goes in and does one more operational check on our expendables. Not just the missiles either; I want the auto-mag shells given a visual check."

"Aye aye, ma'am," Adler said as she sat at her station. "Sending instructions now."

"OPS, inform Engineering I want a comprehensive report on all other ship's systems," Celesta continued. "Have Commander Graham's people interface with the com shops and Flight OPS to make sure their equipment is good to go. We have six hours before potential combat and I want her ready for anything."

Her commands set off a flurry of activity below decks, and no insignificant amount of grumbling and complaining about "busy work." She wasn't just trying to keep her crew distracted, however, as the ship had taken a direct hit by a very powerful weapon. While the damage appeared to be contained to the aft sections, it was simply prudence to make sure there were no surprises waiting for her when the time came for the *Icarus* to fight.

As it turned out, problems began cropping up much sooner than she'd expected. Not even two hours into the ordered systems check it was discovered that the power system had been compromised and that had they tried to fire the auto-mag or the forward laser batteries it would have likely blown out several junctions on the primary power bus, and the secondary bus wasn't capable of allowing both weapons to be fired simultaneously. Apparently when the RDS pod was hit, and subsequently jettisoned, there was damage to junctions where the powerplant fed into the MUX. Commander Graham gave her a running estimate on repairs and it looked like everything would be buttoned up and tested well before she assumed they'd need them. There was considerably less complaining about the workload below decks as the rest of the checkouts were performed.

"All departments have checked in," Barrett said from the OPS station where he was conferring with Ensign Accari. "Power MUX is back to one hundred percent and no other problems were detected during the system tests. Armament has signed off on the forward weapons systems after doing an internal operational checkout, but the chief down there wants permission to do a live fire test."

"Denied." Celesta shook her head. "While we're closing head-to-head with the enemy, firing the forward laser batteries would be giving a bit too much information about our power and frequency output."

"I'll tell him, ma'am," Barrett said. "Loop-back dummy-load tests all checked good, so we know the MUX can handle the current to the projectors. I'll have them button it all back up and get their people out of the forward compartments."

Like all Terran starships, the forward third of the ship was sparsely populated since there were all kinds of nasty sources of radiation and other dangers. All the high-power transmission equipment for the radars and high-power com systems were up there and the RF leakage from the waveguides and transmission lines was a definite health hazard. The munitions magazines were also forward of the centerline, but even the big nukes like the Shrikes were so well-shielded there was little danger from exposure from those.

"Tactical, target and track all enemy ships ahead of us," Celesta ordered as Barrett began moving the rest of the crew back to their battle stations now that all maintenance actions were completed. He also reinitiated the pressure hatch lock-down that was supposed to be in effect whenever the ship was at general quarters. He'd relented to make it easier for the work crews while all the enemy ships were accounted for.

"I want all ships being targeted with each primary weapon by the computer," Celesta continued. "Have it constantly update ranging data."

"Aye, ma'am," Adler said, the request a bit unusual. Normally a ship would be targeted by a specific weapon and the tactical computer would build a firing solution based on that so the ship could be repositioned and properly configured for that particular weapon. To have it tracking all targets and updating to fire all of their primary weapon systems she had to tell it to ignore a lot of conflicting inputs that would just cause it to spit out warnings and alerts non-stop.

"Helm, engines to zero thrust," Celesta said calmly, taking a sip from her coffee, an island in the middle of the hectic bustling as the bridge crew prepped the *Icarus* for the coming engagement. "Steady as she goes."

"Engines answering zero thrust, aye," the helmsman said. "Maintaining course and velocity."

Celesta saw the ship was travelling at .22c, or twenty-two percent the speed of light. That was far above their safe transition velocity envelope so eventually she would need to scrub that speed off, but she wanted to keep their closure rate high enough that the Darshik ships didn't have much of a chance to adjust to any moves she made.

"Aft targets have disappeared," Lieutenant Commander Adler said just as they crossed the imaginary line that meant they were fully committed to the Epsilon jump point. "One target has reappeared in the enemy picket line."

"Keep an eye out for that other—" Barrett never got a chance to finish his sentence.

"Second target has reappeared off our starboard flank! Range is one hundred and twenty thousand kilometers and closing."

"Target the closest bogey, two Shrikes," Celesta said calmly, watching the tactical display and enjoying the fact the target was close enough to get real-time reporting on its position. The ship had angled over and was now accelerating towards them, trying to bring its prow to bear and obviously planning on firing its plasma lance into the *Icarus'* flank. It hadn't fully committed, however, and was crabbing in while maintaining its forward speed and ability to accelerate to match the Terran ship.

"Helm! Full reverse!"

"All engines full reverse thrust, aye!" They were all thrown forward a bit when the *Icarus* groaned and shuddered as the main engines reversed thrust and began hauling them down from their relativistic velocity. It had been a move the enemy ship hadn't expected as it put the Terran ship at greater risk from the ships ahead, but Celesta had no choice: She had to eliminate the closest threat before worrying about those still far out of range.

"Fire at will!" Celesta barked even as Adler adjusted her firing solution while the Darshik cruiser turned in and tried to chop its own speed.

"Missiles one and two away! Stagger fire, three-second interval," Adler called even as the weapon telemetry and status appeared on the main display and the tactical computer added tracks so they could track their progress. Since the *Icarus* was still braking and the Darshik cruiser was still trying to turn in, the missiles closed the gap very quickly. The first missile was

240

defeated by the enemy's point defense, but the second slammed into the cruiser amidships, the hardened penetrator of the Shrike punching clean through the hull. The fission/fusion warhead detonated a moment later and the ship seem to expand slightly and simply disappear on the long-range optics.

"Holy shit!" Barrett said softly. "Must have hit them right in the sweet spot."

"Helm, engines ahead full," Celesta said, watching their velocity continue to drop as they streaked by the expanding cloud of debris. "Nav, begin final course corrections for Epsilon transition. Helm, at ten percent under transition velocity cut the engine thrust to zero." She received a chorus of confirmations as she watched the Darshik picket line redeploy based on what they'd just seen. Their ships were a decent match for the more advanced classes of Terran ships, with comparable weaponry, but the Shrike missiles the humans built to kill a Phage Super Alpha were always deadly if they slipped past the defense screens.

"Their flankers are accelerating down towards us," Barrett said. "They'll begin to turn in once they feel like we won't have the room to reverse course."

Celesta just nodded in agreement. Barrett had been a tactical officer before serving as her XO, and his insights were born from extensive training backed up by combat experience so she rarely found reason to disagree with him, and this wasn't going to be one of those times. It was clear the Darshik ships were moving with confidence as the ships protecting the edges began to push down to cut off any last-minute abort she might have planned.

Over the next six hours the Darshik formation continued to redeploy until they had a single ship anchoring the net and the other five branching out almost equidistant from each other and coming in on

241

them at a shallow angle. It didn't take a tactical genius to see that they were going to try and slowly collapse their formation until the *Icarus* had nowhere to go and could be pounded by the five ships nearly simultaneously.

"Tactical, target the furthest, centermost ship with four Hornets," Celesta ordered. "Then get me an updating fire solution for the auto-mag and stand by. OPS! Let me know when the leading edge of the enemy formation collapses down to the one-hundred-thousand-kilometer range."

"Aye, ma'am," Adler said.

"Numbers coming up on the main display, Captain," Accari said.

Despite the way space combat had evolved in such a short period, it was the timing that Celesta never got used to. Days of nothing, just flying to or fleeing from an engagement and then, as ships came together, it was fast and furious for a few harrowing moments and then back to waiting. It flew in the face of centuries of accepted doctrine in the Terran fleet that all fighting would be done from a safe distance with guided or ballistic weaponry. From the way the Darshik ships seemed to have evolved, and the weaponry they employed, it appeared they'd never considered standoff warfare as a viable option. Nearly all their weapons required their ships to get in very close and try to knock out an enemy at ranges that Terran captains wouldn't consider other than during docking maneuvers.

"Helm, all ahead emergency," Celesta said, watching the ranging data closely.

"All engines ahead emergency, aye." The helmsman deftly disengaged the safety locks and soon the deck was rumbling harshly as Celesta watched her main engines climb to one hundred and thirty-one percent of their designed maximum output. The computers that controlled the engines wouldn't let her destroy them without a secondary safety lockout being overridden from the command console at her seat. They would pull the power back or allow it to climb as it monitored the electromagnetic constrictors, the nozzles, and the plasma pressure in each MPD. All the participants in the battle were close enough that her maneuver had an immediate effect as the *Icarus* accelerated to the point that the flanking enemy ships had to increase their intercept angles and would likely still overrun the destroyer.

"OPS, keep an eye out for any fire from those flankers," Celesta ordered. "Tactical, fire the Hornets and stand by for the auto-mag."

"Firing!" Adler called and four missiles, much smaller than Shrikes, streaked away from the ship from the forward launch tubes. The missiles were all tracking true, but Celesta had no doubt the small interceptors would be destroyed by the Darshik cruiser before they could do any damage.

"Tactical, you are clear to execute auto-mag firing sequence," Celesta said as she authorized the tactical station to take over helm control from her own terminal, pressing her thumb to the screen for a biometric reading.

"Initiating auto-mag sequence, aye," Adler said. "Helm, zero thrust and stand by to relinquish control." The auto-mag was an enormous rapid-fire rail gun that ran almost half the length of the ship. The barrel emerged from the prow along the centerline of the ship and just under the pointed nose of the composite radome that covered the sensor antennas. Unlike the preceding class of destroyer operated by Black Fleet, the *Starwolf*-class only had one cannon and it wasn't mounted on an articulated turret. The entire ship had to be maneuvered to aim it, which wasn't ideal, but the gun was a late addition to the design at the insistence of Jackson Wolfe.

"We're clear to fire, ma'am," Adler said, wanting the final confirmation before unloading with the first of five, five-shot salvos she had programmed.

"Stand by," Celesta said, taking in the tactical picture on the threat board now that all the players were getting within close range of each other. She waited until the range to the forward target ticked just under seventy-five thousand kilometers to ensure the cruiser wouldn't have much room to maneuver while it focused on the four Hornet missiles.

"Fire!"

The deck shook as one-thousand-millimeter tungsten shells with depleted uranium cores were hurled out of the *Icarus* at just over fifteen thousand meters per second. The gun was hard-mounted to the ship's hull so each shot reverberated through the destroyer and the hull rang like a bell. The auto-mag could fire twenty-five rounds before it had to be reloaded, the coils cooled, and the capacitor banks recharged. By breaking that up into five smaller salvos, each correcting aim slightly to make a dispersed pattern, Celesta hoped to catch the cruiser flat-footed and maximize her chance at a direct hit as they were near the weapon's maximum effective range.

"Shots away," Adler said. "Safing auto-mag for a reload and releasing attitude control to the helm."

"Helm, come starboard ten degrees, ahead full," Celesta said.

"One Hornet got through!" Accari called out. "Minor damage to the dorsal surface of the target." They needed no confirmation when the auto-mag shells arrived as close as they were. While the optical sensors couldn't quite pick up the cruiser itself, the brilliant flash of the penetrators ripping through the ship shone briefly like a new star before winking out.

"Target is ... destroyed!" Adler called out. "She's breaking up into four distinct pieces."

"Were they able to get a shot off before our shells impacted?" Barrett asked.

"No, sir," she said. "Course ahead is clear all the way to Epsilon jump point."

"OPS, what are the remaining enemy ships doing?" Celesta asked, standing up.

"Coming about to pursue, but they're completely out of position, ma'am," Accari said. "None will be able to close within weapons range given our current profile on that class of ship."

"Very well. Deploy the warp drive and tell Engineering to prepare for transition," Celesta ordered. "Helm, we're going to maintain acceleration and then decel just before we line up on our jump point."

"Acknowledged, Captain," the helmsman said.

"Nav, verify course and speed," Celesta said. "OPS, prepare the *Icarus* to depart this damn—"

"New contact! Dead aft, two ships just appeared," Adler said.

"Did two of the flanking cruisers jump in?" Celesta asked.

"Negative. Radar profile indicates these are two Ushin ships, same configurations as the two that appeared in-system earlier," Adler said. "They're now accelerating to close the gap."

"How long until we transition out versus the time until they're within assumed weapons range?" Celesta asked.

"Currently five hours from transition, ma'am," the nav specialist said. "That's including decel maneuver."

"Assuming comparable weaponry to the Darshik and that they're at maximum acceleration, they'll not close to within weapons range until we slow for transition, Captain," Accari said. "We could outrun them if we push the engines to flank."

"But then we'll have to shed off even more speed as we near the jump point." Celesta shook her head. "Maintain speed and heading. Tactical, target both Ushin ships with the aft tubes, one Shrike each. Coms, open a channel to our *allies*."

"Broadcasting on last known Ushin channel, ma'am," Ellison said.

"Attention pursuing Ushin vessels, this is Captain Wright aboard the Terran warship, *Icarus*," Celesta said. "Break off pursuit and allow us to leave this system. We have already reported your actions to our leadership ... there is nothing to be gained by further antagonizing this ship."

"*We cannot give you leave*," an artificial voice replied back almost immediately. "*Agreements made must be honored.*" Celesta looked at Barrett in confusion and her XO in turn only shrugged.

"How do you honor your agreement by betraying us and assisting the Darshik?" she asked, not really sure the translation on their side would be up to breaking down what she was asking.

"*A demand has been made. We must comply. Humanity will be made to suffer,*" the voice said before

246

the intercom chirped to indicate the channel had been closed. Ellison shook his head, indicating that it hadn't been him that terminated the conversation.

"At least we have a bit more of a coherent threat," Barrett said. "I have to believe that in the absence of any senior leadership or guidance from the diplomatic corps that we must now consider the Ushin to be an equal threat to the Darshik."

"I'm afraid you're right, XO," Celesta said. She knew Barrett's choice of words was deliberate and meant to not only state his opinion but to put it on official record that the *Icarus* was being forced to defend herself against a force that CENTCOM and the Federation Parliament considered an ally. But they were hundreds of lightyears from the capital and her first responsibility was to the ship and to the crew.

"Tactical … fire the Shrikes."

"Missiles one and two away," Adler said.

Two Shrike nuclear penetrators fired from the aft tubes and fired their engines. In reality they were decelerating from the relative speed they carried from the *Icarus* and waiting for the Ushin ships to meet them, but on the tactical board the tracks showed two missiles racing to their targets.

The Darshik had learned quickly to look for, and intercept, the small Terran missiles that packed such a big punch, but the Ushin were hopelessly ill-prepared for what was coming. Each Shrike slammed into the prow of its respective target, plunging deep into the guts of the cruisers before the warheads detonated. Both ships were instantaneously turned into clouds of expanding debris.

Celesta didn't know whether the Ushin ships could have actually harmed the *Icarus*. She believed the likelihood was low given that the Ushin appeared to be herding the Terran ships to where the Darshik were waiting, but it was a risk she wasn't willing to take given how bizarrely off the rails the mission had gone since arriving in the system.

The helmsman executed the braking maneuver as scheduled and the *Icarus* was slowed down to ten percent below her maximum transition velocity before the engines were shut down and secured. Celesta ordered all the tactical systems safed and the active sensors turned off as she took one last look at the threat board, the Darshik cruisers still pursuing but now too far back to be a threat. She hoped that out of all the com drones and ships that had returned to the Juwel System that CENTCOM would soon be getting a picture of how badly things had gone. She didn't pretend to understand what it all meant, but it was clear the Ushin had been manipulating the situation either on behalf of the Darshik or for their own reasons.

"Stand by for warp transition!" the nav specialist called as the fore and aft distortion rings formed and began to stabilize, arcing out from the lateral emitters until the gravimetric energy created a visual effect on the main display. With a harsh shudder the *Icarus* disappeared from the system with barely a flash of light to mark her passing.

After breathing a sigh of relief at escaping what was behind them, Celesta now had to worry about what was ahead of them.

****

Chief of Staff Marcum sat behind his desk, drumming his fingers and trying to decide if he would take any direct action against Agent Pike or not. The man was protected at the highest levels, that was for sure, but he knew he could dig up enough dirt on the bastard that Wellington would have no choice but to distance himself. Pike may look at the new President as a benefactor, but Marcum knew him to be a politician above all else. He wouldn't risk his new position or power to protect someone who technically didn't even exist.

He'd been sweating bullets on the ride down to the surface and Pike had him half-convinced he was walking into his own execution, but the agent had overplayed his hand and the meeting hadn't gone nearly as poorly as he would have expected. Oh, there was a lot of bluster and cursing from the President, but it was more on being left out of the loop than anything else. Once Marcum had explained just how sensitive the project was due to the Vruahn connection, Wellington had conceded that he'd probably done the right thing.

What had really surprised him, however, was that the project output Wolfe had sent like it was a dire emergency had been largely blown off. The details were almost entirely technical, including some especially dry portions about beta decay and molecular signatures that the President couldn't have cared less about. He wanted a brief synopsis and Wolfe, being the honest idiot he was, had stated that the evidence only suggested one possibility but wasn't conclusive. Marcum had almost been able to see Wellington switch his brain off as soon as he heard that, despite Pike's near desperate pleading that he take another look at the matter.

In the end, Wellington had ordered Marcum to assemble an independent team from Fleet Science and Research to audit Project Prometheus and review Director Wolfe's conclusions before dismissing both he and Pike. The agent refused to even look at the Chief of Staff as he stalked away once out of the office. Marcum had been so preoccupied reflecting on his good fortune that he let the man escape without so much as a word. Not only had Pike been diminished in front of his boss, but Wellington had given Marcum an easy out for getting rid of Wolfe. Again.

He'd had his hands tied at first since the damn Cube would only talk to the former captain, but from the reports he'd been reading other members of the science team and even the administrative staff had been able to develop a rapport with the machine. Wolfe had far overstepped his authority when he had taken Pike on a tour of the facility and even included him on classified communiques. He had enough to actually prosecute him, but he'd settle for just kicking him off the project and yanking his fat director's salary away from him. How could one man so consistently cause so much trouble?

His ruminations were interrupted by an insistent beeping from the secure com link that was sitting on his desk. He picked it up and keyed in, checking the message and frowning as he read it.

"Emergency?" he mumbled, trying to do the math in his head as to when they were supposed to expect word from the taskforce executing the Ushin operation. The message stated he would need to come down to the secure com section to be briefed, another slightly unusual request given that his office was one of the most secure locations on the station. He slowly put on his suit jacket, having opted for civilian clothes as he had been going down to meet with the President as Chief of Staff and not a Fleet Admiral, and secured all his com equipment before heading out the door.

His aide fell in behind him as he walked through the front of his office area, her trusty tile clutched firmly at her side as she followed him through the station. Marcum made sure he walked with a purposeful scowl planted on his face and moved at a brusque pace. He'd found early on after getting his first star that people tended to want to catch him in the corridor to sign off on something minor that they couldn't get an appointment for. If he looked like he was heading somewhere quickly and pissed off, people cleared out of his way like he was on fire.

"You'll need to wait here, Lieutenant," he said, nodding to his aide as he began the absurdly convoluted procedure to get into the secure com section. When he was passed through, and after a five-minute argument after which his comlink was confiscated, he was led down to one of the intelligence briefing rooms. When he walked in he saw that Pike was standing at one corner of the room looking pale and a bit sick. He was about to tear into the agent for wasting his time yet again when he saw the looks on the faces of the other analysts in the room.

"What's happened?" he asked instead.

"We received word from the taskforce. It was a point-to-point com drone from the *New York*. Admiral Wilton personally did the emergency brief," Pike said, handing Marcum a hardcopy sheet of the summary. He read through the two-paged brief twice, his pallor matching that of Pike's as he did so. It was an utter disaster, and not the type that came from bad decisions in the field or poor operational planning ... the type that put people in prison for a long, long time. He couldn't even think about what consequences he might face as he read through the list of ships still missing.

"Fuck me," he said, swallowing hard. "Okay, Pike ... give me a complete brief, everything you have. Then we have to go back down to the surface. The President will need to be informed of this as soon as possible."

"Yes, sir," Pike nodded and began bringing up information on the briefing room's large wall monitors. The agent did most of the talking, acting as an aggregator while funneling in information from the other intelligence specialists in the room as needed. The picture he painted was bleak. Wilton's taskforce flew right into what was apparently a very elaborate trap by the Darshik and, to make things just a bit worse, the admiral clearly suspected that the Ushin were directly responsible. Marcum hoped there were just issues with the translation in that regard, but he couldn't deny that if the Darshik set a specific trap for the Terran taskforce *someone* had to tell them they were coming.

"So far that's all we know," Pike said, wrapping up his report. "The information from Wilton wasn't as inclusive as it could have been because the *New York* was covering the withdrawal of the Forth Fleet destroyers and she was taking fire. The Seventh Fleet destroyer, *Atlas*, is likely lost. The *Icarus* was deep down in the system and Senior Captain Wright reported that she was going to try and draw the enemy further down to allow the *New York* and the destroyer *Hyperion* to hit the jump point.

"Admiral Wilton stuck to the plan with the opening salvos coming from his heavy-missile cruisers, but then he had the foresight to send them back through the Juwel jump point once they'd spent their payload. This actually could have been much worse given the fact you cut back the size of the taskforce being deployed and Admiral Wilton was able to save the bulk of his fleet."

"Saving most of the taskforce was indeed a stroke of luck thanks to Wilton's competent command." Marcum nodded slowly. "But this wasn't just a trap to destroy a bunch of Terran ships for the sake of it; they were trying to reduce our forces significantly in one decisive action before we could even figure out what the hell was going on. This sort of gambit can only be followed by one thing."

"That being, sir?" an analyst asked.

"An invasion." Marcum tossed the pages he'd been nervously rolling up back onto the table. "Call your boss, Pike. We need to be on top of this as fast as we can."

"Yes, sir." Pike nodded and went to one of the secure com terminals.

****

Pike didn't see any further use in antagonizing Admiral Marcum. Everything he'd said about the man to his face still held true, but he was still the CENTCOM Chief of Staff and the highest ranking military officer in the Federation. That alone accorded him a certain amount of respect and they would all need to work together now that the mission had changed from a simple routing out of an occupying force to protecting Fed planets along the Ushin/Darshik frontier.

There was also the fact that Pike himself had known about the plan to use Starfleet to expand the Federation's territory by assisting the Ushin militarily. Granted it was ill-gotten knowledge and he'd had nobody to report it to as the Federation's bureaucracy got its feet under it, but that did nothing to assuage the guilt he felt as Celesta's ship was currently unaccounted for and had last been spotted deep in a system completely blanketed by the enemy.

It wasn't his place to question what the elected leadership did, or didn't do, when it came to the application of force to secure a political goal, and he had to admit that at the time it seemed like a decent trade-off. The Fleet flies in, kicks a weak holding force out of two systems, humanity gets their two dozen or so planets, and there's even the feel-good story of freeing new allies from evil invaders. It was the sort of stark morality tale that played well in the press and to the public, the vast majority who had never even been to orbit or seen a starship in person. To them it was always something happening so very far away, but Pike knew how meaningless the distances were from watching the Phage crawl across the Frontier, wiping out planets at will.

Everyone involved in the Ushin deal should have seen clearly they were being manipulated. Events had happened too quickly and too conveniently, hindsight being what it is, and now it seemed they might be inextricably mired in a situation they were not prepared for. That excuse held water when the Phage had appeared out of nowhere and begun razing planets, but to have it happen this soon afterwards didn't give Pike a lot of hope for the species.

"What the hell's going on?" The voice almost startled Pike as he rounded the corner heading for the docking-arm complex.

"What do you mean?" he asked innocently.

"We're getting back-channel rumors that the taskforce we just deployed was wiped out," Amiri Essa whispered. "What the—"

"Lieutenant Commander, I would suggest you forget anything you've heard regarding any deployed Fleet ships for the time being," Pike said, all traces of his usual sardonic humor gone. "I'm not kidding. The shit is about to hit the turbine, and it's a *lot* of shit. I'd hate to see you get splattered with any of it."

"I guess that's all the confirmation I need," Essa said. "How about you, Agent? You going to stay squeaky clean as usual?"

"Amiri," Pike began in exasperation.

"Got it." Essa held his hands up. "Just watch your back, Pike."

"Always."

Chapter 21

The *Icarus* shuddered back into real-space in what seemed like the middle of nowhere. The navigational data provided by the CIS assets had put them just inside the heliopause of the target system, and at that range the primary star wasn't much brighter than some of its nearest neighbors.

"Position confirmed, ma'am. We're as far out as we can get and still be considered in the star system," the chief at Nav reported.

"OPS and Tactical, begin full spectrum passive scans immediately," Celesta said. "We are under strict emission security protocols, everybody. I don't want a damn thing that has a direct connection to an antenna even powered up except for the passive detection systems. OPS will coordinate all requests through CIC, but for now just assume that your equipment is on that list and tell your backshops to sit on their hands."

"We're already receiving a lot of thermal and RF energy that indicates a heavy presence down there," Adler said. "Can you confirm, OPS?"

"Confirmed," Accari said. "CIC is processing the initial returns and building a profile of probable ship placements based on what we know about this system."

"Which is next to nothing." Barrett frowned. "Ma'am, would you rather I go down to CIC to help them chew through the incoming data?"

"You're not trained as an analyst, Commander," Celesta chided him gently. "I need you up here, XO. Nav, I want you to plot me a reciprocal course to utilize this jump point as our egress. OPS, tell Engineering I want the engines prepped for a quick start, but keep them cold for now. Let's just be a hole in space for a bit and see what we see."

There had been some argument among her senior staff when she'd informed them they had hit the Epsilon jump point for a reason other than escape. She intended to complete the reconnaissance of the second star system the Ushin had tried to lead them to in order to get some answers CENTCOM would likely need about the entire debacle.

From the nav data the CIS had provided, she had decided to transition in as far away as she could and stay cold for as long as possible. The *Icarus* wasn't a Prowler and the destroyer didn't run very cold when she was underway. She had again cursed the bad luck of losing the damn RDS pod, something that would have allowed them to get in close with minimal risk of detection, and had her people working on a practical plan to allow them to capture the much-needed intel without risking the ship. While it was true they needed to know as much about the Darshik, and apparently the Ushin, as possible, she wasn't about to risk the *Icarus* or her crew doing something foolish like trying to play spy with a mainline warship.

"Maintaining general quarters; we need to rotate watches soon," Celesta said to her XO. "We may have come in undetected or they could be sending an intercept for us right now. With the passives it's just too difficult to tell. Either way we need to rest the crew."

"I'll handle it, Captain," Barrett assured her. Celesta nodded her thanks and went back to staring at the threat board as the tactical computer struggled to identify anything from the small bit of light and radiation captured by the passive array. She needed to come up with something drastic or the entire trip would have been for nothing. With one final look around the bridge, she handed over command to her executive officer and went for a quick meal in the wardroom, hoping against hope that the passive scans would turn up something interesting over the next few hours.

****

"We're sure about this?" Celesta could hardly believe what she was being told.

"This is the one thing in this system the tactical computer has a *very* specific model for," Lieutenant Commander Adler nodded. "There's a Phage Super Alpha sitting down in that system."

The Super Alpha was the first type of combat unit the Phage had sent against humans in the first probes before the war cranked up in earnest. Although it was still connected to the hive, or the "core mind," it had a much larger neural mass than the standard Alphas and a bigger profile. Their shapes were all somewhat irregular due to the growing process the Phage used when producing them, but the sheer mass and rough shape wouldn't have been something the computer would have mistaken for something else. The thermal signature of the object was also an identical match for a Super Alpha that wasn't trying to hide. With a ninety-seven-percent probability the computer had picked up on one of the Phage's most devastating combat units sitting down in a Darshik star system.

"Let's look at this logically," Barrett said. "We knew that there were Phage combat units still floating through space after we killed the core mind, essentially alive but without direction. Is this thing maneuvering or showing any other signs of activity?"

"Negative, sir," Adler said. "It's in a high, stable orbit over the third planet and appears to have a lot of unidentified ship traffic around it."

"Not to get off subject," Lieutenant Commander Washburn said, actually raising her hand, "but the third planet is most definitely inhabited and shows signs of an advanced society. EM radiation is about what we'd expect from one of our more heavily populated planets, and we've detected lit cities on the dark side."

"Let's talk about that for a moment and then come back to the Phage ship," Celesta said. "This system's location was supplied to us by the Ushin. Given that we're assuming the last, uninhabited system was a trap, what do we think this is?"

"We know there's a connection between the Phage and the Darshik from our initial intel brief, ma'am," Accari said. He was the most junior officer in the room, which raised a few eyebrows, but Celesta knew that he sometimes saw things the others missed. "Our mission profile stated we were to come here second, but if we assume we weren't meant to survive the trap set in the Tango System, I think the most likely conclusion is that the knowledge of this system was either mistakenly given or they wanted another Terran force to make its way out here when we didn't make it back home."

"Without even a rough psychological profile of the Ushin from CIS, Fleet R&S, or the Fed diplomatic corps, I think trying to guess the Ushin intent with that degree of accuracy may be a waste of time," Celesta said. "Let's just operate under the assumption we were fed this location on purpose, and when we get here it just so happens to have one of the combat units that killed millions of people from an enemy that almost wiped out the species."

"If we lend credence to the theory that the Darshik were changed by their encounter with the Phage—that they began to deify it—that could be our answer," Barrett said. "Maybe we were brought as a sacrifice."

"That's wildly primitive thinking for a species that has interstellar travel capabilities," Celesta said, controlling the urge to roll her eyes. "But you could tell me they brought us here as cattle stock to feed the masses and I wouldn't be able to refute your theory. Let's keep this conversation to what we do know."

"So far that's very little," Washburn said. "The passives at this range will need a lot of time focused on a single spot to begin getting a detailed picture."

"Then I think the obvious spot would be that Super Alpha." Celesta stood up, in turn causing all her staff to leap to their feet too. "Keep the sensors trained on that spot and begin getting me a picture of what in the hell is going on down there. Lieutenant Commander Adler, I'd like you to turn over that task to CIC. I need you doing your primary job and protecting the ship. You're authorized to bring the redundant passive array online to scan local space and make sure nobody sneaks up on us again."

"Should we deploy the gravimetric detection system?" Adler asked, referring to the six small autonomous drones that could form a laser grid that detected minute changes in gravity, alerting them that something with mass was moving close to them.

"I'll keep that option open, but not right now," Celesta shook her head. "The system broadcasts a constant telemetry signal to the ship that will alert them that *somebody* has snuck into their system. We're still going to maintain strict emission protocols for the time being."

"Yes, ma'am." Adler nodded.

"Lieutenant Commander Washburn," Celesta continued. "After you get the CIC settled and collecting every scrap of intelligence that comes from that planet, I want you working on some outside-the-box ideas to get us a better look down there. You're free to pull in other departments as you see fit. If nobody has anything else? Dismissed."

They all filed out of the conference room and back to their duty stations, while Celesta leaned back in her chair and closed her eyes for a moment. The stress of the situation was building and she had to admit that she was not only scared beyond belief but had no idea what to do next. She briefly wished for a moment that the ship she was sitting on was the *Ares* and she was still the XO ... but then she remembered what Captain Wolfe had told her about all those insane situations they'd flown into during the war.

After his retirement, as his last bit of advice to his former XO, he said that he'd been scared shitless during at least eighty percent of the combat hours his ships had logged. Despite appearing cool, calm, and relentless he was quaking in his boots, but he knew that if they were to have any chance of making it through then the crew couldn't know that. The ship could only have one captain and any perceived weakness on the bridge invited debate and insolence in the crew. He'd compared a starship crew to a pack of dogs, and while his metaphor had been crude, it was apt: There could be only one alpha, and if she wasn't it someone would challenge her for it in situations like they found themselves in now.

With strengthened resolve, she walked out of the conference room and back towards the bridge. She'd find a way to get the *Icarus* back home safely and bring CENTCOM any intel she could glean in the process that would help in what was looking like an inevitable war.

****

"Good morning, Cube," Jackson said as he walked in. The other technicians and researchers were already getting up and preparing to leave the room since recently any time the director came down to talk to the research subject it was always of a highly classified nature. "Thanks, everybody." Jackson nodded to his people.

"What would you like to discuss today?" Cube asked after the hatch to the cargo hold clanged shut.

"I want to expand on our previous talks about the species that calls themselves the Darshik," Jackson said, rolling a chair over to where he could see the lit terminal on the Vruahn machine and sitting down. "In light of recent events I'd like to move away from the more abstract information in your database and see if you can't dig up something a little more practical."

"The Darshik have moved against you. I warned you of this."

"You said that they were militaristic," Jackson corrected. "As far as we knew the Darshik only knew of us through their connection with the Ushin. The Phage connection was just a theory of yours."

"What's happened, exactly?" Cube asked. Jackson pursed his lips and thought hard about what he was about to say next. The news of Starfleet's engagement against the Darshik-held worlds, and what appeared to have been a disastrous ambush, was highly classified. He didn't think telling an alien machine would be the wisest thing to do, but the rub was that out of every intelligent being in Terran space the Cube was the only one that had ever even heard of either species.

"Fleet sent a taskforce out to two systems the Ushin claimed were theirs and the Darshik were occupying." Jackson decided to go for broke. "The first system ended up being an overly elaborate trap that only dumb luck allowed most of our ships to escape from. I need to know if we can expect some sort of retaliatory strike or if you can provide any context as to why the Ushin would apparently help the Darshik."

"I have told you everything my memory holds on both species," Cube said simply.

"But you and I both know that sometimes different lines of thought will jar loose some facts in there you may have failed to mention the first time I asked," Jackson said.

"Your tone of voice and body language implies you think I deliberately withhold information from you."

"The thought has crossed my mind," Jackson said. "Come on. Give me something useful."

The panel on the Cube went dark and it fell silent. Jackson was used to these gaps in the conversations, some lasting as long as thirty minutes. He attributed it to either lingering effects of the accident that had formed the Cube's intelligence or, more likely, pouting, as they always seemed to happen when he was pressing or implying that he didn't believe it.

"The probability is strong that the Darshik will come," it said finally. "It is their way, although that wasn't always the case. Their interaction with the Phage at an early stage in their societal development may have caused this—"

"It couldn't have been that early if they already had interstellar flight capability," Jackson interrupted.

"The Darshik did not develop their interstellar travel technology," Cube said.

"Now we're getting somewhere," Jackson muttered. "So where did they get it?"

"The species you call the Ushin provided the technology that the Darshik have then modified on their own."

"That's a pretty damn important thing to leave out, isn't it?!" Jackson strained to keep his temper in check. Explosions usually resulted in the Cube going dark for a few days. "Please tell me exactly what you mean by that."

"I am sorry, Director Wolfe," it said. "My files only included summary information regarding the surrounding species in the area that you might have encountered in the final stages of the war. I often have trouble connecting individual and separate facts together into a coherent line of thought. I apologize."

"No need to apologize," Jackson said with a sigh. "We're doing the best we can. Let's take it from the top and try to piece something together that Fleet can use. If the information I have is accurate, the Darshik may already be heading to any Terran worlds they're aware of."

"I will do my best," Cube said.

Chapter 22

"Commander Graham, may I have a word with you?"

"Lieutenant Commander ... Washburn, isn't it?" Graham said, wiping his hands on his utilities. "You work in CIC?"

"Yes, sir," Washburn said.

"What can I do for you?" Graham seemed distracted and busy, but Washburn needed his expertise and advise before presenting her idea to the captain.

"Captain Wright has tasked me with finding a way to get more direct intel from the Darshik planet in this system without risking the *Icarus*," she said. "I have one I think has promise, but it will require some modification to a Jacobson drone and one of our com drones."

"Intriguing," Graham said, pushing aside his tile and giving her his undivided attention. "The Jacobson makes sense, but why do you need a com drone?"

"I don't think the captain is going to want to risk having the *Icarus* waiting around to receive the broadcast from the drone, verify it, and then try to accelerate to transition velocity while only having the passive sensors to detect incoming threats," Washburn said as she followed along after Graham motioned to her with his free hand.

"My thought is to program a com drone to listen as the Jacobson relays the data it collects in a single burst, then transition out of the system to get the data to

New Sierra," she continued. "Actually, the intel would beat us back by more than a week."

"Two problems I see right away," Graham said as he ushered her into his office and out of the noisy engineering bay. "We have no more point-to-point drones left aboard, and the standard com drone doesn't have the fuel to make it from here to the DeLonges System. The best we could hope for is that, barring any interstellar obstacles, it makes it back to the Juwel System and relays the data through the standard network.

"Second, the com drones aren't designed with this sort of tasking in mind. While it has the requisite receive and transmit hardware, it doesn't have the computational power to set it adrift with the sort of intricate programming it would take."

"So ... back to square one?" Washburn looked crestfallen.

"No problems are insurmountable, Lieutenant Commander," Graham smiled. "Just difficult. I think the idea is solid, but we'll need to bring more people into the loop before presenting this to the captain. Commander Severn down in Flight OPS will need to be included as soon as you can manage it. We'll need to coordinate between his department and mine to see if a drone can be modified to do what you want it to. The Jacobson is no issue ... those little beauties are so flexible it won't take but twenty minutes to program it for the mission."

"I'll get everybody moving right now, sir." Washburn was already standing up. "Captain Wright won't want to be sitting in this system any longer than she has to."

"We're agreed there," Graham nodded his head. "She won't risk this ship for something that can be obtained by the CIS later as a worst-case scenario. I'm putting myself at your disposal, Lieutenant Commander."

"Thank you, sir," Washburn said, already through the hatchway.

****

"How quickly can this be accomplished and what percentage do you give it for success?" Celesta asked, clearly skeptical.

"Two days with all hands on deck." Commander Graham shrugged. "After that, the whole thing is fairly straight forward. I'd say we have better than an eighty percent chance that it goes off as planned."

"What we can't account for, however, is the Darshik reaction," Washburn said. "We're assuming they'll be so disoriented and surprised that we'll be able to slip back out of the system, but that's just my best guess. I feel I'd be negligent if I didn't point out that the Ushin did give us the location of this system and they appear to be working with the Darshik ... or at least for them. We could very well have been under observation the moment we transitioned in."

"I'll take your concern under advisement," Celesta said. "It's definitely something we should keep firmly in mind when it comes time to move the *Icarus*. We'll need to plot out a wide, circuitous course to bring her back around to this jump point and there are more than a few times we'll be at risk.

"I'm approving this plan as you've brought it to me so far, but I think I might want to expand on it. The ramifications of what I want to do, however, could be profound. We just don't know enough about this species to even guess what would happen if I take this one step further and, even more concerning, we don't know if we're just seeing the tip of the iceberg when it comes to Darshik military strength. They could have a much larger fleet, and we have no way of knowing whether the Ushin-provided intelligence should be discounted completely."

"What do you have in mind, Captain?" Barrett asked.

"Something to respond in kind to the warning we were given in the Xi'an System," Celesta said. "The *Ares* was dragged from an ultra-secret location just to be detonated in an unnecessarily dramatic display meant to either frighten or dishearten us ... or both. We have a chance to do something similar here, but it could be akin to kicking the hornet's nest, as Captain Wolfe used to say so often."

"What do you need from us, ma'am?" Commander Severn asked, his feral smile clearly showing what he thought of the prospect of figuratively jabbing a stick into the enemy's eye.

Chapter 23

Celesta walked down the port main access tube, past Engineering, on her way to the drone launch bays. Unlike the shuttle launch bay on the starboard side of the ship, the drone bay was built so that individual craft could be pulled into a pressurized maintenance area without the hassle of bringing them in through an airlock. Even the largest drone, the Jacobson, was small enough that Flight OPS crews would simply seal the launch hatch and pressurize the entire launch tube before pulling the holding cradle into the bay. The *Icarus* currently only had four drones left onboard thanks to the Darshik showing up before she could recall them from her impromptu sensor network, but they were Jacobsons and they had plenty of mission modules aboard so her plan was still technically feasible, if just.

When she walked into the main unmanned space/aero vehicle (USAV) maintenance hangar, Commander Severn's crews already had both Jacobsons sitting in the middle of the floor on their cradles, access hatches open and cables snaked into the machines from the associated support equipment that had been moved into place. She could also see the sealed crates that held the scalable mission modules had already been brought up from storage and were being inspected by another team of techs. The meeting hadn't let out all that long ago and Celesta appreciated the sense of urgency with which Flight OPS was going about their business.

"Captain on deck!"

"As you were," Celesta shouted to be heard over the noise in the hangar. "Where is Commander Severn?"

"Tech center, Captain," a spacer third class called out and, unnecessarily, pointed to a closed hatch near a bulkhead that had cables passing through and running over to the waiting spacecraft. Celesta waved her thanks and walked over to the hatch.

The tech center was a quiet, isolated room where specialists could work in relative peace to complete the often-complicated programming that went into a drone prior to launch. It also allowed them to monitor the spacecraft once it had been handed off to the CIC or OPS on the bridge.

"Captain," Severn nodded as she walked in. "We're compiling the program for the first drone and my people are working on the second. That one is a bit less involved so I expect it to be done shortly. We'll be running the programs through the simulators and then, if they check out, installing them in the Jacobsons."

"And the com drone?"

"I have a team inspecting the drone itself and Lieutenant Commander Washburn's people are helping program that one along with Commander Graham's team," Severn said. "My coders don't have any experience with that system."

"Of course," Celesta nodded. "I'm not here to needlessly harass your people, Commander. I just want to be plugged in on every aspect of this operation. There could be … ramifications … if we pull it off successfully and make it back to Terran space."

Severn motioned for her to move away from the furiously working programmers and near the hatchway.

"If I had any doubts about the plan, the ship, or you, Captain, I would have relieved myself from duty," he said quietly. "We know the stakes, ma'am. We're with you."

"I never had a doubt, Commander," Celesta said without a smile. "So now the part where I *do* lean on you … how much longer until we can get the Jacobsons on their way?"

"Twelve more hours, ma'am," Severn said with confidence.

"Very good, Commander," Celesta said. "I will leave you to it."

"You might want to stop by and talk to Commander Graham, Captain," Severn said as she reached for the hatch handle. "His people could use a little encouragement … they have the more difficult task in this project." Celesta just nodded to him and left.

She still had some doubts about what it was she was planning to do. It was unsanctioned and risky … but being a starship captain meant taking bold, decisive action when the opportunity presented itself without wringing one's hands or fretting over lack of direction from leadership. In spite of her doubts this *felt* right. She'd make a stand here, and if this was the hill she died on, literally or figuratively, so be it.

****

"Flight OPS and Engineering reports all ready," Accari reported. "CIC has also checked in and is standing by."

"Very good." Celesta stood in the middle of the bridge, breathing in the relative calm for a moment before setting things in motion that could not be reversed.

"OPS, tell CIC they are clear to execute. They are authorized to launch all needed spacecraft and weapons on my authority."

"Aye aye, ma'am," Accari said. "Operation is live; starting the mission clock."

"Tactical, how's the neighborhood?" Barrett asked.

"Passive sensors indicate local space is clear, sir," Adler said.

"Jacobsons have departed the *Icarus*," Accari reported. "Coms drone has also been launched. All drones are moving away on maneuvering jets. CIC says weapons will launch in three hours."

"Very good," Celesta said. "Stay sharp and stay loose, everybody. We have a long watch ahead of us, and we're still behind enemy lines."

After the mild flurry of activity of launching spacecraft and coordinating across departments, the bridge settled into a tense quiet with station operators talking quietly to their backshops through headsets. Celesta watched the main display as the drones began thrusting down into the system, firing their plasma engines in the lowest stable output mode they could to avoid detection. The acceleration profiles meant it would take a long time for them to get into position, but it greatly minimized the likelihood they'd be detected.

"Weapons firing," Lieutenant Commander Adler announced just under three hours later, startling Celesta slightly as she'd been wholly focused on the threat board. "Shrikes one, two, and three are away and carrying launcher velocity only, no engines."

"Now the real wait begins," Barrett said softly. "Twelve hours before the Shrikes fire their engines, nearly two full days for the Jacobsons to get in position."

"OPS," Celesta ignored her executive officer, "inform Engineering that we're ready to begin prepping the mains for start. We'll be moving the *Icarus* soon and we cannot afford any slips in schedule due to malfunctions."

"Aye, ma'am," Accari said.

****

"All sections have checked in, Captain," Barrett said as he put down his com link. "The *Icarus* is ready to get underway."

"Not a moment too soon," Celesta said. "Helm, come about to your first course change; ahead one-quarter and maintain low-output mode on main engines."

"Ahead one-quarter, low-output, aye," the helmsman said. When he throttled up the mains the vibration was so muted through the deck that it could hardly be felt. The course her nav team had plotted out kept the *Icarus* in open space and away from any stellar body that the Darshik might be using to hold a detection satellite in orbit. They would fly out in a long, lazy arc down within the orbit of the seventh planet before coming about sharply and surging to transition velocity. If they timed everything right, their engine thermal bloom might be overlooked when things kicked off down near the Super Alpha.

They'd been able to confirm through the passive sensors that the Phage combat unit was surrounded by some sort of grid or scaffolding, and that there were at least fifteen other ships parked in orbit very close to it, some active and some looking like nothing more than derelicts. The presence of other ships had given her pause when it came to executing her plan, but ultimately she pressed ahead. It wouldn't be long now ... the drones and weapons had been cold-coasting through the system for the better part of two days, and so far there was no indication they'd been spotted, but Celesta took no solace in that. A Darshik cruiser had managed to sneak up right behind them without the passives detecting it, so the fact there wasn't any overt sign down in the system that they'd been spotted didn't lessen her anxiety.

"Executing next course change," the helmsman said without prompting nearly seven hours later, veering them down into the system and beginning the wide loop that would eventually bring them back around with just enough room to accelerate, deploy the warp drive, and transition out. So far so good. It wasn't that Celesta really expected to escape undetected, but their only option was to fly back through the system they'd just fled from, so she decided to roll the dice and hope against hope that the *Icarus* could sneak back out without the ships still in that system getting advanced warning.

"Ma'am, we have an ... anomaly ... down near the Super Alpha," Adler said as the *Icarus* slogged through her lazy turn. "Passives have been able to tentatively identify one of the ships near that lattice structure; the computer is making it as a *Foster*-class heavy cruiser with a forty percent degree of accuracy."

"The *Leighton*," Barrett said. "They brought her here."

"Is that ship under power?" Celesta asked sharply.

"It doesn't appear so, ma'am," Adler said. "The anomaly is reading as cold. No engines, no thermal exhaust, no discernable lights."

Celesta frowned. Like most Terran starships the *Foster*-class was capable of running "cold" for a limited time, but under normal operations an older ship like that would have a visible thermal plume from the cooling systems as well as the regular discharge of plasma over-pressure from the powerplant. She couldn't imagine that the *Leighton* still had any survivors on it if it was reading as cold as surrounding space. Even if they had inexplicably decided to switch over to closed loop cooling right as the *Icarus* transitioned in, there would still be hot patches on the hull that wouldn't have cooled that quickly. The ship just wasn't designed or built for that level of stealth.

Her presence did throw Celesta's plan into flux, however. She could assume that there was no living crew aboard the *Leighton*, but she couldn't assume that they were all dead. It was equally likely they'd been removed from the ship and were detained somewhere else. What would happen to them when her operation went live? She could still quietly recall her assets and just hope the small burp of EM radiation that required would escape notice, but then what? There was zero chance the *Icarus* and her small contingent of Marines could find the crew, effect a rescue, and escape so deep in Darshik territory, but would their operation sign their death sentence?

All these questions flitted through Celesta's head in less than a second as she realized there was still really only one option open to her. The crew of the *Leighton* had signed up for the same dangers her crew had, and while they deserved every chance for a rescue, there wasn't a chance for that with one destroyer.

"The op is still a go," she said. This drew a few looks from her crew, some incredulous, others concerned, but she ignored them.

"You heard the captain," Barrett said sharply. "That ship is a derelict and we all know it. We have work to do, so let's get to it."

This seemed to snap everyone out of their stunned silence and got them moving in the right direction again. Celesta understood the emotions they were feeling and even shared them, but her responsibility was to the Federation and to humanity as a whole ... she had a chance to deliver a hard blow if her guess was correct, and she couldn't shy away from that based on nothing more than a slim chance the *Leighton* crew was still alive. She sat back in her chair, the weight of her decision seeming to press her down into it as she thought about what might happen if she were wrong.

****

"*Your aggression is unwarranted. Your attacks were unprovoked. We will not allow you to continue. Like the Phage, you will learn a hard lesson of what happens when you attack humans. This will be your only warning.*"

The message was being broadcast at full power across the system from a Jacobson drone streaking at full speed in a heliocentric orbit just past the fourth planet. It had been loaded with multiple transmission modules and was spitting out the message on every frequency in both Standard and what their Ushin translation matrix had given them.

"Second Jacobson has gone active," Accari reported.

"Helm, all ahead emergency," Celesta ordered. "Bring the *Icarus* to transition velocity. OPS, stand by to deploy the warp drive."

"All engines ahead emergency, aye!"

"Shrikes have fired their second stage boosters, weapons going active," Adler said as she watched the mission clock. The *Icarus* was so far out that they had no idea if anything was actually happening save for the message being broadcast by the second drone since it had actually reached them. The rest was just assuming everything was working as it had been designed.

"*Icarus* is at transition plus ten! Engines to zero thrust and securing from flight mode," the helmsman called out.

"Warp drive deploying, emitters and transition capacitors fully charged," Accari said. "Turning over control to Nav."

"Stand by for warp transition!" the chief at Nav practically bellowed. With a hard shudder the destroyer vanished from the Darshik system without waiting to see what havoc they'd wrought.

****

"*Your aggression is unwarranted. Your attacks were unprovoked. We will not allow you to continue. Like the Phage, you will learn a hard lesson of what happens when you attack humans. This will be your only warning.*"

The Jacobson drone was still cheerfully broadcasting its message as its active sensors detected a Darshik ship crossing the pre-programmed threshold. It sent a burst transmission of its entire flight log to the waiting com drone and initiated a self-destruct, the powerful explosives it normally carried having been swapped out for a fusion warhead. The blast wasn't enough to damage the ships closing on its position, but it was more than enough to ensure the Darshik wouldn't be collecting anything big enough to study.

The second Jacobson drone, the primary, had all sensors trained on the small flotilla and lattice structure that surrounded the Super Alpha when three Shrikes slammed into the organic hull of the Phage combat unit. The tertiary boosters flared briefly to further imbed the warheads before the powerful nuclear devices detonated, annihilating the Super Alpha. In turn, everything in the vicinity was also destroyed. The drone transmitted everything it had recorded and then began a real-time telemetry stream to the com drone until a Darshik ship finally came around and began to bear down on it. The Jacobson sent one last confirmation and then self-destructed.

Once it received the final confirmation from the remaining Jacobson drone, the com drone, flying under an entirely new set of operational parameters, fired its plasma engine. The tiny spacecraft streaked up to transition velocity in less than three minutes and vanished in a little wink of light, leaving behind a system roiling with chaos and weapons fire.

****

"Transition complete, position verified. We're in the Juwel System."

The words were met with an almost audible sigh of relief on the bridge. It had been a long, long flight fleeing from the Darshik system. They'd entered the Tango system and had an easy enough time outrunning the three cruisers still there, skirting around the periphery without them being able to get even close. Celesta had fired her remaining Shrikes on the way out, but they'd already hit the Juwel jump point before the weapons intercepted the Darshik ships. What had alarmed her was that they seemed to already be putting the trap back together; three dummy formations had been flying around the target planet's orbit just like those that had lured them in.

"OPS, go ahead and fire up all our transponders and reconfigure the *Icarus* for normal flight," Celesta ordered. "Coms, get a sitrep as soon as you can."

"Aye, ma'am," the two officers said in unison.

Celesta was mentally and physically exhausted and they weren't even close to being back to home port. The com drone should have passed through here already as it was much faster than a starship, but there was no way to know since once it hit the platform and forwarded its data package it would be reprogrammed, refueled, and deployed to wherever the automated system sent it. She knew it wasn't even worth the trouble to try and see if their particular drone had hit the platform.

"Ma'am, we have a message coming in from CENTCOM," Lieutenant Ellison said. "They must have sent it as soon as they received our transponder signal. It's text only."

"That's never good," Barrett mumbled, rubbing his bloodshot eyes.

"Send it to my terminal," Celesta said, pulling her monitor around. The message was short and to the point and left little doubt that her com drone had indeed managed to get its content out of Darshik space.

Senior Captain Wright – you are ordered to proceed to New Sierra Platform at maximum sustainable speed. No contact is to be made with Fleet personnel in the Juwel System unless emergency technical assistance is required. –CENTCOM Routing Office.

The message was properly formatted, if terse. While the Fleet com section wasn't known for its eloquence when dispatching orders, the next part of the message cleared things up a bit more.

Wright ... get your ass back here immediately. The data you sent has leadership concerned, to put it mildly. You are ordered to talk to NO ONE about your mission. –Marcum

"OPS, does the *Icarus* have enough consumables aboard to make it directly to the DeLonges System?" Celesta asked, rubbing at her temples.

"Yes, ma'am," Accari said after a moment. "We're well within our operational envelope to make it all the way back with air, water, food, and propellant to spare."

"Fantastic," Celesta said, her voice completely flat. "Nav, set a course for the DeLonges jump point and clear it with Juwel's flight control. Helm, you're clear to execute new course when you receive it, all ahead full. We need to be through this system as quickly as possible."

"Our com drone made it through?" Barrett asked.

"I have to assume so looking at the message Admiral Marcum sent," Celesta said. "What I can't tell is what sort of welcome we'll receive when we step off the gangway."

"Well ... at least we have the long flight back home to think it over," Barrett said sourly.

"That's the spirit, Commander," Celesta said.

Chapter 24

"Welcome aboard the *Pontiac*, Admiral."

"Director," Marcum said with a nod as he took Jackson Wolfe's proffered hand.

"I'll admit to some surprise that you're here personally," Jackson said carefully. "Was there something in particular you're wanting from Prometheus?"

Marcum just smiled at Jackson in a way that made his stomach drop. The Chief of Staff held his hand out and his too-young aide put a tile in it.

"Jackson Wolfe," Marcum said, reading off the tile, "you are hereby relieved as Director of Project Prometheus. You will forfeit all pay and privileges associated with your assimilated rank and are terminated from civil service, effective immediately."

"I suppose I should have expected this," Jackson said. "You must really be taking some perverse pleasure in this seeing as how you've flown here personally to fire me."

"I'm not done," Marcum said, flicking his finger over the tile to bring up another document. "Jackson Wolfe, under the war powers authority vested in the President of the United Terran Federation, you are hereby recalled to active military service. Your last-held rank of Senior Captain is reinstated and you will report immediately to CENTCOM HQ, New Sierra Platform, for assignment and orders. There's some other technical stuff in here about bringing you back into the fold, but you get the point ... Captain."

It took a full second for what Marcum was saying to sink in.

"This isn't possible," Jackson shook his head. "I retired. I'm not subject to recall."

"The Devil is in the details," Marcum said with the same oily smile. "Your retirement was under the old Confederacy charter. The Federation has had much more foresight in drafting its new relationship with CENTCOM and Starfleet. It's also retroactive. Come on, Wolfe ... you're too young to be retired anyway."

"You think this is funny?"

"No, Captain, I don't," Marcum said, his voice hard. "But let's both face facts for a moment; you're not a researcher, you're not a scientist, and you're a mediocre civilian administrator at best. This project isn't where you belong and it no longer needs you now that the damn Vruahn machine is talking to your assistants. What you are is a starship captain and, as much as it causes me physical pain to say this, you were a damn good one. At least so far as fighting your ship in a war was concerned." He stopped himself in what looked like mid-tirade and blew out a slow breath.

"We're against the ropes again, Wolfe," he went on. "With the ESA planets breaking away and refusing any contact from Fed-loyal worlds we're in a bad way. Drafting you back in to take you away from your family isn't something we would do if we felt it wasn't absolutely necessary. Arcadia isn't invulnerable. The Darshik could pop up here just as easily as they did in the DeLonges System."

"Low blow, but your point is well taken," Jackson said. "What do you need me for?"

"I'd like you to start analyzing the Darshik engagements," Marcum said. "If we could—"

"No," Jackson said, holding up his hand. "I could do that here and, more to the point, the Cube would be faster and better at it than I would be ... as it's already proved if anybody would bother reading the reports I send out. I know that legally I could fight this, so if my conditions aren't met I'll simply refuse your orders and tie it up with lawyers so neither of us gets what we want."

"What are your conditions?" Marcum asked suspiciously.

"I actually have only one," Jackson said. "If you really think you need to drag me back into service then there's only one place that makes sense for me to be. You said so yourself: It's what I am."

"I suspected as much," Marcum sighed. "Very well, Captain Wolfe ... you will be reassigned to Black Fleet and put on the bridge of a starship again. You've got a couple weeks here and then I need you on your way to New Sierra. There's a lot you need to be brought up to speed on, and I want you there to meet the *Icarus* when she finally makes it back so you can debrief Captain Wright. She's kicked up a hell of a storm and it won't be long before the Darshik come at us again."

****

"*Icarus* departing!" the Marine sentry bellowed from the top of the gangway as Celesta walked through the starboard boarding hatch, drowning out the computer's identical announcement.

She was dressed impeccably in her dress blacks and had instructed all her officers to do the same as they departed the ship. Once they disembarked, the crews on the New Sierra Platform would probably drag her over to an enclosed heavy maintenance berth so they could begin to address the hull damage. All told, the *Icarus* had come through another battle relatively unscathed save for a missing RDS pod. As she walked off the gangway and stepped onto the platform, she was greeted by Admiral Pitt and a handful of other officers, but no Marine guards or platform security. She took this as a good sign.

"Welcome home, *Icarus*," Pitt said loudly, walking forward and returning Celesta's salute before offering his hand. "And congratulations on a successful, if off-script mission, Captain. We're still reviewing the data your com drone brought back, but we'll get to all that in debrief."

"Thank you, Admiral," she said. "To be perfectly honest, I half-assumed I would be arrested on sight."

"It was either give you a medal or arrest you," Pitt said with a straight face. "Obviously the details of your mission have been deemed classified. We'll discuss it later."

"Did the *New York* make it back?" Celesta asked.

"Yes ... barely," Pitt nodded, indicating she should follow him. "She's still being evaluated as to whether it will be easier to fix the damage or scrap her. Captain Lee did a fine job keeping the ship out of Darshik hands and his crew alive. The damage to the ship was nothing short of shocking considering there were so few casualties aboard."

"That's something at least," Celesta said, wanting to say more but not able to as they were walking along an unsecured corridor.

"All I can tell you is that you're being commended for your quick thinking," Pitt said. "We'll debrief you tomorrow to get the missing details from you and your crew while memories are fresh, but then you'll likely be cooling your heels for a few days. Admiral Marcum wanted to be here when we really started digging through your mission data."

"Where is the admiral?" Celesta asked idly.

"Recruitment mission," Pitt said cryptically.

The next week went by in a blur as the bridge crew and officers of the *Icarus* were run through what felt like a criminal interrogation. CENTCOM and CIS plainclothes operatives would ask questions, circle back and try to trip them up, and then present any inconsistencies with the triumph of having caught them in a lie. It was exhausting and enraging, and by the fifth day Celesta had had enough. She calmly asked if she, or any of her crew, were under arrest or under investigation for anything illegal, and when the CIS representative grudgingly answered that they weren't, she marched out.

Once her officers learned she was refusing to play their games, they also opted out of any further hostile interrogations while ordering their subordinates to not cooperate. Celesta knew this was likely to have further ramifications as the people questioning them would surely complain to her superiors, but after all they'd been through she was more than a little offended at the treatment. Even at the height of the Phage war she couldn't remember CENTCOM being so adversarial with Fleet personnel.

"I understand you're no longer cooperating with the debriefing staff," a voice said from the open door to her temporary office a full day after she'd called off any further sessions. Since the *Icarus* was now fully under control of the repair crews she'd been assigned a temporary block of generic offices so she could handle the administrative duties that didn't stop just because a ship was in port.

"Are we calling it a debrief, or an inquiry, sir?" Celesta asked, rising to her feet to greet Admiral Marcum.

"It was necessary, but I do apologize." Marcum walked in, closing the door behind him. "The CIS people in particular seem to forget we're all on the same side."

"Yes, sir," she said, still standing.

"Sit down, Captain," Marcum said, taking a seat in front of the desk. "I'd like to commend you for your performance in the Tango system. Between you and Admiral Wilton, we managed to save the bulk of the taskforce from that trap the Darshik had set."

"So what's the next step, sir?" she asked.

"We bring you fully up to speed on everything we've learned so far on the Darshik and the Ushin while the *Icarus* is repaired," Marcum said. "And there's a lot. I wouldn't be overstating things if I said we may have bumbled into a horrifically bad situation here. We're still unravelling the relationship between the two, but it looks like the Ushin and Darshik have a link to each other that predates even the Phage. One of our outside intelligence projects uncovered that their ships, while different in appearance, are unmistakably from the same source of engineering and materials. The fact the Ushin led us into a Darshik ambush further confirms that."

"Offshoots of the same species?" she asked.

"We don't know that for sure yet," Marcum said. "The organic remains from the battle in this system are still being analyzed by Fleet R&S, but they're confident that having samples from both an Ushin and Darshik ship will give us a conclusive answer on that."

"That's something at least," Celesta said. "So can we put these ridiculous questioning sessions to rest and get down to business, sir?"

"It's why I came personally to see you." Marcum stood up, prompting her to do the same. "Your presence is required down on the surface tomorrow at 0900; you can ride down in the shuttle with me. Have your crew stand down on the station here for R&R." He shifted around uncomfortably for a moment before simply nodding and exiting the office.

Celesta just shook her head at the odd behavior and wondered what fresh horrors would be revealed at the upcoming briefing. Since it was on the surface, she had to assume members of the new civilian oversight would be in attendance.

****

The uncomfortable ride down to the surface in the Chief of Staff's personal shuttle was soon forgotten when Celesta saw who was standing on the landing pad waiting for them. Like a ghost from the past, resplendent in his dress blacks, was Senior Captain Jackson Wolfe. She heard a chuckle as Admiral Marcum seemed to be thoroughly enjoying her shock.

"I was going to tell you yesterday but I didn't want to ruin the surprise," he said. "I went to Arcadia personally and reactivated him."

"I bet that pissed him off ... sir," she said, looking at the scowl on her former mentor's face.

"A safe bet," Marcum nodded as the shuttle touched down with a bump. They waited until the atmospheric engines spooled down and then the six passengers climbed out and walked towards the greeting party.

"Sir, it's a pleasure to see you again," Celesta said, saluting. It wasn't a necessary courtesy as she was with two fleet admirals and she held the same rank as Wolfe, but she did it anyway as an overt sign of respect. Jackson returned her salute crisply and shook her hand.

"Likewise, Captain Wright," he said, almost smiling. Any further conversation was interrupted as the flag officers accompanying Marcum wanted to crowd in and talk to the legendary starship captain and have an opportunity for a picture or two. Celesta was reminded of something that Wolfe had said to her as she watched the bizarre spectacle: *All* flag officers were politicians at heart and all had aspirations of higher office, and everything they said or did had to be viewed through that filter. At the time Celesta had just thought her boss was a world class cynic, now she understood what he'd meant.

They were ushered into a secure briefing room that more resembled an arena and, as she'd expected, a dozen Parliament members as well as the President and his staff all entered from the other side. Once they were all seated, Admiral Pitt took to the lectern and began a dry, detailed briefing of the Ushin operation that had ended in disaster.

Little was brought to light that Celesta didn't know about save for the fact that Jackson Wolfe had been the chief administrator of something called Project Prometheus and that it was responsible for a good portion of the cultural data they had on the Ushin and the Darshik, including the fact that the Darshik likely deified the Phage after their own run-in with that species. It was that very fact she had used when destroying the inert Super Alpha in a warning as equally dramatic as the one they'd received in the Xi'an System. At the Jacobson's sensor data showing her Shrikes blowing up the Phage unit more than a few high-ranking officials and officers nodded in her direction or gave thumbs up of approval. One thing she saw that she hadn't been aware of was the fact the Ushin ships in the system were immediately attacked by Darshik cruisers after the *Icarus* had transitioned out. It was glossed over quickly, but Celesta intended to find out what the analysts thought about that interesting aftereffect.

Once Pitt concluded his overview there were a few other presenters, including Wolfe himself, to give a bit more detail as to the nature of the fight they found themselves in. Despite the matter-of-fact presentation, Celesta couldn't help but feel like she was watching a performance. Something was ... off ... and she couldn't put her finger on it. She made a mental note to speak to Wolfe about it after it was over if she could get him alone.

"That concludes the joint session of this briefing. We'll now be dividing into subgroups based on areas of responsibility and specializations to begin further breaking down the Darshik problem," Admiral Marcum said five long hours after the brief had started. Celesta saw someone walk quickly over to the President and whisper in his ear, and it took her a moment to realize that it was Pike, dressed as his alter ego Aston Lynch. The President's eyes widened and he visibly paled, looking shaky as he rose from his seat.

"Mr. President?" Marcum interrupted his own comments as the Chief Executive walked slowly up to him and pulled him aside. The admiral's reaction to whatever was said mirrored President Wellington's and he nodded, stepping back.

"I've just received word that a com drone has entered the system with greatly disturbing news," the President said, leaning heavily on the lectern. "A week ago the Darshik returned to Terran space. The Juwel System has been overrun and the enemy has landed ground troops on the planet. I'm now declaring a state of emergency ... we are once again at war with an alien species."

Prologue:

"Can you tell me what Project Prometheus is?" Celesta finally asked, swirling her drink around in her glass. After the immediate chaos created by the news that the Darshik had invaded Terran space and were landing assault troopers, she had finally pulled Captain Wolfe away for a private word. The two were sitting in the lounge of his well-appointed quarters on the New Sierra Platform splitting a bottle of very expensive bourbon from Earth.

"It's an emergent AI project," Jackson shrugged. "It didn't really have much practical application until the Darshik dragged my old ship back from the outer regions and blew it up. I'm still pissed about that."

"So how does a starship captain get involved in an emergent AI project?"

"It asked for me," Jackson said, his words slurring ever so slightly between the ess and kay sounds of the second word. Other than that you couldn't tell he'd polished off more than a third of a bottle in less than an hour and a half.

"If you don't want to tell me then just—"

"The principal was an object you carried aboard the *Icarus* for a time," Jackson interrupted her. "It had been in storage and somehow ... woke up. It asked for me."

Celesta was about to snap back at him that his answer wasn't any more helpful than it had been before when she realized what he was talking about.

"The Vruahn stasis pod?" she asked in shock. "It's ... *emerged*?" Her alcohol-addled mind couldn't find a more appropriate term before she said it.

"Emerged and still able to remember a lot of what the Vruahn had programmed it with about local space," Jackson said. "It also ran the analysis that discovered the link between the Ushin and the Darshik. That probably would have been useful *before* our new President and esteemed Chief of Staff rented the fleet out to the Ushin in return for a couple dozen planets."

Pike had stopped by earlier, before the pair had really decided to drown their frustration, and quietly told them of the conversation he had "overheard" between Marcum and Wellington.

"About that—" Celesta said, not finishing her question.

"It's not the flimsiest reason we've ever used to go to war as a species," Jackson said. "In fact, most wars are started on false pretense. At least territorial expansion is an idea I can wrap my head around even if I don't agree with it."

"So you're not going to try and expose the fact we've lost people and ships based on a lie?" she asked, surprised.

"Well, the Darshik *did* attack us first," Jackson said. "We don't know what the real motivation is for the Ushin right now. Given that they provided you with the coordinates for one of the Darshik's main star systems, I would have to assume that anything else they've done was under duress. The Darshik did open fire on the Ushin ships after you destroyed that Super Alpha."

"Maybe," Celesta said doubtfully. "They are aliens, after all, so we have no frame of reference. Hell, we can barely talk to them."

"We have to accept that we've entered a new age for our species," Jackson said. "We've had close neighbors all this time and the further we expand the more we're going to brush up against them. We'd better figure out exactly what our policy will be for first-contact scenarios from here on out, but in the meantime I don't think there's any avoiding an all-out war with the Darshik."

"Changing subjects to something less depressing, somewhat, how is Jillian taking the fact Marcum conscripted you into this?" Celesta reached for the bottle again.

"About like you'd expect," Jackson said. "She understands, but she's pissed. With the twins she also realizes there's zero chance that she can try and petition to be reinstated herself."

"Do you think they'll let me keep my current rank now that you're back?" she asked, trying to make it sound like a joke. "I've gotten used to the pay bump."

"Sorry, Senior Captain ... you're stuck where you're at," Jackson said with a smile. "I'm not coming back to Ninth Squadron. I've yet to get an assignment other than I know I'll be attached to Black Fleet again. Admiral Pitt was adamant that you not be displaced. Hell, knowing Marcum I probably won't even be commanding a warship. It's equally likely I'll be flying the resupply ship and ferrying munitions and propellant to your ships."

Celesta just nodded, suppressing the shudder she felt at the legendary Captain Wolfe being relegated to flying a cargo hauler. It would be a criminal waste of a needed resource. She was also torn between being relieved that CENTCOM, or at least Admiral Pitt, thought enough of her to keep her in command and wishing to dump the mess into Wolfe's lap.

"Well then, here's to being back together again." She raised her glass. "It's too bad it had to be another bloody war to make it happen."

"Together again," Jackson toasted her before draining his glass.

****

"This is a fucking disaster," Wellington said, swirling a very expensive scotch whiskey from Earth in his cut-crystal tumbler. Even though he was from Columbiana he preferred the real thing, damn the cost.

"It's an unintended consequence, certainly," Marcum said as he looked down into his own drink. The pair was sitting in the study at the President's new official home, so recently built that it still smelled of fresh paint and new furniture.

"Shut up, Marcum," Wellington said disgustedly. "I didn't bring you here to commiserate or to sing me platitudes. We need to be on the same page about this. Ambassador Cole is presumed missing since the *John Arden* was destroyed in the Juwel System, and we have to figure out how to best present this to the public."

"I'm not sure I understand, sir." Marcum frowned.

"Let me spell it out for you," Wellington said. "Noble intentions aside, the bottom line is we've gotten ourselves inextricably drawn into a war because we—*I*— was too stupid to tell the Ushin we would not act militarily until we had independent verification of their claims. Now I've already gotten Starfleet personnel killed and a Terran system invaded. What the fuck was I thinking, trusting some alien without question?

"My point being is that we need the public's support on this while we figure out a way to end hostilities as quickly as possible. Wright's stunt of blowing up that Super Alpha they were worshipping complicates things, but we need to see if there's still a diplomatic solution on the table."

"Sir, they still technically attacked us first," Marcum said. "I don't think even the opposition-friendly press will be able to pin this on you and make it stick."

Wellington just looked at Marcum like he was dumber than the chair he was sitting on. "I'm not talking about my political career you dolt!" He had to keep from shouting. "People are dying. Details or not, best of intentions or not, that is largely on me. I would resign today if it wouldn't cause more harm than good, and I *will* step down when this is over as it is obvious my judgement is compromised. What I want from you is a strategy to make sure Fleet's morale and focus remains where they need to be to finish this ASAP. It's why I told you to go drag Wolfe out of mothballs and stuff him back into a command chair."

"I think I understand what you want, sir," Marcum said, showing no indication he took offense at being called an idiot by his boss.

"Make sure you do," Wellington said, reaching for the ornate crystal decanter.

****

Pike leaned back in his seat on the flight deck of the Broadhead II, having listened to the entire exchange between his boss and the CENTCOM Chief of Staff. After a moment's hesitation, he reached over and deleted the message he'd been composing to be sent from an anonymous message account to a friendly source in the media he'd used before. He would give Wellington the benefit of the doubt that he meant what he'd just said … for now.

Thank you for reading *New Frontiers,*

Book One of the Expansion Wars Trilogy.

The story will continue with Book Two:

Iron & Blood

Due in winter of 2016

Subscribe to my newsletter for the latest updates on new releases, exclusive content, and special offers and connect with me on Facebook and Twitter:

www.facebook.com/Joshua.Dalzelle

@JoshuaDalzelle

Also, check out my Amazon page to see other works including the bestselling

Omega Force Series:

www.amazon.com/author/joshuadalzelle

From the author:

Thanks for reading the newest installment of what we're loosely calling the "Black Fleet Universe." For those starting with this book: welcome. As has been talked about after the last book in the original trilogy I had wanted to write a book centered on Celesta Wright. In fact, my original plan was to leave Jackson Wolfe out of this book altogether but I knew I wanted to bring him back in future books in some capacity so I filled in a bit of his backstory to explain what he's been doing since leaving the military.

The story was a bit of a challenge to flesh out from its original outline for a couple reasons. I wanted these books to become a bit more focused and on a smaller scale and by "Counterstrike" I was seeing things creep towards having too many moving parts to be able to deliver a novel with a concise plot. If every book deals with the absolute survival of the entire species I feel like it diminishes the drama of the series as a whole and takes away from all the individual storylines. So for this book I tried to zoom in on only a few key aspects of what might happen after something as traumatic as the Phage War if another group of aliens popped up.

At this point I see no harm in talking about a few things that will, or will not happen, in the second two books of this trilogy. First, the Phage will NOT be coming back other than as the tangential storyline introduced in this book. That particular entity was killed and I won't be bringing it back to life in future books. Second, Wolfe will play a more pivotal role in the next two books, which was something I had planned already but my beta readers specifically asked. Thanks again for continuing on with this series. I plan on releasing "Iron & Blood" next before getting back to work on Omega Force. Cheers!

Josh

Made in the USA
Monee, IL
11 July 2022

99431813R00173